The Riddle
of the Sands

D1483967

The Riddle
of the Sands

Geoffrey Knight

CLEIS
PRESS

Published in the United States.
Cleis Press Inc., P.O. Box 14697, San Francisco, California 94114

Printed in Canada.
Cover design: Scott Idleman
Cover photograph: David Vance
Text design: Frank Wiedemann
Cleis logo art: Juana Alicia
First Edition.
10 9 8 7 6 5 4 3 2 1

ISBN 13: 978-1-57344-366-1

Library of Congress Cataloging-in-Publication Data

Knight, Geoffrey, 1969-
The riddle of the sands / by Geoffrey Knight.
    p. cm.
ISBN 978-1-57344-366-1 (trade paper : alk. paper)
1. Gay men--Fiction. 2. Adventure and adventurers--Fiction. I. Title.

PR9619.4.K57R53 2009
823.92--dc22

                                        2009025535

For my dad,
who is nothing like the fathers in this book.

Thanks, Dad!

I

Laptev Strait Prison, Siberia

THE OCEAN WAS A DARK, SINISTER GRAY AS THE BLIZZARD cut across the barren Siberian shores and tore whitecaps off the Laptev Sea.

Across the water, the prison lay almost flat to the ground, a vast windowless concrete slab built next to a breakwater, low enough to withstand the fierce Arctic wind. This part of the world spent six months of the year in darkness and six months in blinding white, so it was easy to deny the prisoners any natural light. Recently, human rights activists had tried unsuccessfully to shut the prison down on the ground that a lack of natural light was a form of starvation for the human body. It was not the first time the prison had been threatened with closure. In the winter of 1986 a blizzard had buried the entire building. Two rescue military helicopters were sent in but crashed in the storm. Eventually a ship was dispatched, but when it finally reached the prison, half the inmates and wardens had frozen to death.

Yet the prison remained open for one very good reason: in all of Russia and Siberia, government officials could find no better place to keep their worst criminals as far away from civilization as possible.

The cruiser battled the waves, dipping into troughs and tipping over foaming crests. The ex-military boat had been retired from service by the Russian Navy and was now used as convict transport. Needless to say, comfort on board was minimal. Every time the boat took off from the crest of a wave, it gave an unsettling groan. When it landed in a trough, it let out a thud as loud as a sonic boom.

Shane and the Professor shared this disconcerting voyage with the stubble-jawed, cigar-smoking captain of the floating bucket and a young pale British foreign correspondent who was gazing with some alarm at the sleet-slicked window. Shane was certain the guy was about to throw up at any minute.

"How far away are we?" the correspondent asked the captain in broken Russian.

"You sound anxious," laughed the captain with a smoke-filled smirk. "Don't worry, she's only sunk once before."

At that moment, a giant wave smashed into the bow of the vessel. The cruiser pitched to port and the correspondent lurched straight into Shane, who managed to catch him but couldn't stop their heads from butting together.

"Ow! Jesus!" Shane growled, pushing the young man aside.

"I'm so, so sorry!" the young man stammered in a distinct British public-school accent. "I'm not very good on boats." He offered Shane his hand by way of introduction—and apology. "Daniel West, foreign correspondent for the *London Town Crier*." Shane looked vague. "It's a newspaper," Daniel explained.

Daniel was in his mid-twenties and handsome, in a geeky kind of way, with black-rimmed glasses and short slicked-back hair. But he was neither frail nor feeble. Years of being bullied at school had taught him how to fight and he'd won many a schoolyard battle. Shane had felt the tough, solid body underneath that heavily coated exterior.

"Shane Houston," Shane said in return, shaking Daniel's hand with one hand and rubbing his forehead with the other.

The young reporter adjusted the glasses on his nose and turned to the Professor. "And you must be Professor Fathom. You're on your way to see him too. He asked for you personally, didn't he?"

"Who?" the Professor asked, feigning ignorance.

"Caro Sholtez. The minute I heard someone had been granted access, I did everything humanly possible to tag along for the ride. Is it true what they say? That he burned down an entire village in Papua New Guinea, simply because they wouldn't allow him to enter their sacred jungle?"

The Professor answered softly, carefully, not feeling the need to raise his voice above the rumble of the blizzard crashing against the boat. "New Guinea is a remote place. Those reports are…unsubstantiated."

"But it's true he plundered and murdered his way across four continents before U.S. forces tracked him down. And it's true the United States government paid the Russians a small fortune to buy Sholtez a one-way ticket to Laptev Prison, right? Yet nobody knows what Sholtez was after. He went to jail without a lawyer."

"A lawyer would have sold his secrets."

Daniel's eyes narrowed with suspicion. "You know, don't you. You know what he's looking for. You know what drives him." The young reporter's hands dipped into the pockets of his jacket, pulling out a pen and notebook.

The Professor paused. "Yes. I know what Caro is looking for. And yes, I know what drives him: obsession. But if you don't mind, Mr. West, please put your notebook away. Correct me if I'm wrong, but you're not here to interview *me*."

"Sorry, it's a reflex action, I'm afraid. I've been doing stories on poverty, prostitutes, and the coal miners of Vorkuta for the last two years, and suddenly I'm staring down the barrel of a cover story. I guess I'm just a little excited. Not to mention nervous."

The cruiser shuddered and groaned, and Daniel West swiftly took his seat.

"By the sound of your voice, I'd say *extremely* nervous," the Professor said.

"It's this boat. Or rather, the water. I can't swim," Daniel admitted openly.

"I think, in this part of the world, it's not drowning you have to worry about. It's freezing to death."

"Twenty-nine degrees Fahrenheit," Daniel said, nodding. "Or if you like, minus one point eight degrees Celsius. I read that somewhere. I suppose I have a knack for trivia and puzzles."

"Puzzles?"

"You know, crosswords, memory games, that sort of thing."

"I imagine that might come in handy for you someday," the Professor offered up encouragingly.

The captain of the vessel suddenly pointed through a starboard window and shouted in broken English, "Gentlemen, say goodbye to the world you know—and hello to Hell. Welcome to Laptev Prison."

The boat landed and a gangplank slippery with icicles bridged the gap between the rocking cruiser and the concrete wharf that led to the prison block, which resembled a massive bunker. Two stern Russian guards—sporting thick hooded military coats and Kalashnikov assault rifles with underbarrel grenade launchers—escorted Shane, the Professor, and Daniel West along the wharf.

On the way to the prison entrance they passed a small wire pen with four silver huskies caged inside. A sled was strapped to the roof as an excuse for shelter. The howl of the trapped dogs competed with the howl of the wind. Shane shot an angry glare at the guards.

The Professor instantly sensed Shane's disapproval and murmured softly to him, "Now, now. We're simply visitors here. Let's not give them any reason to invite us to stay."

They reached a huge steel door which opened from the inside as they approached, and were briskly escorted into a corridor where the only source of warmth was the buzzing fluorescent lights overhead.

As the steel door closed behind them, a guard snapped at the three clearly unwelcome visitors, shouting in angry Russian and waving his rifle to the left.

"He wants us to follow him," Daniel translated.

With one guard behind them and one leading the way, the Professor, Shane, and Daniel walked past several prisoners, whose faces were twisted wrecks of silent rage. They squatted in the shadowy corners of their cells or sat perched on their bunks like strange, wild birds. Only one stood at the bars as they passed.

Actually, he didn't just stand at the bars. He stroked them, rubbed himself against them, *licked* them.

His scabbed lips were bent in a cracked, wicked grin. His long, rotting yellow fingernails clicked against the cold bars. And a laugh, guttural and primal, slid from his salivating mouth.

"I...want...eat...you!" he guffawed loudly in broken English.

A chill shot up Shane's spine. "Please tell me that's not Caro Sholtez."

By way of a response, the guard snarled at the prisoner. "He is Vladimir Voltar," the guard spat, then struck the bars with the butt of his automatic. Voltar barely flinched. He just continued to stare hungrily at the visitors. Dribbling. Laughing.

"He's one of the worst serial killers in recorded history," the Professor informed Shane quietly. "He tortured and mutilated one hundred and eight men, women, and children across Eastern Europe. And they're just the ones whose bones they found. He killed them mercilessly, and then ate their flesh. He is, by every definition of the word, a monster. That's the kind of place this is. A monster's lair. I suggest we keep moving."

Next door to Vladimir Voltar was Caro Sholtez's cell.

Despite Shane's heated objections, the Professor was sent into Sholtez's cell alone while Shane and Daniel were ordered to wait outside.

Inside the sparse cell, a guard sat the Professor down rather brusquely in a chair at a table in the center of the room. The Professor heard a voice opposite him. "Take it easy! The man's blind, can't you see? Treat him with some respect."

The guard snorted, left the room, and slammed the door behind him.

Once they were alone, the Professor turned to the voice opposite and said in a cool, even tone, "Hello, Caro. It's been a long time."

"Too long," said the voice. "I'm beginning to think you don't enjoy my company anymore."

"I don't," the Professor said bluntly.

Although the Professor could not see, Caro Sholtez made a mocking frown. He was the same age as the Professor, with silver hair, silver eyes, and a face lined with intelligence, but not a glimmer of kindness. "Oh, come now, Max. You make it sound as though I've harmed or offended you in some way."

"The harm you bring to others offends me. Simply to get what you want."

"Simply?" Caro asked, a little stunned, eyebrows raised. "There is nothing simple about what I seek. The only thing simple about it is the lives that get in the way. How can you compare a pathetic human life here or there to the most important discovery in history? I thought you of all people would appreciate that, Max."

The Professor shook his hand. "No, Caro. History is the story of life, not the destruction of it."

"Oh, I forgot," Caro Sholtez chuckled. "Max the merciful. And me, Caro the killer. That's all you think I am, isn't it? A murderer."

"Have you ever kept count of the people you've slaughtered?"

Caro laughed again. "Of course not. That would be morbid. People would start to put me in the same class as my dear friend next door. You met Vladimir on your way in, no doubt. Poor thing. He has the IQ of a stray dog—and the appetite of one too. I don't doubt he'll be studied and written about in history books for decades to come. Me, on the other hand—I intend to *rewrite* history books."

Caro Sholtez leaned forward then and said in a low, serious voice, "Max, I've found the first piece of the clock."

Outside the cell, Shane paced anxiously up and down the corridor while Daniel checked his camera settings. Suddenly a third guard came thundering down the corridor. A worried exchange took place among the prison staff. Shane felt the skin on the back of his neck prickle with alarm. Daniel caught a single word: *Karosta.*

Inside the cell, the Professor sat up. He couldn't help but ask, "The clock? Are you sure? Where? Where did you find it?"

Caro sat back and smirked. "You can't help yourself, can you, Max? For all your honesty and integrity, you want to find it as much as I do. You just want me to do all the hard work. Rather thankless of you, don't you think? Now it's my turn to sit back while you and your boys get your hands dirty. Which is why I asked you here. I want you to find the other pieces."

"I cannot and will not become involved in your search, Caro. I made that clear long ago."

"Come now, Max, you can't possibly resist. I thought your days of denial were over. If you turn your back now, you'll regret it forever—and forever is a very, very long time."

The Professor shook his head, slowly, determinedly. "Once upon a time I might have helped you. But you've become a murderer, Caro. You're nothing but a terrorist now. Denying you and your ways is something I could never regret."

Caro let out a long, cold sigh. "Very well, then. I didn't want to have to do this, but it seems you give me no choice."

"Do what?" the Professor asked suspiciously.

"Leave you behind, along with my good friend Vladimir. You see, I promised him that if you refused my offer, he'd have more than enough food to last him the rest of the Siberian winter... Starting with you."

Outside the cell, Shane grabbed Daniel as two more guards bolted down the corridor. Their frantic shouts echoed off the cold walls. "What are they saying? What's going on?"

Daniel was trying to catch every panicked word and translate them. "Karosta, it's an old war port in West Latvia, overrun now by rebels known as the Liberdade Army. Apparently they've just stolen a KA-52 Werewolf—"

"A what?"

"A military helicopter. An assault chopper with antitank missiles. It's a flying arsenal." Daniel turned to Shane. "The Russian Air Force has managed to track it. It's headed this way!"

Shane spun to the cell door of Caro Sholtez in sheer horror. "It's a prison break!"

Outside the prison, through the thick concrete walls,

the shrill howl of the wind transformed into another ear-piercing sound—a whine, a deafening mechanical squeal.

Sitting opposite Caro Sholtez, the Professor moaned, his voice filled with dread. "Oh, Caro, what have you done?"

"I suggest we get down," Caro whispered beneath the deafening whir. The Professor could almost hear the smile in Caro's voice.

In the corridor, Shane rushed at the cell door, shouting and slamming his fist against the small glass panel to try to warn the Professor, just as—

KA-PHOOOOM!

The outer wall of the prison exploded in a giant blast.

Massive chunks of concrete flew through the air.

The door in front of Shane blew off its hinges and slammed him against the far wall.

Glass shattered.

The metal bars of cells pierced the air like javelins.

It seemed that the entire prison was under attack, then, suddenly, the lights flickered and died, sending the whole building into complete darkness.

Shane coughed dust up from his lungs, pushed the door off him with all his strength, and sat up, hearing the groans and cries of guards and prisoners alike echoing in the blackness. "Professor!" he called.

There was no answer.

He staggered to his feet and tried to feel his way along the smashed walls, tripping over rubble and the occasional soft, heavy form of an unconscious guard.

"Professor! Professor, can you hear me?"

"Shane?" came a voice from behind him. It didn't belong to the Professor.

"Daniel? Are you okay?"

"I think so," came Daniel's rattled voice, somewhere in the dark.

Suddenly, Shane heard a horrific scream in the distance,

accompanied by a hideous cackle, then laughing squeals from the cells followed by the unmistakable clang of snapped metal bars being used as bats and hammers.

The prisoners were escaping from their shattered cells.

"We gotta get outta here," Shane said ominously.

"How? I can't see a thing."

"Any way we can. I think the animals are loose in the zoo." Shane quickly stumbled his way toward Daniel's voice. "Keep talking so I can find you!"

Daniel's head was scrambled. "What do you want me to say?"

"Start by telling me what a goddamn chopper is doing all the way out here! I thought helicopters couldn't fly in this weather."

"It's not that they can't, it's that their pilots *won't*."

"I guess if you want something bad enough."

"You think Sholtez has done a deal with the rebels?"

At that moment Daniel felt something tug at his neck as Shane lifted the camera off him. "That'd be my guess," Shane answered, "but I ain't stickin' around to find out."

In the next moment, the world went from complete darkness to blinding illumination as Shane—now with Daniel's camera around his own neck—popped the flash so they could see their surroundings.

What they saw in that split second was the twisted, crazed faces of a dozen escaped prisoners, rushing down the corridor toward them like vampires exposed to the sun. Leading them was a grinning Vladimir Voltar. As darkness swallowed the light, Shane and Daniel heard the erratic hungry stampede coming for them. Shane pressed the shutter button again.

Flash!

The sight of the ruptured doorway leading into the holding cell imprinted itself on their retinas.

"Over here." Shane grabbed Daniel's arm and dragged

him stumbling behind him. He kept popping the flash, both ahead of them and behind, to piece together the route of their escape and keep the prisoners at bay with the blinding flares.

Flash!

They jumped over the rubble into the shattered holding cell.

Flash!

Shane glanced behind and saw the demented face of Voltar bearing down on them, getting closer and closer, only a few feet behind Daniel now.

Flash!

In front of him he saw the shards of the table where Caro Sholtez and the Professor had been sitting. Sholtez was nowhere to be seen, but under the broken tabletop lay the unconscious body of Professor Fathom.

Shane snatched up a split plank from the tabletop, and as Vladimir Voltar came screaming into the cell, Shane pushed Daniel out of the way and swung the piece of wood in the direction of Voltar's blood-curdling cry.

There was a loud *thwack!*

Voltar's scream turned into a gagging grunt.

Flash!

The maniac fell backward through the doorway, eyes wide and dazed, blood gushing from a broken nose. He crashed into several other clambering inmates, creating a bottleneck in the doorway.

Shane dropped to his knees. "Professor! Wake up!"

The Professor shook his groggy head and felt Shane's face with his fingertips. "What happened?" Then, suddenly recalling it all, he added, "Where's Caro?"

At that moment, Daniel grabbed Shane, who eased the Professor to his feet. "Come on, there's wind coming from this direction. I think it's a way out."

They scrambled over the rubble, pushed past some

broken bars, and saw a beam of light filtering in through the bombed outer wall of the prison.

Behind them, Vladimir Voltar tried to push himself off the other bumbling inmates. As he fell on top of an unconscious guard, he found the cold barrel of an AKM assault rifle lying by his side.

Freezing air and sleet blasted Daniel's face as he emerged from a breach in the wall into the stark Siberian daylight. Shane pushed the Professor through the hole, then pulled himself to freedom, just as the deafening whir of a military chopper appeared overhead. The chopper hovered a short distance off the ground, watching their escape.

Shane, the Professor, and Daniel shielded their faces against the downdraft that lashed at them. The pilot of the chopper wore a black helmet and black fatigues. And in the passenger seat—his face grazed and a little bloody—sat Caro Sholtez, laughing.

Suddenly the wall a few feet behind Shane shattered with a loud blast that came from a grenade *inside* the prison.

Shane, Daniel, and the Professor ducked as rubble once again flew through the air.

Without a moment's hesitation, Shane pulled the Professor up by the arm. "Let's move!" he shouted at the top of his voice, and the three of them bolted for the wharf.

Behind them, the breach crumbled wide open with another grenade blast, and Vladimir Voltar came staggering out, cackling and grinning and waving his new assault rifle like the lunatic he was.

At the end of the wharf, the captain of the old transport vessel—cigar clenched grimly in his teeth—was frantically untying his boat and casting off the lines. He glanced back at the prison in horror: smoke billowed from its razed walls; dazed guards stumbled from the ruins and were attacked, disarmed, and killed by deranged escapees; and through it all, Shane, Daniel, and the Professor raced toward the end of the wharf, calling and waving desperately in an attempt to get the captain's attention.

They succeeded, but the captain wasn't waiting for anybody. Nothing was going to stop him from getting the hell out of there.

Well, almost nothing.

In the Werewolf, Caro Sholtez turned to the pilot and said into his headset, "Show them what you can do, my dear."

Beneath the black helmet the pilot nodded, and with a majestic sweep, the chopper flew directly over the heads of Shane, Daniel, and the Professor and down the length of the wharf.

The captain cast off his boat, gunned his rickety motor, then stared in terror as he saw the Werewolf zoom over the wharf toward him. His mouth fell agape and his cigar tumbled to the floor as the antitank missile hissed through the air.

It slammed into the hull and the cruiser exploded.

Shane shielded the Professor as all three of them slid to the icy surface of the wharf, staring in shock at the huge orange and black fireball rolling into the sky and the shards of the disintegrated boat splashing into the frozen sea.

"Oh, God," Daniel whispered.

Shane glanced back at the prison, thinking fast.

Vladimir Voltar was charging through the sleet toward them, his assault rifle in hand.

That's when Shane heard the bark and howl of the huskies.

Voltar fired another grenade, but in his frenzied state he missed his target completely. The grenade blasted into the ocean.

Shane bolted back down the wharf, toward Voltar and the burning prison, reaching the kennel before Voltar could fire off another shot.

He pulled the sled down and opened the cage door, and the four silver dogs stopped barking and came to him as if he was their mother, joyously licking his hands and face. "Hey, you guys. We need you to get us outta here."

In the blinding white sky above, the chopper swept across the sea and headed back toward the wharf. Inside, the pilot turned to Sholtez and said in a distinctly female Russian voice, "You want me to finish them off?"

Sholtez shook his head. "Let Vladimir take care of them. If I'm going to leave him here to die, he might as well die on a full stomach."

Shane, Daniel, and the Professor all ducked as the chopper passed close overhead and swiftly vanished in the blizzard.

On the wharf, Daniel helped the Professor onto the sled as Shane harnessed the dogs. There was another shot from Voltar's rifle, and a grenade soared between Shane and Daniel and landed in the empty dog pen.

"Get down!" Shane cried.

The three of them dropped, and the grenade blew. Shredded wire and metal filled the air. Not wanting to waste another second, Shane jumped on the front of the sled and Daniel on the back, and with the Professor sandwiched tightly between them, Shane snapped the reins and called, "Yiddy-up!"

The dogs responded instantly to Shane's voice and leapt into motion.

The sled lurched and began sliding quickly along the icy wharf, heading back toward land.

Shane held the reins tight, aiming straight for Voltar, who was running at them, rifle in hand, head rocking with mad amusement. He fired once more, and the grenade passed so close to Shane's head he felt its burning hot shell brush his hair.

It exploded behind them just as Shane steered the huskies directly into Voltar, knocking the crazed cannibal clear out of their way.

Voltar crashed onto his back on the concrete. His rifle slipped from his hand, skidded across the wharf, and splashed into water.

By the time he scrambled to his feet, the sled was racing past the smoking prison and disappearing into the sleet.

But Vladimir Voltar was not as stupid as people thought. He knew that once every morning and once every night, the guards did a routine check of the prison's perimeter. And he knew what mode of transport they used and exactly where they kept them.

Making their way south of the prison, the huskies were like a streak of silver lightning, pulling the sled swiftly through the snow.

Daniel looked back and saw the bombed prison vanish in the white haze of the blizzard. For a moment he didn't see anything else.

Then, through the snow, a single yellow dot appeared. A headlight. Getting closer and closer. And with it, over the sound of the wind, he heard the buzz of an engine straining to go as fast as it could.

"He's back!" Daniel yelled.

Shane glanced behind, then gave the huskies another "Yiddy-up!"

"Can we outrun him?" the Professor asked.

Shane shook his head. "No, but we can outsmart him."

As the whine of the snowmobile grew louder and louder, Shane veered the sled to the right, taking them up a long, icy slope. The dogs ran as hard and as fast as they could. The wind caught Voltar's drool-filled laughter and carried it past Shane and Daniel and the Professor.

"I...want...eat...you!" the monster raved.

The dogs yelped as they ran, as though they could smell Evil bearing down on them.

The snowmobile sped closer and closer still, so close that Daniel, sitting at the rear of the sled, could see Voltar's yellow eyeballs boring into him. He could see the saliva freezing around the edges of his scabbed lips. He could see blood foaming in Voltar's mouth; the killer was so hungry, he had started eating the insides of his own cheeks.

"I...*want...eat...you!*" he screamed in a spray of icy blood.

"Can we go any faster?"

As if to answer, the sled cleared the crest of the slope and gravity took over. Suddenly the dogs couldn't pull the sled fast enough. In fact, the huskies were now struggling to keep ahead of it.

Shane quickly unhooked the harnesses and the freed huskies veered away, out of the charge of the speeding sled. They snapped their restraints and dashed into the snow, a liberated pack now.

"The dogs! Are you crazy?" Daniel cried.

"Maybe. It's a one-way ticket now," Shane called back.

"What do you mean?"

Shane pointed.

A few hundred feet ahead of them, the snow-covered land abruptly ended, dropping away into the white haze—into what could only be the Laptev Sea. The out-of-control sled was heading straight for it with no way of turning and slowing.

Suddenly the snowmobile rammed into the back of the sled, hitting it with a jolt that almost knocked all three of them overboard.

Voltar cackled and spluttered on his own blood.

He steered the snowmobile along the right-hand side of the sled.

Shane turned around and grabbed the Professor by his jacket. "Sorry, Professor, but you'll thank me for this later. Remember to roll."

"Roll?" the Professor asked, but just as it dawned on him what was coming, Shane threw the Professor off the left-hand side of the careening sled.

The Professor landed and rolled and skidded and toppled, sending snow and ice flying into the air all around him. Inertia carried him for a good thirty feet before he slid to a halt, covered in snow and gasping in shock.

Voltar threw an angry gaze back at the Professor, safe in the snow, then started squealing and ranting. "Eat, eat, eat, eat!" He quickly turned his attention back to Shane, who quickly turned to Daniel.

"You're next."

Daniel glanced ahead at the fast-approaching cliff and nodded, but before he could make a move, Voltar veered hard alongside the sled. Both sled and snowmobile rocked as the blade of the snowmobile snagged the rim of the sled, locking the two vehicles together.

Voltar suddenly pounced, leaping from the snowmobile onto the sled.

He lunged at Daniel with his mouth wide open, aiming for his face, his nose, his lips, whatever he could bite off and eat. But before his teeth could sink themselves into Daniel's flesh, Shane planted a hard, swift punch directly into Voltar's already broken nose.

The killer's head flew backward and his hands lost their grip on Daniel, but he was back for the attack within seconds.

Shane had already seized Daniel's coat and pitched him overboard.

Voltar tried to grab the young reporter's ankle as he flew into the air, but Daniel hit the ground in a splash of snow and was gone.

Shane glanced ahead.

The cliff was coming.

He knew distances. He had twelve, maybe fifteen seconds before they hit the edge. He knew if he jumped too soon, Voltar would jump with him. But if he left it too late...

He turned back to the monstrous murderer, whose wide eyes now turned to him, whose parted, cracked mouth now drooled blood and saliva for him.

"You want a piece of me?" Shane shouted.

"I...want...eat...you!" Voltar nodded.

Shane bunched up his fist. "Eat this instead!" And with that, he threw the hardest punch he could, his knuckles landing square in Voltar's face.

The Russian's head jolted sharply and his arms whirled like propellers as he lost his balance and fell backward onto the sled.

Shane looked up and saw the cliff speeding toward them. He jumped.

But just as he did—

—Voltar's hand shot out.

The killer grabbed Shane's boot and held on tight.

Shane hit the ice, landing on his back, and continued sliding behind the sled, Voltar clinging to him.

Voltar laughed.

He reached for Shane with his other hand, dragging him back onto the sled by both feet.

Shane couldn't reach him, couldn't punch him, couldn't pull himself out of his grasp. Then, suddenly, he remembered the camera. Daniel's camera was still hanging around his neck.

The cliff was twenty, fifteen, ten feet away.

Shane grabbed the camera and pulled it from around his neck.

Voltar pulled him closer, pulling them both toward their doom.

Shane lifted the camera up, as close to Voltar's face as he could manage, an inch from the killer's eyes, and whispered, "Smile."

Flash!

After countless days of concrete walls, dim, faltering

fluorescents, and no sunlight at all, the flash of Daniel's camera so close to his feeble, yellowed eyeballs was literally blinding.

Voltar screamed.

He let go of Shane with both hands.

The cannibal's clawlike fingers clutched at his eyes, plucking at them uncontrollably. His nails jabbed and gouged at his burning eyeballs.

Then, suddenly, the sled and the snowmobile—with Voltar on board—launched themselves off the edge of the cliff—

—as did Shane, still sliding at top speed along the ice plain until he slid straight off it.

Voltar sailed far into the air, still scraping at his eyeballs, drifting free of the sled and the snowmobile in midair as they disappeared into the blizzard.

Following close behind, Shane overshot the cliff before—

Snap!

—he was suddenly pulled back.

Pulled back by the camera in his hands.

Its strap had snagged on the rocky, icy edge of the cliff.

Momentum threw him out into the air.

The camera strap swung him back toward the cliff face, which he slammed into with all his weight and a grunt as the wind was knocked out of him.

Clutching the camera as tight as he could, he glanced up and saw the strap caught on a jutting rock above him. He looked down and saw nothing but the cliff face fading into white in the distance far below. Through the howling wind, he heard two distant splashes and knew that Voltar and the interlocked sled and snowmobile had just made contact with the freezing Laptev Sea. And then he heard—

"Shane!"

He glanced up. Daniel was leaning over the cliff's edge.

He had already grabbed the camera strap. He was already pulling Shane to safety with all his strength.

"Hold on," he said. "Don't let go."

Shane shook his head. "I don't plan to."

A Russian naval frigate on a routine training exercise in the Laptev Strait picked up the distress call first and arrived at the burning prison within the hour to evacuate survivors.

Shane, Daniel, and the Professor were abruptly escorted aboard the ship along with half a dozen wounded guards. The rest were already dead or deemed by the Russian forces not worth saving.

"You can't just leave them here to die!" Shane argued with one of the officers, but he was shouted down and shoved into the cargo hold of the ship.

"He said, with this weather, they'll be dead in an hour anyway," Daniel translated.

The gangplank was yanked aboard. The frigate's engines roared, churning up the deep, freezing water, and the ship pulled away from the concrete wharf of Laptev Prison. It was the last time anyone would ever set foot there.

That was when the Professor felt the cell phone in his jacket vibrate.

II

John F. Kennedy International Airport, New York

JAKE FOUND SAM LYING IN THE BATHTUB.

He pulled the poison dart from the kid's chest.

He found the note and pocketed it.

He helped Sam, still stunned and confused, out of the tub, dressed him quickly, shoved some clothes in a backpack. His fingers fumbled as he set the stopwatch running on his watch: one hundred and twenty hours. He grabbed a pen out of his backpack, emptied the ink cartridge, and slipped the poison dart inside. He rummaged frantically through a drawer and found Sam's passport.

Sam had turned eighteen one month earlier, and while Jake reluctantly agreed to no longer call the kid Sammy, Sam in turn agreed—upon Jake's insistence—to get a passport. Without ID, it was too easy for a kid on the street to fade away, to fall prey to the night, to disappear without a trace. Jake believed if Sam had proof of his own existence—proof that he was part of society, not a victim of it—then he would always have a chance at a better life.

Jake felt Sam's forehead, his pulse. "How do you feel?"

"A little dizzy, but I'm okay. Where are we going? I ain't goin' to the cops!"

"Relax! We're not. We need real help."

At the airport, Jake sat Sam down and told him to stay put, then moved out of earshot and dialed a number in his phone. "Professor?"

"Jake?" came Professor Fathom's voice, although it was difficult to hear.

"Professor, I got a big problem. Perron's back. He's poisoned Sam. I got home and found a dart in the kid's chest. Some kind of poison blow dart."

"Is he alive?"

"Yeah, but not for long, according to a note Perron's goon left me." Jake pulled the note from his pocket.

> Dear Mr. Stone,
> You want your little friend to live, and I want a new treasure to replace the mansion you sent to the bottom of the Grand Canal as well as the finger I've lost! Your precious Sam has a rare poison called Deldah-sha running through his veins. It is slow and lethal. He will die in precisely 120 hours, roughly 5 days, unless of course he receives the antidote, the only known bottle of which is in my possession. I will happily trade it for the location of the Lost Pyramid of Imhotep.
>
> Yours truly, P. Perron.

Jake added through gritted teeth, "That son of a bitch!"

"Do you have the dart?" the Professor asked.

"Yeah. I'm at the airport, with Sammy. Ready to jump on a plane to Cairo."

"No," the Professor said. "Don't go to Cairo yet. Meet us in Paris. Eden can analyze the poison, see what we're dealing with. Jake, we need you and Sam in Paris. We'll fix this together. Trust me. Meet us at the Hotel Descartes."

Jake quickly agreed, "We'll be there as soon as possible." He glanced back at Sam, who had been watching Jake the whole time, his face frightened, yet trusting.

"I don't want him to die, Professor," Jake said softly into the phone, turning his back to Sam to give himself time to fight back the tears.

"He won't," the Professor assured him. "We'll find the Lost Pyramid."

III

San Diego, California

WILL STOOD FACING THE BLACKBOARD, CHALK IN HAND, in Professor Nathan James's small college office. He was completely naked, and already hard, when he felt an enormous measure of lubricant land at the top of his ass crack. The cool gel snaked slowly between his cheeks—a sensation that turned his nipples into small, hard buds in anticipation—before being stopped halfway down his ass, then smeared generously, by Nathan's thumb and middle finger.

Will had been drawing on the board. "According to Professor Chamberlain," he said slowly, trying to concentrate, his voice quivering a little, "the internal design of the pyramid consists of a main chamber with three passageways branching out from it. Only one of them leads to—"

He suddenly caught his breath as Nathan's middle finger pushed its way firmly inside his hot, ready ass. Will pushed hard against the board and the chalk snapped in two.

He exhaled slowly, eyes closed for a moment, and finished his sentence in a whisper. "—the ascension shaft."

Nathan's finger slid in and out of Will's ass, relaxing him, opening him up. "According to Chamberlain's theory," breathed Nathan, "there should be a hieroglyph above the entrance to the tunnel that leads to the shaft. What is it?"

Soft groans began to creep into Will's voice as he drew on the board. "A snake. A horizontal semicircle. A horizontal rectangle. A circle on top of a cross." Will sighed as Nathan pulled his finger from his ass. "Living forever."

He heard the snap of a condom being stretched, and then rolled over Nathan's cock.

"What's the purpose of the ascension shaft?"

Will felt the swollen head of Nathan's cock nudge gently against his entry. He gripped the sides of the blackboard with both hands to brace himself, then straightened his back and pushed his ass out, hungry for Nathan's cock.

"It's a passageway. A passageway for the souls of the entombed. A path to the h-h-h—" Will gasped.

Nathan's cock, huge and hard, plunged itself inside Will's desperate, burning ass. The blackboard rocked on its easel with the weight of Nathan and Will pushing against it.

"—heavens," the young student finished.

Nathan pulled his cock out halfway, then pushed inside Will even harder, quickly building up a rhythm. His left hand settled on Will's hip and held on tight. His right hand, still wet with lube, reached around Will's tight, muscled stomach and edged its way down till he found the young man's stiff, pulsating cock.

He clenched it in his slippery fist and began stroking it hard.

Will gritted his teeth as short, sharp grunts of pleasure escaped him.

Nathan picked up speed and began to thrust harder, faster.

Will fell forward but caught himself by placing his hands against the board in front of him, smearing the chalk diagram of the pyramid's chambers.

Nathan quickened the pace of his stroke on Will's cock, his hand pounding it now, sliding swiftly from the head down the length of his shaft, slapping against Will's balls, then shooting back up again.

Will looked down and watched. "Faster," he breathed.

Nathan's hand was moving so quickly it became a blur.

The head of Will's cock swelled even larger, ready to explode, bursting with a bright purple plum color. A small spurt of precum pumped out of it. He clenched his teeth even harder, holding himself back, resisting the urge to come with all his strength.

Inside him he could feel Nathan's hammering cock grow more and more engorged.

Nathan panted harder and harder, his breath hot on the back of Will's neck. He tightened his grip on Will's hip and pressed himself flat against Will's back now, moving ever closer to him, pushing even deeper inside him.

Will felt the sparse hair of Nathan's chest and stomach brush against his back.

Their sweat mingled. Nathan's hips clapped frantically against Will's buttocks. He began to groan, as if in pain. "I can't...hold..." Suddenly Nathan let out a loud, ache-filled "Fuck!"

Will felt a scorching hot burst filling the condom inside him as the head of the rubber ballooned with not one, not two, but three sizzling surges.

A split second later Will unclenched his jaw, opened his mouth wide and let a great coil of cum spring from his loins. It shot up from his balls, up his shaft, and spattered against the blackboard.

Will groaned.

Nathan gave the young man's cock one last hard stroke

and squeezed it tight at the base, forcing out a second wave of cum that shot even higher than the first. White spools landed on Will's smeared depiction of the pyramid's tunnel system before sliding slowly down the board in glistening trails.

For a long moment the two men stayed where they were, locked together, heaving and panting.

Then, exquisitely slowly, Nathan pulled himself out of Will's passage.

The young student let out another small gasp as Nathan slid from his ass, then turned in time for Nathan to plant a long, hard kiss on his lips.

"This isn't on the curriculum, you know."

Will smiled. "You'd be my favorite subject if it was."

Nathan pointed to the blackboard, panting. "I'm talking about the pyramid. The Lost Pyramid of Imhotep. Why the sudden curiosity? It's a myth, you know. There's no proof it actually exists—or ever did."

Will pulled on his jeans, smiled, and gave a coy shrug. "But if it did, if I wanted to know more, how would I find out?"

"You're being very mysterious, Will Hunter."

"And you're dodging the question, Professor James."

"There's no shortage of books on Imhotep. The guy was a high priest, an engineer, an architect—hell, he was the holiest man in all of ancient Egypt, second only to the pharaohs. Scholars and academics have been writing about him for thousands of years, all the way back to Herodotus. But the legend of his Lost Pyramid… There's only one man who ever turned that subject into a life's pursuit." Nathan gestured to the board. "Professor Henry Chamberlain."

Walking naked over to one of his bookcases, Nathan ran his fingers along the spines of numerous old and frayed volumes. "Ah, here it is. *The Riddle of the Sands,* by Henry Chamberlain."

Nathan pulled a thick book from the shelf and handed it to Will. It was heavy, bound by an aged leather strap that had been wrapped around it several times and looped securely around a metal stud on its cover. Will unraveled the strap and flipped through the book. Its pages were filled with maps and text and handwritten excerpts and diagrams, much like the one he'd drawn on the blackboard, only in more detail.

"It's a fascinating read," Nathan said. "But everything in that book is theory, Will. Chamberlain tried to publish a second book, but nobody believed in his ideas. Nobody, including Chamberlain himself, could prove that the Lost Pyramid is anything more than an Egyptologist's fantasy. The more Chamberlain searched, the more people thought he was nothing but a crackpot."

"Is that what you think?"

Nathan shook his head. "I'm obsessed with archaeology. It'll be the death of me one day, I know it. We all cross boundaries. We all push the limits. If Chamberlain's a crackpot, then we're all crackpots. But half his findings, half his ideas, have never been published. If you really want to get inside Chamberlain's head, there's only one way to do it. Go see him."

"He's alive?" Will asked, somewhat astonished. "He must be—"

"Old?" Nathan nodded. "Very. Like everything else in Cairo."

"Cairo? Chamberlain lives in Cairo?"

Minutes later, Will was clambering down the stairs of the History department as fast as he could, trying frantically to button his shirt and dial a number in his phone at the same time.

Someone on the other end of the line answered his call almost immediately.

"Professor? It's Will. I'm on my way to Egypt now."

IV

Berlin, Germany

IT WAS HERR ERNST SCHRODER'S FIRM BELIEF THAT THIS particular café on this particular street served the best coffee in Berlin. And Ernst Schroder would know. He was, after all, a man of the world, and everywhere he went—whether he was tracking down lost jewels in Dubai, misplaced bank accounts in Monaco, or wayward heiresses in Armenia—he always stopped to taste the coffee. Now, as he sat at his usual table in this particular café on this particular street in Berlin, polishing off his second cup and pretending to read his newspaper, he couldn't help but wonder why the handsome stranger in sunglasses four tables away hadn't so much as sipped his own coffee—for the entire time he'd been here.

Ernst Schroder knew a lot of people, both the dangerous and the dull. But one thing he knew, better than anyone, was that staying informed and staying well connected relied on one skill over all else: staying alive. He decided to pay for his coffee and promptly leave. He turned down the street and walked at a casual pace. At one point he stopped to pat a cute, fluffy dog on a leash, taking the opportunity to glance back at the tables outside the café. The stranger was gone.

Ernst picked up his pace. He rounded the corner of an alley and was suddenly seized by the scruff of his shirt and shoved up against a wall, behind a Dumpster, and out of sight from passersby.

"Whoever you are," Ernst breathed, "we can negotiate—"

But the handsome stranger plucked off his sunglasses and put his fingers to Ernst's lips. "Shh, it's okay. I'm not going to hurt you."

Ernst looked at the young man and recognition set in. The young man took his hand away from Ernst's lips, and Ernst spoke. "You. You're one of Max's boys."

"My name is Luca," he said, nodding. "I need your help. I need to find someone."

"This isn't the way I normally do business."

"No," Luca said, straightening Herr Schroder's shirt for him. "I'm sorry."

Ernst was intrigued by Luca's desperate actions. "Who is it?"

"A clown," Luca answered directly. "Named Valentino. That's all I know."

Ernst couldn't help but smile. "A clown? Are you looking to settle a score?"

"No," Luca shook his head. "I'm looking for my past."

For a moment, Ernst said nothing more. He moved away from the wall and walked to the entrance of the alley. Before he stepped out onto the street, he turned back to Luca. "I'm staying at the Berlin Grand. Give me one hour."

One hour and three minutes later, Herr Ernst Schroder crossed the lobby of the Berlin Grand and whispered to an anxious Luca, "The Cirque des Trompettes. It won't take you to the end of your journey, but it will lead you in the right direction. They're performing in Warsaw for the next few days."

"Thank you!" Luca said sincerely, then rushed out of the hotel.

He sprinted through the streets of Berlin and along the river Spree as fast as he could. He reached Berlin's Hauptbahnhof—the city's monumental, glass-shrouded central train station—and bolted up to the ticket desk. "Please, I need a ticket to Warsaw, Poland," he panted.

The girl behind the counter tapped at her keyboard. "Sir, we can connect you through Poznan. There's a train leaving in"— she checked her watch—"three minutes. Do you have luggage?"

Luca shook his head. Above the noise of the station, he heard the phone in his pocket ring. He saw the caller ID and answered it quickly. "Professor?"

"Luca, we have an emergency. We need you in Paris, right away."

"Paris? But I—"

The woman overheard. "Paris? I'm sorry sir, I thought you said Poland."

"I did. Warsaw, Poland," Luca answered quickly.

From the speaker of the phone, he heard the Professor's concerned voice. "Luca, are you all right? You sound—"

"Sir, the connecting train to Poland is boarding now," the woman told him.

"Luca?" the Professor asked. "Is everything all right?"

"Sir? Is it Paris or Poland?" the woman insisted.

Luca looked at the train departure board, then back at the woman behind the counter, and sighed. "Paris," he told the woman.

He paid for his ticket to France, then said into the phone, "Professor, I'm on my way."

V

Paris, France

ELSA HATED FRUIT BOWLS. "PSSH-PSSH! THEY CALL THIS food? You boys are going to need real food, not fruit! Fruit is for bats!" She seized the large bowl—stacked neatly with apples, strawberries and Chinese gooseberries, compliments of the management of the Hotel Descartes—and shoved it in the closet. Then, from seemingly nowhere, she produced a box of glistening strudels.

"Don't strudels have fruit in them, Elsa?" Shane asked cautiously.

"Of course, but with all that sugar and pastry, it's no good for you at all! Just what growing boys need!"

"If I didn't know better, I'd swear you were trying to fatten us up."

Elsa shook her finger at Shane like a schoolmistress. "When you boys stop running around, I'll stop giving you things to run off! Don't try my patience, Shane Francis Houston. I thought you were supposed to be keeping the swelling down on the Professor's face."

"He's busy. In there." Shane pointed to the closed door of the bedroom. "And I'm sorry if he sustained a little... slight...bruising."

"Little! Slight! He could have broken a hip!"

"Well, next time a serial killer is chasing us on a snow-mobile through Siberia, I'll think of a more gentle way to save the Professor's life."

"I hope so. Otherwise I'll kick your *Hinterteil* till it's *Schweinwurst!*"

"Elsa, the guy was drooling! He wanted to—"

Elsa shook her finger again. "*Schweinwurst!* You hear?"

Shane sighed and nodded his head like a naughty schoolboy. "*Schweinwurst.* I don't even know what it means, but I hear."

"It means pig sausage," Jake said. "She's gonna kick your ass till it's pig sausage."

Jake had been pacing ever since he and Sam had arrived. He hadn't spoken a word since he'd left Sammy alone with Eden and the Professor in the other room so they could do tests and a blood analysis.

Elsa turned to him, relieved and happily surprised. "It's good to hear your voice again. We've been worried. Are you okay?"

Jake nodded. "I'm fine. You and, er, Shane *Francis*, don't you worry about me." He glanced anxiously at his watch and pointed to the closed door. "It's him in there, he's the one we all need to worry about."

Behind the door—out of sight—Sammy lay on a bed while the Professor sat beside him and Eden worked furiously. It was a makeshift science lab—microscope, syringes, vials, gauzes, bandages, open books—but Eden had performed in far worse conditions; at least here the sheets were clean and he could boil the water.

"It's Deldah-sha, all right," he said, lifting his head from his microscope and looking gravely at the Professor. "He'll be fine for a couple of days, but then the fatigue will set in. Then nausea and vomiting. And then..." Eden said no more.

The Professor was leaning over Sam, concerned. "Samuel, my name is Professor Fathom." He patted Sam on the leg and smiled encouragingly. "Why don't you hop up if you can. I don't believe in keeping secrets from those I trust, and it's time we find an answer to your problem."

Sam said with a grim frown, "Am I gonna die?"

"Not if we can help it. Go on, Jake and the others are waiting to see you."

The moment Sam stepped out from the bedroom, Jake rushed up to him and hugged him. "Sammy, are you okay? How do you feel? Do you feel sick?"

Sam shook his head, annoyed, looking around at the others like an embarrassed kid. "Jake, I told you not to call me that!"

Jake ignored him and looked to his trusted friend Eden. "Tell me he's gonna be okay. Tell me what we need to do."

Eden had with him several books. He pushed aside the box of strudels and spread the books out on the table. Everyone gathered, including Sam.

"The bad news is, Perron wasn't bluffing. Sam does have Deldah-sha in his blood. It's one of the rarest poisons on the planet. It's also one of the slowest acting. Which means Perron wants his prize more than he wants Sam dead."

"His prize being?" Elsa asked.

Jake produced the scrunched-up note. "The Lost Pyramid of Imhotep."

"Will is already on his way to Cairo," the Professor informed them.

Jake shook his head. "But what if the pyramid is a myth?"

"Any problem can be solved in a number of ways," said

the Professor. "We have two alternatives, five very capable men, and five days to find a solution."

Jake checked his watch. "Four days," he corrected. The fact was, they had even less than that now, but Jake didn't want to say it. He didn't want to believe any of this was real.

"What are our two alternatives?" Shane asked.

Eden answered, "The first is, we find the Lost Pyramid."

"And the second?" Jake asked.

"The second," Eden replied, "is that I go to Brazil and find the Deldah-sha orchid. It's a native flower of the Amazon. If I can find one, if I can bring back the pollen from its anther... Placed under the tongue in its natural form, it's twenty times more effective than any manmade antidote. It's an instant cure for the poison."

"Then let's go!" Jake hastened. "What are we waiting for?"

"It's not as simple as that," Eden said.

"It's just a flower!"

Eden shook his head. "It's a flower that hasn't been seen since the nineteen-thirties. Given the rate of destruction of the Amazonian rain forests, it could well be extinct by now. There's only one man who may be able to help: an American botanist living in Manaus, in the heart of the Amazon."

Concern swept across the Professor's face. "You mean Alexander Thorne? Eden, be careful. His methods and ethics are questionable at best. All he cares about is money and fame."

"He's a botanist. How dangerous can he be?"

"He's a horticultural pirate. Nothing more than an orchid hunter, and a wealthy and ruthless one at that."

"He's our only lead to the Deldah-sha," Eden pointed out. "I'll be okay."

"Take me with you," piped up Sam. "I want to help you find it."

"No," Jake and the Professor both said sternly at precisely the same time.

"Why not! I can help! I'm young, I'm strong, I don't feel sick at all."

"You will," the Professor warned. "Sam, you need to stay here with Elsa and me, out of harm's way. In the meantime, Shane, I want you to take Jake and meet Will in Cairo." The Professor turned to Eden. "If you're sure you can handle Brazil on your own..."

Eden smiled confidently. "Professor, I'm Brazilian. I'll be back with the orchid before you even notice I'm gone."

Across the room, Jake was pacing again and shaking his head. "I'm not leaving Sam. I don't like the idea of not knowing where he is."

"He'll be here with us," Elsa said, nodding as reassuringly as she could.

"But what if something happens? How will I know where he is? If he's safe?"

The Professor was already moving toward a locked writing bureau in the corner of the suite. "I've already thought of a solution for that. "His feeling fingers traced their way to a small key, turned it, then opened the lid of the bureau to reveal the cracked computer screen from his room at the Royal Hotel in Vienna. It was on, hissing and buzzing unnervingly. The blurred image of a digitized map jittered and jumped on the broken screen. It was a map of Paris. In the middle of the map was a red flashing dot.

"That's you, isn't it," Shane observed, a little incredulous. "That's us, right here. Right now."

The Professor nodded.

"You're telling us that the tiepin...?"

The Professor nodded again. "Yes, the tiepin tracking device. It's still lodged somewhere inside me, which doesn't at all surprise me. I'd ask Eden to remove it, but I daresay it could serve us well. And since this monitor doesn't have much life left in it"—the Professor opened a drawer in the bureau and pulled out five sturdy-looking digital watches—"I have a gift for each of you."

He gave a watch each to Eden, Jake, and Shane. The three took their old watches off and strapped the new thick digital watches onto their wrists.

"There's a global tracking system on each of them, synched up to the device inside me. It's accurate to within two hundred meters. So long as you have your watch with you, you'll know my exact location, anywhere in the world. And so long as Sam is with me—"

"I'll know where he is," Jake said, nodding.

Figuring the technology out quickly and logically, the boys turned a small dial on the right side of their watch faces to reveal a map of the world. A small set of crosshairs quickly scanned a grid of the globe and zeroed in on a map of Paris—the same digitized map as the one on the broken computer screen. A small red dot began flashing over the Hotel Descartes.

The Professor handed a fourth watch to Shane. "Give one to Will when you meet him in Cairo," he instructed. "I'll give the fifth one to Luca."

"Where is Luca, anyway?" Shane asked.

"He's on his way here now," the Professor assured them all. "And, I've no doubt, he'll turn up when we most need him."

VI

The Office of the London Town Crier, London

"WHAT THE BLOODY HELL DO YOU CALL THAT?" NEVILLE Sackville, chief editor of the *London Town Crier*, snatched up his coffee mug and threw the photograph across his desk. It slid to a halt in front of Daniel West, who stood facing Sackville, his look of hope quickly turning to despair and desperation.

Daniel grabbed the photo and pointed. "It's an eye! The eye of a killer!"

Neville shook his head, finding it impossible to shake the doubt out. Indeed, the photograph was very close up and extremely blurred. Unfortunately, it was also the only photograph that had survived the Laptev Prison escape. "You know what your problem is, West? You don't know how to get close to the story!"

"I was close! There was a rocket launcher!"

Neville Sackville snorted dubiously, then got up from his desk and stormed out of his office, charging past his personal assistant, Miss Parsons, who caught his coffee mug as he slammed it down on the edge of her desk.

Daniel chased after him, still waving his one and only picture, racing through the labyrinth of cubicles and the tappity-tap symphony of nimble fingers busily punching out stories for the daily news—music to Sackville's ears.

"But this is big news!" Daniel's voice, on the other hand, was not music to the chief editor's ears. "This is a cover story! Caro Sholtez busted out of prison!"

"If that's the case, then, unfortunately for you, God was the only one who saw it. Where's the proof, West? I want to see proof!"

"I'm your proof! I was there!"

"Not according to the Russians. They've got no record of you ever visiting Laptev, nor have they submitted any reports to the Foreign Council or even the press of any kind of incident occurring there."

"You don't believe me?"

Sackville stopped marching and sneered at Daniel. "I don't believe in fairies, no matter how hard I clap! And without a shred of evidence to back your story, England won't believe a bloody word you write."

Sackville continued walking through the maze of reporters, Daniel West in tow, until he had done a full circle of the office. Arriving back at Miss Parsons's desk, he snapped up a photograph of a plump regal corgi. "Sorry, West, but your cover story just went to the dogs. There's been a shooting accident out at Windsor Castle. Sources say it was that reckless prince again, completely tanked off his knockers and showing off with his rifle. Now the queen's got one dead corgi on her hands and I've got a story that'll sell shitloads of newspapers!"

With that, Sackville stormed back into his office and slammed the door shut. The glass pane in the door rattled, as did both Daniel and Miss Parsons.

"Dammit!" Daniel threw his blurred photograph on the ground.

"Are you okay, Daniel?" Miss Parsons offered up timidly.

"No! I just spent the last two years of my life in Russia freezing my arse off, and now I just blew my one chance at a..." Daniel's voice slowly trailed away as he spoke. Something had twigged in his brain.

Miss Parsons looked at him, concerned. "Daniel? Last chance at what?"

"...a cover story..."

As the words came out, Daniel suddenly remembered the phone call Professor Fathom had received aboard the Russian frigate. The engines were loud and the adrenaline was still pounding through his head after their narrow escape from Vladimir Voltar, but Daniel clearly recalled hearing something about a lost pyramid. Something about poison. Something about—

"Cairo!" Daniel blurted suddenly. "Miss Parsons, do you have access to any hotel guest lists in Cairo?"

"Of course not," she muttered, as though she had no idea what Daniel was talking about. "Why would I have access to any hotel guest lists, anywhere in the world? That would be a violation of every privacy law in the country!"

Daniel smiled, leaned in close, and whispered in Miss Parsons's ear. "A violation that could be our little secret. Just yours and mine."

Miss Parsons looked around nervously. She quickly started shuffling papers on her desk and rearranging pens, pretending to ignore Daniel. But the truth of the matter was, she'd always had a thing for him, something of a secret girlish crush, what with those eyes and that schoolboy smile and...

For a moment Miss Parsons stopped pretending to busy herself and looked up at him. The second she did so, she didn't stand a chance.

"For me?" His shining blue eyes pleaded. "I promise I won't tell a soul."

VII

Cairo, Egypt

THE ENTRANCING MELODIES OF NEYS AND MIZMAR FLUTES danced and swirled through the heat and dust as Will made his way through the noisy, bustling side streets of Old Cairo. The air was thick with the pungent stink of donkeys and the dizzying scents of spices and sweet, exotic perfumes. Noisy men gathered in the *ahwa baladi* and coffee shops of the old town, laughing and arguing and abusing each other over their chugging shisha pipes.

Will's backpack was slung over one shoulder, and it weighed as heavy as it looked. He checked an address scribbled on a piece of paper he pulled from his pocket, then paused in front of a tall, narrow door nestled between a rug vendor and a crowded coffee house.

The door was red and battered. Will knocked, thinking his knuckles might take off more of the chipped paint. Indeed, a few red flakes fluttered to the dust. The moment they settled, the door opened dramatically and a portly old man in a caftan, shawl, and glasses abruptly blasted, "Who the bloody hell are you?"

"My name's Will Hunter. I'm looking for Professor Henry Chamberlain."

"What for?"

"I'm looking for an answer," Will replied, pulling his backpack off his shoulder and unfastening the buckles.

"An answer to what?" The old man was becoming increasingly irritated by the handsome young stranger, but his eyes widened when he saw what Will had just pulled from his backpack.

"An answer to the Riddle of the Sands," Will replied, holding the huge old book of the same title in his hands.

After a stunned silence, the old man said, "Well, then, I suppose you'd better come inside."

The old man wheezed and panted all the way from the front door to the mosaic-tiled courtyard that was situated in the middle of the house.

In the center of the courtyard was a fountain—the small statue of a young Egyptian boy, presumably from ancient times, kneeling in the middle of a bubbling spring, pouring an endless flow of water from a reed basket.

"Water is life," the old man commented, noticing Will looking at the fountain. "Welcome to Egypt, the Mother of the World, or *Umm al-Dunya,* as the locals like to call it. It's the greatest civilization in all of history and it wouldn't be here if not for the Nile. Water is the answer to everything. Without it, there is no life, no creation."

The old man plunked himself down at a petite table that sat on one side of the courtyard, indicating for Will to join him. "So, you have a copy of the book."

"Yes," Will said, sitting down and placing the book on the table.

The old man inspected it. "There aren't very many of

these left, you know. Have you read it?"

Will nodded. "On the plane over here."

"Over here from where?"

"Are you Henry Chamberlain?"

"Young man, you never answer a question with a question."

"Well, you never told me who you were when I introduced myself."

The old man eyed him for a moment, his gaze an odd mix of contempt and growing respect. "I am. And if you've come to talk about the riddle, I think we both need a drink." Suddenly he shouted at the top of his voice, "Mikal!"

Will jumped with a start, then from within the house he heard the frantic shuffle of a pair of soft-soled shoes. A thin little man came running into the courtyard.

"You called, Dr. Chamberlain?" he breathed in a panicked voice.

"Have you been napping again?"

The man wiped his bleary eyes. "No, Dr. Chamberlain." It was a very unconvincing lie.

Henry Chamberlain turned to Will with a frown. "Mikal here has a habit of falling asleep in the sun every time I send him upstairs to water the roses on the rooftop garden. He claims the smell of the flowers sends him to sleep. Still," he sighed, "I don't know what I'd do without him."

As if to prove the point, Mikal asked, "Have you had your pills yet this morning, Dr. Chamberlain?"

The old man grumbled like a bear. "Why don't you stop nagging me about it and just go fetch the damn things." Mikal managed to take three steps before Henry Chamberlain added, "And bring us the shisha—and some scotch!" He glanced at Will. "Is it too early for scotch?"

Will looked at his watch. It was just after ten in the morning. "I don't mind, I'm on a different time," he said with a polite shrug, not wanting to offend his host—or spoil his chances of finding out what he needed to know.

Henry Chamberlain burst out laughing. "That's been my problem too—for the last fifty years!" The old man's laughter soon turned into an uncontrollable hack, and Mikal came running out with a glass of water and a cocktail of different-colored pills in a small paper cup. Henry poured them into his throat all at once. Slowly the coughing fit faded away and gasp by gasp Henry managed to calm himself down again.

"Should I get the oxygen?" Mikal asked, concerned.

"Christ, no! I'm still waiting on my bloody shisha and scotch! And so is Mr. Hunter. Now chop-bloody-chop!"

Mikal scurried away, then Henry turned to Will and with a sly grin said, "So, you want to find the answer to the Riddle of the Sands. May I ask why?"

"Does it matter?"

"You're doing it again—answering a question with a question."

"That's why I'm here, to ask questions. To find out if the Lost Pyramid of Imhotep really exists, and if it does, find it."

Henry's smile broadened. "You have passion, I see. I like men with passion. And if they're young and handsome, well, needless to say I like them even more."

At that moment, Mikal returned with Henry's shisha and two glasses of scotch on a tray.

"Ah, my shisha!" Henry exclaimed. "Mr. Hunter, you must smoke with me."

The shisha was large and ornate and looked like a cross between a mechanical octopus and a colorfully elaborate bong. Mikal lit it, Henry put one of the many pipes to his lips and inhaled, and the shisha bubbled and gurgled and let out a gentle plume of smoke. Henry handed Will a tentacle.

"I'm not really much of a smoker," Will said politely.

Henry laughed. "My pretty young friend, this isn't smoking—this is living!"

Will took a timid puff. The smoke was sweet and strong, and he let out a rasping cough.

Henry laughed raucously and handed Will his scotch. "Here. This'll help wash away your innocence!"

Will gulped his drink.

Henry did the same. "Trust me, the first puff is always the hardest. After that it gets much, much easier. Before you know it, it'll be like breathing air."

Will inhaled again, even more cautiously than before, but Henry was right, it did go down easier—then easier again with each puff.

"There you go," Henry said, nodding encouragingly, like a father teaching his young son how to ride a bike. "How old are you? Nineteen?"

Will nodded.

"He would have been your age, you know—perhaps a little younger—when all the trouble began."

"Who?"

"Ahnu. Imhotep's son."

Will thought for a moment that perhaps he had missed one or two of Nathan's lectures. "I didn't know Imhotep had a son called Ahnu."

Henry took another puff on his shisha pipe and Will followed suit. "Nobody knows," Henry said, pursing his lips and blowing two perfect smoke rings into the warm air. "That's where the riddle begins."

"You never mention Ahnu in your book."

"That's because the Egyptian authorities ordered it removed. That's what they've been doing for thousands of years—removing all trace, all evidence of Ahnu from history. It was one of Imhotep's eternal commands. The poor boy was literally erased from time. The real tragedy is that even Ahnu himself had a hand in it." Henry took a swig of his scotch, then inhaled his shisha pipe again. He noticed that Will looked intrigued, confused, desperate for more. "Perhaps I should start from the beginning," the old man said, smiling, then settled in for his story.

"Besides Pharaoh Djoser, whom he served, there was no man in all of ancient Egypt more powerful than Imhotep. He lived during the Third Dynasty, around twenty-six hundred BC, a man of many talents: history's first known architect, not to mention a physician, a sculptor, a holy man, a poet, a philosopher, as well as the designer of the Pyramid of Djoser, built two centuries before the Pyramids of Giza. He was one of the greatest minds in the history of humankind. But in his lifetime, there was one greater. His son Ahnu."

"Let me guess," Will said. "The father–son relationship was a tad strained."

"You sound like you speak from experience."

Will simply shrugged.

"Perhaps 'strained' is putting it mildly. You see, it wasn't enough that Ahnu's inventions and designs were more remarkable than Imhotep's, but to make matters worse, when Ahnu turned eighteen, he confessed to his father that he was, in the words of the ancient Egyptians, impure."

A chill shot down Will's spine. "What do you mean, impure?"

Henry raised one eyebrow. "Have you heard of the Book of the Dead? And yes, I know I just answered a question with a question, but this is my story and these are my rules."

Will nodded. Maybe it was the morning scotch, or maybe it was the heady sweet smoke from the shisha, but he was beginning to like this humorous, pushy old man more and more every minute. He took another puff on his pipe. "It's a compilation of texts used for burials."

"Not texts. Spells. To protect the dead on their journey to the kingdom of Osiris, god of the afterlife. But protection could only be granted on the condition that the dead had not performed any acts of impurity, including murder, blasphemy, and homosexuality."

"Ahnu was gay." Will made the logical jump.

Henry nodded. "Egyptian society, both ancient and modern, deems homosexuality one of the greatest of sins. Make no mistake, it exists. Not even religion can stand in the way of nature. But it is kept behind closed doors. Unfortunately, not only was Ahnu guilty of such a sin, he had also fallen perilously in love with Khay, one of Imhotep's slaves. Khay was Ahnu's muse and inspiration. Ahnu was in the midst of designing something truly incredible when Imhotep learned of his son's love affair with a slave."

"What happened? What did Imhotep do?"

Henry sighed. "Imhotep was as close to being a deity as any mortal man in history. Such power can be blinding. Who knows if Imhotep ever loved his son. What I do know is that Imhotep loved his career more."

Will's head was spinning from the smoke, all the while trying to push thoughts of his own father out of his mind.

"When Imhotep stormed into the chamber," Henry continued, "Ahnu didn't see the dagger in his father's clenched fist, only the hatred and betrayal in his eyes. By the time Imhotep plunged the dagger into Khay's chest, it was too late. Imhotep then turned the weapon on his own son, but Ahnu managed to fight him off. The young man took the body of his dead lover and the papyrus scrolls containing his designs and fled into the desert."

"Did Imhotep go after him?"

"Oh, yes," Henry said, nodding. "Relentlessly. It became his obsession. For years he sent his minions out to scour the desert in search of his son. Not to bring him home, but to destroy him. To clean away the stains Ahnu had left on his legacy. It took five years to find him, but in that time something remarkable had happened. Ahnu had gathered his own army of followers. They lived in a hidden oasis in the desert, all of them homosexual slaves who had heard of the terrible murder of Ahnu's lover. They built a small city around the oasis—a City for the Impure—and together they constructed Ahnu's greatest achievement. His very own pyramid. A tomb for himself and Khay. Their final resting place."

"But Ahnu wasn't dead at that stage."

"He planned to be. He knew his father would track him down eventually, and when that happened, Ahnu planned to end his own life and be forever with his lover in the realm of the dead."

"Ahnu killed himself?"

Henry nodded. "At twenty-four years of age."

"But suicide isn't the answer to anything," Will said, suddenly enraged despite his light-headedness. "And being gay isn't something to run away from, it's not something to be ashamed of! We have to enjoy it, live it, be who we are!"

Henry smiled warmly. "Ah, there's that passion again. I like it a lot. But these were different times." The old man drained his scotch and Will did the same; then, with a little effort, Henry stood from his chair. "Come into my study. I want to show you something."

Henry and Will left the bubbling shisha and their empty scotch glasses and entered Henry's study through the large glass doors.

Inside, the walls were lined with shelves crowded with books, artifacts, and pictures of tombs, dig sites, and desert temples. There was an old wooden box with a latch and lock sitting on one of the shelves. Henry took it down. Gently. Respectfully. As though he was handling a priceless treasure.

He placed it on the desk in the center of the room, but left the box locked while he continued his story. "It took five years for Ahnu to build his monument in the middle of the desert. When Imhotep and his army finally found the City of the Impure, he razed it to the ground and drove the slaves into the desert, but as his chariot was consumed by a giant shadow, he stopped and stared up in wonder at what had suddenly blocked the sun. It was Ahnu's pyramid—the largest, most magnificent structure Imhotep had ever seen, and undeniably the greatest achievement in man's history up to that day. Imhotep saw a single figure disappearing into the pyramid. It was Ahnu. He was drenched and left a trail of wet sand in his wake. Imhotep charged after him, followed by several other chariots, but then something astonishing happened: before his very eyes, the pyramid began to vanish. The earth moved. A terrible wind blinded Imhotep and his men. The sand shifted beneath the wheels of the chariots and the hooves of the horses, and as Imhotep's men screamed for mercy the desert swallowed several of the chariots whole. Somehow Imhotep managed to race to safety. When he looked back—the pyramid was gone."

"How?" Will asked.

"That, my friend, is the Riddle of the Sands. How do you make a pyramid simply disappear? It was a question that drove Imhotep to the brink of insanity, the puzzle he could never solve. It was Ahnu's revenge. Not only had he robbed his father of the chance to kill him, but he had built something awe-inspiring, something his father could never replicate, although he tried and tried till the day he died. Nobody ever returned to the City of the Impure for fear that it was cursed. And needless to say, it could never go down in history that someone like Ahnu—a man of impurity—could have built something of monumental proportions and magical capabilities. Such achievements were left to the pharaohs and the gods. And so Ahnu's genius, his very existence, was erased from Egyptian history forever. Even Khay's family were killed to maintain silence."

"But you said so yourself, murder was an act of impurity too. With all that blood on his hands, Imhotep could never have received the Book of the Dead."

Henry shrugged. "In Egypt, sometimes even the truth

gets buried. Whether or not Osiris let him enter the after-life, that's another riddle altogether."

"But how? How do you know all this if everything's been destroyed?"

"Lost stone carvings. Forbidden etchings. Scripts. Texts. Favors. Bribes. A little trickery here. A little illegal paper-work there. Over the decades I've pieced together thousands of clues, tiny pieces of the biggest secret in Egyptian history. But now I'm simply too old, and far too ill, to ever find the answer."

"I can," Will said with such confidence, such conviction, there was no doubt in Henry's heart that this young man could solve his mystery—or at least try his damnedest.

"You can't do it alone," Henry warned. "There is unimaginable danger."

"I have friends," Will said. "And I have you."

Henry chuckled and spluttered at the same time. "I can't bloody go with you. Look at me, I'm falling apart like an old mummy! I wish I could go, I wish I were sixty years younger. But no, my days of searching are over, I'm afraid."

Will placed his hand firmly on top of Henry's, then smiled and looked him square in the eye. "Then come with me in spirit. Tell me everything you know. Tell me all the clues. Tell me where to start. And I'll find your pyramid."

Henry looked into Will's excited face, then down at the young man's hand, which sat gently on his own, which in turn rested on the top of the wooden box.

"You need a key. And a map. And you need to know what's in this box."

Will looked down, then reverently took his hand off Henry's so he could open the box.

Henry unlocked the latch. He opened the lid. And from inside the box, he carefully pulled out what looked like a cube, ornately carved out of wood. "I had this model built from diagrams I drew myself."

"What is it?"

Henry tipped the cube on an angle, so that one tip pointed up and another pointed down, and suddenly the model took shape. "It's Ahnu's pyramid," he whispered.

Will could see that the top half of the tilted cube indeed looked like a four-sided pyramid. "And this?" he asked, pointing to the bottom half of the cube, which was essentially an upside-down mirror image of the pyramid. It had helical grooves carved all the way down its length, like a screw.

Henry grinned like a child with a secret. "Leonardo da Vinci invented the helicopter. Jules Verne gave us the modern-day submarine. I believe Ahnu constructed the world's first automated drill, on a massive scale." Henry elaborated, "You see, the top half of Ahnu's construction is a normal pyramid, but underneath it is a giant screw." Henry turned the top half of his model counterclockwise. As he did so, the bottom half rotated clockwise. "It's not just a tomb, it's a machine. Able to rise above the surface—"

"Or disappear into the desert, before Imhotep's very eyes," Will breathed, mesmerized. "And become the Riddle of the Sands."

Henry sighed. "That's my theory. One I've never been able to prove."

"But how does it work? What activates the machinery? What makes it rotate so it can rise and sink?"

"My guess is that Ahnu used the physics of the landscape to shift the weight of the pyramid, setting the machine in motion. Precisely how, who knows? But knowing what I know of Ahnu, and what I know of the ancient Egyptians, the secret can be unlocked with a key." Henry raised one eyebrow then and asked, "Will, do you know who Min is?"

Will's thoughts scurried through the corridors of his giddy head. "The Egyptian god of fertility. Always depicted with his right arm raised, holding a flail, and in his left hand..."

Henry smiled. "Go on, you're on the right track."

"In his left hand he held his erect penis."

"As a god of fertility, it's widely believed that Min, like most Egyptians, was not a fan of homosexuality, since homosexuals are, by virtue of their desires, incapable of breeding. Yet legend has it that a gold key in the shape of a small statue of Min emerged from the desert a short time after Imhotep's return from the City of the Impure. It is said this key will unlock the Riddle of the Sands."

"But if Min didn't approve of homosexuals, why would Ahnu make the key to his pyramid in Min's likeness?"

"Ah, more riddles! And the only way to answer them is to find the key."

"How? Where do I begin?"

"The Museum of Egyptian Antiquities. Here in Cairo. It is the world's finest collection of ancient treasures. There are more than one hundred and thirty thousand artifacts and relics on display. The basement of the museum is a labyrinth, a trove of hundreds of storerooms containing hundreds of thousands more treasures. Some of those artifacts have never seen the light of day. Some of those rooms have remained locked for decades. One of them is a storeroom dedicated to Min. He's not one of the museum's favorite poster boys, you know. They like to keep him down there in the dark."

"Why?"

"Because Egyptologists are a bloody prudish mob, that's why—with the exception of screwballs like me, of course. Over the years, several statues of Min have been castrated or destroyed altogether. And so in an effort to spare as many as possible, the museum's curator packed the majority of existing Min statues into a storeroom and locked the door. I believe the key you're looking for is inside that room."

"How the hell do I find a key in the shape of a statue of Min in a room filled with statues of Min! How do I know what I'm looking for?"

"You're smart, you'll figure it out. But one problem at

a time, my friend. First, you have to get into that room, which is no mean feat in itself. I've tried to gain access to it a number of times but without success. You, on the other hand, you're younger, and much more handsome than I ever was! Youth and beauty go a long way in this town—if you talk to the right people. And I know exactly the man you need to talk to. He's attractive, shrewd, and quite likable—and he has connections in every royal palace and every dark alley in Cairo. Although, be warned, he may want to do more than talk, if you catch my drift."

Will did not balk. "I want to find the Lost Pyramid. I need to solve the Riddle of the Sands. I'll do whatever it takes. But I thought you said Egyptians were intolerant of the gay lifestyle."

"They are. But what is said in the daylight, and what is done in the shadows, are two very different things. In Egypt—as in many cultures—homosexuality may not have a face, but it most definitely has its place."

"Who is this man?"

"He is known as Moro. Every afternoon at three o'clock he goes to a place called the Blue Hamam. It's one of the city's more traditional bathhouses, situated south of the Citadel and north of the City of the Dead. I can arrange for you to meet him there this afternoon. The rest—is up to you."

"And when Moro gets me into the museum...and I get my hands on the key..."

"You mean, if you get your hands on the key."

"What then?" Will asked.

"The key will get you into the Lost Pyramid. Before that, you have to find the location of the City of the Impure."

"How?"

"Imhotep built a temple dedicated to Min near Koptos, north of Luxor. I'm not talking about the Temple of Min and the goddess Isis in the middle of the town. There is another temple, twelve miles west of the city, in the middle of the desert. Abandoned because it is impenetrable. Inside this temple is a chamber that has never been opened. It is sealed tight, and nobody knows how to get in. According to several ancient scrolls found in Saqqara, where Imhotep is believed to be buried, a map to the City of the Impure lies within that sealed chamber."

Will rubbed his forehead. "Wait, wait, my head's spinning."

Henry laughed again. "That's the shisha! You've either had too much or not enough! It's all very simple." He coughed. "First, steal the key from the Museum of Egyptian Antiquities. Second, figure out a way to open the secret chamber in the Temple of Min near Koptos and find the map inside. Then follow the map to the City of the Impure and use the key to find the Lost Pyramid."

"You call that simple?"

Henry spluttered some more, then, exhausted, he sat himself down in the large leather chair behind his desk, shook his head, and sighed. "No, you're right. If it were simple, I would have found the pyramid long ago. God knows I tried."

He reached out then and laid his weathered old hand on Will's forearm.

"If you find it, when you step inside it, when your eyes see what nobody has seen for almost five thousand years— think of me," he whispered.

"What will my eyes see?" Will asked, in a voice as hushed as Henry's.

"Some say gold, some say silver. I say the truth. The treasure you'll find inside is the truth that Imhotep had a gay son who was the single greatest man in all of ancient Egypt."

At any given time, Jake Stone was fully aware of his surroundings, wary of every questionable face, suspicious of every sideways glance. But the countdown was on to save Sammy, and Jake's attention to detail was not up to its usual well-honed standards. Otherwise he might have noticed the tall French-Algerian man on the plane he and Shane caught from Paris to Cairo; he might have spotted the same formidable character shadowing them through Cairo's bustling airport terminal; and he would most certainly have remembered him as the man he'd seen in the elevator of his warehouse apartment in New York—the same man who had shot Sammy with the poison dart.

But Jake didn't see him at all now. He was too busy keeping his eye on his ticking stopwatch. "Less than eighty-nine hours to go," he told Shane, his voice short and his movements anxious.

"He'll be all right," Shane assured him as he adjusted his cowboy hat on his head and scooped their luggage off the baggage claim belt. They hurried toward the exit. "We'll find the pyramid, Eden will find the orchid, and Sam will be fine."

"Shane! Jake!" At that moment, Will rushed through the terminal doors toward them, embracing them both fiercely as they met. "Hey, you guys okay?" He aimed the question squarely at Jake.

"We'll be a whole lot better if you tell us you have a lead."

Will nodded. "I found the start of the trail, but we have to hurry. We've got an appointment at a bathhouse called the Blue Hamam in twenty minutes."

Shane raised one eyebrow tentatively. "Will, we don't have time for—"

Will winked. "It's a rendezvous. Trust me. You want to find the Lost Pyramid? I'm trying to fast-track the whole thing."

"Speaking of tracking," said Shane, handing Will his new digital watch. "A present from the Professor. A global tracking device. So we know where he is."

Will strapped on the watch, twisted the dial, and beamed at what he saw. Then without wasting another second, he gestured toward the exit. "Come on, I've got a cab waiting outside."

The three of them hastily made their way out of the busy terminal. They didn't see the large French-Algerian stride steadily, purposefully after them.

Nor did Shane notice the handsome, bespectacled Englishman follow them outside and jump into the car behind them. The Englishman pulled out a small English–Arabic phrase book and translated as best he could, "Follow that cab."

The steam was like a floating white veil. Will, Jake, and Shane followed the Master of the House through ancient narrow corridors, their walls wet and sticky with mist, into one of the bathhouse's many guest rooms.

"Please undress," he said in a soft, calm voice. "Completely. Your belongings will be safe here. I will return shortly."

As the Master left them alone for a moment, Jake looked around the small stone-walled room warily. "You better not be wrong about this, Will."

Will was already pulling off his T-shirt, his chest and abs quickly beginning to glisten in the humid air. "We need to find a key, and then find a temple, so that we can uncover a map so that—"

"Whoa, whoa, whoa!" Jake cut him off. "You call that fast-tracking things?"

"Jake, listen to me. This is more complicated than any of us ever realized. Perron might be after the treasure, he might be looking for glory, but finding this pyramid will bring to light a missing chapter in the history of civilization."

Jake peeled off his shirt and unbuckled his belt. "You

can rewrite history all you like, all I care about is saving Sammy."

"We all do," Will said, taking Jake's shoulder in his hand and squeezing the large, tense muscles beneath his glistening skin.

As the slow, hypnotic currents of steam swirled and circled their bodies, Will, Shane, and Jake stripped bare. T-shirts, boots, jeans, socks, all landed on the floor in a heap, leaving the three men standing naked—their large chests gleaming, their rippled stomachs shining, their ample cocks brimming with confidence despite the strange, ancient surroundings.

"Your robes," the Master of the House said, reappearing in the doorway and offering Jake, Will, and Shane a thin white robe each. "Please, follow me."

Dressed in their robes, the three followed the Master farther into the misty depths of the building, down a set of ancient stone stairs, and along several more narrow, twisting corridors. The sound of water dripping and trickling emerged from unseen crannies and dark corners, and the eerie wail of a distant chant mingled with the drifting, swirling steam. Soon they arrived at an open door that led into a large room filled with looming shadows, stone pillars, and dozens of burning candles, their flames dancing and flickering in a thick shroud of mist.

"Please, sir," he gestured for Shane to enter. "This is the Room of Tranquility. Relax. Meditate. Be at one with your surroundings. You may be pleasantly surprised at what you discover."

Shane entered the room, then the Master of the House turned back to Will and Jake. "Let us continue on."

They ventured farther along the narrow corridor, then down a spiral stone staircase, steep and dark, to arrive at a second open door. Inside was a stone table with a sheet draped over it. At one end was a flat, square pillow, at the other a folded towel. The Master gestured for Jake to enter. "The Room of Touch. Lay yourself down on the table and let us take away all your worries and fears."

Reluctantly Jake entered the room, while the Master of the House gestured for Will to follow him even farther into the labyrinthlike building.

They turned countless corners left and right before arriving at a third open door. It led into another large room dancing with watery ripples. In the middle of the room was a luminous green pool set deep into the stone floor. Steam drifted up from its shimmering surface. The Master indicated for Will to enter. "Please, sir. The Room of Deep Waters. This is where you'll find the answers you seek."

Will took a deep breath, then stepped inside the room. "I'm supposed to meet—" He turned back to the doorway, about to tell the Master of the House that he was here for a rendezvous with a man called Moro. But the Master was gone.

"Henry was right," a voice suddenly announced inside the echoing chamber. "You really are something of a treasure."

Will spun around, startled, his eyes scanning the room from wall to wall.

The voice laughed. "Down here."

Will quickly looked down, into the green pool, and saw the handsome, wet face of an Egyptian man in his early thirties. His black hair was slicked back and his thick eyelashes blinked away huge beads of water. He swam gently to the edge of the glowing pool and emerged from the water completely naked, ascending a set of submerged stone steps.

As the man rose from the pool, Will saw that his chest was strong, with a sparse forest of hair, his stomach was flat and toned, and his uncut cock was well on its way to revealing what promised to be a bulging, hungry head.

"You must be Moro."

The man's eyes were a brilliant emerald green—like the color of the pool itself—hypnotic, enchanting, exotic. It was easy to see the charm and power of this man. At that moment, there was not a doubt in Will's mind that Moro did indeed hold the keys to Cairo.

"And you must be Will Hunter."

Confidently Moro strode directly up to Will, untied the young man's robe, lifted it off Will's shoulders, and let it drop to the floor. Will couldn't contain himself; his cock pounced upward, stiffening into a full erection within seconds.

Moro smiled. "I understand you need a hand with something."

The shroud of steam was so thick, so heavy, that Shane couldn't see a thing except the white mist all around him and the yellow flames of the candles flickering through the dense veil of vapors.

But then he saw something else: a shadow, somewhere at the far side of the room, moved through the mist.

Shane stopped in his steps. "Is someone there?"

There was no answer, no sound, nothing. And then—

The shadow moved again, closer this time.

Shane froze. Unease turned to alarm. "Who's there?"

Again there was no response, nothing but the faint, faraway melodies of the neys in the streets outside.

Shane listened intently. His eyes were wide, scanning his steamy surroundings. He rolled up the sleeves of his robe, ready to defend or attack, whatever the need might be. Suddenly he heard a footstep, directly behind him.

He spun in a swirl of mist.

He saw the figure of a man.

His fist shot through the steam and he felt his knuckles impact on someone's jaw. The figure of the man staggered backward, but before he was out of reach Shane landed a second punch in the man's chest.

He heard a loud grunt, then a pained "Shane!"

The figure collapsed, winded. A pair of glasses flew off his face.

Shane swooped in. "Who are you!"

"It's me... Daniel... Daniel West."

Jake entered the Room of Touch and turned with alarm at the sound of a pair of feet scampering across the floor. He sighed with relief when he saw a small man carrying a tray of oils, lotions, and wet cloths. He had entered from another door and had scurried across the room to the stone table. He busily set his bottles and towels down, then smiled at Jake, gesturing for him to lie down on the table.

"Please, take off your robe." The little man seemed harmless enough and Jake did as he was instructed, letting the robe drop to his feet.

As he stood there naked, he felt small, light fingers begin to dance over his body—his broad shoulders, his large chest, his ripped stomach, his thick thighs—as the little man intently observed every inch of his subject's flesh.

Jake felt himself harden yet again. He was not attracted to the little man in any way, but his attentive touch and such intense scrutiny and focus on his body begged for a physical response. The little man didn't even seem to notice.

"You have a wound that you did not allow to heal properly," the little man observed, examining the scar in Jake's side.

"Time is a luxury I can't afford," Jake replied.

"You should learn to relax."

"It's kinda hard in my line of work."

"If you relax, you'll live a long, uncomplicated life."

Jake couldn't help but smirk. "That's kinda hard in my line of work too."

"Let me help." The little man indicated toward the table.

"Please lie facedown. Eyes closed. It is time for healing."

Jake lay down on the table. He felt warm oil drizzle slowly over his tense back. He felt the little man's nimble fingers spread across his bare skin and begin to knead his bulging, knotted muscles. His eyelids slowly sank over his eyes, and although his concern for Sammy didn't leave his mind for a single second, there was a moment, albeit brief, when Jake Stone felt his fears and anxiety disappear.

It did not last.

The little man took his hands away as Jake lay on the table, his back warm and slick, his tired muscles crying out for more.

Then the hands returned, laying themselves flat and wide upon his skin, inching their way toward his neck.

Only they were bigger than before. The fingers were longer and stronger. The palms wider.

And they weren't warm anymore. In fact, they were freezing.

Jake's eyes shot wide open a split second before those large cold hands closed in on his neck, pressing him down hard and locking him in a stranglehold.

Jake tried to push himself up, he tried to struggle free, but the hands were clasped tightly around his throat now. He gasped and gurgled for air, and tried to twist his head around to get a glimpse of his attacker.

Out of the corner of his eye his saw a large black man.

Smiling. Grinning. Laughing.

The two men were locked together. Will stood with his back to Moro. The handsome Egyptian gently massaged Will's cock with one hand, and held his jaw and throat in the other, caressing the length of his neck. Will threw his head back and groaned, and Moro's lips moved in to kiss the young man's throat.

Will felt Moro's chest and stomach pressing against his back. He felt the stiff, thick rod of Moro's cock nuzzling its way between his ass cheeks.

"It's not impenetrable," Moro breathed as his lips and tongue danced up and down Will's long, tender throat. His cock pushed harder, finding the warmth of Will's crack and locating the rim of his anus. "You just have to be brave. Show a little courage. And move swiftly, for, once inside, you don't have long."

Moro squeezed the base of Will's hardened cock in his fist, then stroked it so firmly and slowly it was almost excruciating.

"Tell me more," Will murmured.

Moro smiled, then released Will's cock and stopped kissing his neck.

He stepped away, his cock sliding out from between the young man's ass cheeks. Will thought for a second he'd said something wrong; he thought for one panicked moment he'd blown his one and only chance to find the Min key. He watched Moro stride across the Room of Deep Waters and stop at a robe hung up on the wall. He reached into a pocket of the robe and pulled something out.

Moro turned then, his hard cock angled high, and waved a condom packet for Will to see. "I can get you inside the museum's basement rooms, but first, I want to get inside you."

Will stood ready and willing, his own cock stiff and bursting for some action. "I'm up for it."

"Indeed you are," Moro observed with a satisfied smile. Across the room, the Egyptian tore open the condom wrapper and placed the circle of rubber over his cock's bulging head before unrolling it all the way down his shaft.

He approached Will, and when he was within arm's reach he took his hand and led him down the steps of the luminous pool. They descended into the warm water up to their chests, then Will instinctively turned his back to Moro once more, taking the stone edge of the pool in both hands.

It was the position Moro wanted him to take. He pressed his body against Will's back. He kissed Will's shoulder. "You're beautiful," he said, reaching around to caress Will's chest and tug gently at his nipples before his probing hands slid under the water and down Will's sides. One hand came to rest on Will's left hip, the other moved around to his ass to part Will's cheeks once more. "Tell me," he said, guiding the stiff rod of his cock to the opening of Will's anus, "are you as handsome in a dinner jacket as you are naked?"

"Why do you ask?"

"Because that's what all the waiters will be wearing at the Curator's Ball tonight, which happens to be at the Museum of Egyptian Antiquities."

Will snatched his breath as Moro slid his long, thick cock into his ass.

Shane snatched his breath, his mind racing. "Daniel West?" He dropped beside the man he'd just flattened and the mist parted to reveal Daniel's face, wincing and gasping. Shane's less-than-fond memories of Laptev came flooding back. "Daniel! What the hell are you doing here?" He noticed Daniel was fully clothed. "Did you sneak in here? Have you been following me?"

"Yes," Daniel admitted openly, wheezing as he crook-edly placed his glasses back on his face, "something I'm quite regretting at this point. You've got one hell of a right hook!" Daniel touched his fingers gently to his jaw with grave concern. "Do you think you broke it?"

Shane helped Daniel to his feet. "You wouldn't have to ask if you didn't creep up on me like that!" he replied, a little annoyed. Nonetheless, he pulled Daniel's hand away and touched his own fingers gently to the English reporter's jaw, tenderly feeling for damage. "No, it's not broken. But you're gonna have a heck of a bruise. Now, would you mind telling me what the hell you're doing following me here—from Siberia!"

"I didn't follow you *all* the way from Siberia," Daniel argued, toying at the buttons on his shirt. He was starting to feel the temperature in the room. "At least not directly. I went to see my editor. About the Laptev incident. But evidently a dead corgi sells more papers than a terrorist prison break these days. That's when I remembered overhearing your Professor Fathom talking on the phone about someone being poisoned and a lost pyramid. I'm sorry, Shane, but it sounded like a story. And don't get me wrong, I appreciate the concern, but I think you can take your hand off my jaw now."

Shane didn't even realize he was still tenderly cradling Daniel's jaw in his fingers, even while Daniel was talking. The cowboy snatched his hand away quickly, a little embarrassed, then turned the conversation back to the subject at hand. "You shouldn't have come. Someone's life is at stake. This isn't a scoop for your goddamn newspaper, Daniel! You should go!"

"Not until you tell me more about this lost pyramid you're looking for!"

"I don't know a goddamn thing about the lost pyramid!"

"You must know something," Daniel pressed, then distractedly added, "Dammit, it's hot in here!"

"Then take your damn shirt off!" Shane snapped.

"Okay, I will!" Daniel snapped back. The young Englishman tugged desperately at his shirt buttons, arguing as he did so. "But don't stand there and tell me you came all the way to Egypt without knowing why!"

"I'm telling you, I don't know anything about the pyramid," Shane insisted.

"And I'm telling you, I'm not an ambulance chaser."

Daniel managed to peel the shirt off his sweaty, muscular torso. He was in reality more muscular than his clothes made him look—his pecs were round and smooth, his stomach tight and toned. He threw his shirt to the ground and looked Shane earnestly in the eye. "I want the truth to be told, Shane. There are some stories that the world deserves to know."

Shane said nothing, but instead stood looking into Daniel's intense, honest gaze. He thought about Will's words. That the discovery of the lost pyramid would forever right a wrong. That finding the pyramid would rewrite history.

And suddenly Shane realized that to rewrite history—

—they'd need a writer.

Shane also realized something else in that moment. He realized how damn attractive Daniel really was. Without another second's hesitation, without a hope of stopping himself, Shane broke the gaze between them, opened his mouth, and planted his lips on Daniel's.

Jake opened his mouth and gasped desperately for air.

He finally recognized the man standing over him—the man with his large hands wrapped firmly around his throat. It was *him*. The man who shot Sammy with the dart.

Jake snapped his arm back and jabbed his elbow upward, away from his body, with as much force as he could muster. His elbow thumped the attacker square in the chest. It was a hefty blow. A gust of air escaped the large man, and his grip on Jake's throat loosened long enough for Jake to pull free and roll off the stone table.

His attacker lunged and grabbed for him, but missed.

Jake landed with a heavy thud, flat on his bare stomach, but jumped to his feet almost instantly.

The two squared off quickly on either side of the table.

Jake glanced down and saw the little masseur lying still on the floor. A dart protruded from his neck. Wide-eyed and angry, Jake looked back at the man opposite him. His assailant was fully dressed in black trousers and a long, black coat and stood grinning at Jake's vulnerable naked state.

"Don't worry," said the man in a thick accent. "He's not dead. Just sleeping. Think what you will of me, but I don't kill people unless I have good reason to."

"Like Sammy?" Jake spat.

The large man grinned. "Your little friend Samuel is not dead either—at least, not yet. But if and when he does die, it will be for gold. Priceless ancient jewels. A prize beyond imagination. Personally, I can't think of a better reason to kill someone."

"Who the hell are you, anyway? How much is he paying you? I hope it's worth it, because if Sammy dies, I'm gonna—"

"My name is Ra," the large man interrupted, his smile unwavering. "And I can assure you, whatever you intend to do to me, the deal is worth it. You see, Monsieur Perron has contracted my services for free—in exchange for fifty percent of whatever treasures lie awaiting inside the Lost Pyramid of Imhotep."

"So what the hell are you doing here? I hate to tell you this, but killing me ain't gonna get you to the pyramid any faster, pal."

In an instant, Ra's smile dropped into a savage sneer. His hand disappeared inside his coat pocket and produced his long, thin, wooden blowpipe. He raised it to his full, dark lips.

Will parted his lips and let out a cry. Moro's cock was longer than he first thought, something he realized with a wave of pain and pleasure as the elongated shaft forced its way all the way up the length of the young American's rectum. Will held his breath and gritted his teeth—his chest muscles clenched tight and his stomach tensed—as the cock penetrated him. Then, as it came to a halt deep inside him, he exhaled slowly and steadily, releasing all the air from his lungs.

Moro held himself there for a long, lingering moment, his entire shaft held firmly in the grip of Will's strong anal muscles.

"The Curator's Ball begins at eight tonight," Moro breathed quietly into Will's ear. "I'll set you up with a contact inside the catering company. How many of you are there?"

"Three." Will quickly caught his breath as he felt Moro's cock retreat, almost as painfully as it had entered. He looked down through the distorting green surface of the pool and saw his own cock, hard and stiff and throbbing in the water, completely turned on by the intrusion of Moro's shaft.

"I will arrange a way for you to access the basement," Moro said through clenched teeth. He withdrew his cock almost completely, leaving only the head inside Will, then thrust his entire length inside the young man's rectum once more. Faster this time. Harder.

Will grunted audibly. Water splashed against the wall of the pool as Will's body was forced forward.

Moro pulled out, then pushed inside him again. "But be warned—once you enter the storerooms you'll trigger an alarm."

Moro's thrusts had by now become faster and more furious. He was building up a powerful rhythm, making waves that smacked and splashed against the wall of the pool. Will was listening as hard as he could, gasping and moaning and rocking with the force of Moro's body inside his.

"How long?" he groaned. "How long do we have?"

"It's big, the museum. They are many storerooms, many chambers," Moro panted. "The guards know the basement well. They move swiftly. Once they discover that someone has accessed the area, you'll have two, perhaps three minutes to find the room containing the Min artifacts, locate the key of Min and get out before the guards catch you."

"Or else?"

"Or else next time someone's fucking your hot, tight, American ass, it'll be inside an Egyptian prison."

At that moment, all Daniel West could think about was getting his hands on Shane's hot, tight, American ass.

All Shane could think about was tearing the clothes off the handsome British reporter's body. He pulled frantically at Daniel's belt buckle, unsnapping it and ripping open his pants. Their lips were still locked, their tongues now probing and pushing and hungrily lapping up every inch of each other's mouth. Shane pushed down Daniel's trousers and underpants and a thrill shot through his body.

A beautifully shaped, quickly swelling cock bounced out from between Daniel's muscular legs.

Shane pulled himself out of the kiss and stole a moment to watch Daniel's cock stiffen and rise with each passing second. Frantically, he untied his robe, letting it drop to reveal his hardened cowboy's body, his own cock thick and stiff.

Daniel's glasses instantly steamed up. With a quivering hand he swiftly snatched them from his face to get a better view. It didn't last.

Shane was already dropping to his knees, as though he was about to pray, but instead of joining his palms together, he seized Daniel's upwardly curved cock in a fistlike clench. The Texan opened his lips wide and took the head of Daniel's cock in his watering mouth.

Daniel let out a groan, still trembling slightly, and tilted his head back. His hands reached down. One found a tuft of Shane's short blond hair, the other settled on Shane's thick shoulder and squeezed it hard as the cowboy devoured first his head, then his entire shaft with no shortage of expertise or assurance. As Shane began to slide his wet, warm, welcoming mouth up and down the young reporter's cock, Daniel realized that Shane had done this before—many times.

The Texas cowboy began to play with his own cock. It was wet and slippery with all the steam in the room and his fist slipped back and forth quickly and easily. He could taste Daniel's precum in his mouth now, sweet and salty and slightly sticky, and it made him even harder. He began thrusting his head back and forth faster. He took Daniel's cock into his throat as far as it would go, his chin tapping against Daniel's large round balls. He pulled back quickly and teased Daniel's head with his tongue, then swallowed the shaft again and again and again. At the same time, Shane was slapping his own wet cock as hard and fast as he could, making a loud clapping sound that echoed off the stone floor.

Daniel didn't hear it. His ears were filled with the deafening roar of his own adrenaline pounding through his head. He groaned again as Shane began to grind his lips— his teeth—up and down the length of Daniel's cock.

"Oh, God! Harder!" Daniel panted. The pain was dizzying, the ecstasy excruciating. He was doing his best just to keep his knees from buckling beneath him. He wasn't simply trembling anymore, he was beginning to quake all over.

He felt his balls tighten and quickly ascend.

He felt the head of his cock balloon, ready to explode in Shane's throat.

And just when Daniel thought he couldn't take any more, Shane swiftly ran his free hand up Daniel's inner thigh, between his ass cheeks, and plunged two slippery wet fingers straight up into his anus.

Daniel's entire body lifted—

His balls erupted—

And with one almighty blast after another, he blew four hot, huge loads of cum directly into the back of Shane's throat.

"Fuck!" Daniel cried. "Oh, *fuck!*"

Shane locked his lips around the base of Daniel's shaft, trapping the fluid like a reservoir of cum and swallowing it down as fast as he could in giant gulps. It was thick and spicy and slid down his throat in great juicy globules.

The taste was all Shane needed to fire off his own load.

The first jet of Shane's cum shot between Daniel's legs and slapped against the stone floor. The second and third loads catapulted even higher, splashing against Daniel's shins and inner thighs.

Shane gave a muffled grunt—his mouth still full with Daniel's engorged cock—and an extended, ecstatic sigh escaped his nostrils.

With Shane's fingers still fixed firmly up his tightly tensed ass, his cock swollen and spent in Shane's mouth, and the Texan's cum all warm and sticky against his legs, Daniel slowly lowered himself down from the tips of his toes.

Delicately, tenderly, Shane eased Daniel's cock from his mouth and slid his finger out of Daniel's ass.

Around them, the steam swirled and slowly settled once more into a soft, still, white veil. Shane rose from his knees and stood before Daniel, both of them panting and smiling. "Are you sure you want to know more about the pyramid?"

Their lips met once more, now with the sweet flavor of semen, then Daniel whispered, "If you're off in search of something, I'll follow you wherever you're going."

Sweat raced down Will's face. Moro was pounding so hard into the college quarterback now that the young man's entire body was charged with pain and pleasure. Will's fingers clung to the edge of the rock pool, his fingernails digging desperately into the roughly laid stones. The water lapped and slapped against his back and Moro's chest in a torrent between their merging and converging bodies. With every thrust of Moro's cock, a strained, enraptured cry escaped Will's lungs.

"Harder," he whispered breathlessly. "*Harder!*"

But the heaving Moro could go no harder. Nor could he go much longer.

He felt the surge of cum swell in his balls. He groaned, sensing the closeness of his orgasm.

Will too knew the moment had come. He gripped the rock ledge firmly, bracing himself, and watched his throbbing, unrestrained cock through the tumultuous green water. Its head bulged, making way for an inevitable underwater eruption.

Suddenly, from behind him, Moro let out an orgasmic cry.

He grabbed a firm hold of Will's hips in both hands and rammed his cock all the way inside the young American as an uncontrollable jolt rocked his body.

Will felt the already burning temperature rise deep inside him, as the head of Moro's condom filled with his fiery fluid.

At the same time, Will's body quivered and spasmed, and an explosion of cum jetted from his cock through the wild green water. He watched the white stream twist and dance through the pool, one long ribbon of cum followed by another—followed by another.

Will cried out, his chest heaving with pleasure.

Moro's arms suddenly wrapped themselves around him, his cock hard and full inside the young man, his lips close to Will's ear, his breath brushing past Will's hair. "Tonight. Eight o'clock."

The first dart whistled through the air and brushed past Jake's hair, missing his ear by a fraction of an inch.

Naked and unarmed, Jake backed up fast, but there was nowhere to run and no place to hide in the small stone room.

Ra quickly slipped a second dart into his long, thin blowpipe and pressed it to his lips.

Jake realized he had only one option: charge, and do his damnedest to fight him off before he cornered him like a rabbit.

He kicked into action, sprinting as fast as he could toward his attacker. He dodged the second dart, then leapt over the stone table in the center of the room, vaulting over it like a gymnast before slamming straight into Ra's chest.

Both men went crashing to the ground.

Ra landed with a heavy thump. The blowpipe flew from his grip and rattled across the floor. Jake grabbed for it, but Ra seized the American's wrist and twisted it. A cry of pain echoed through the chamber.

Before Ra could snap his wrist bones, Jake managed to plant his foot directly into Ra's nose.

The large man's head rocked back on his neck. The blow was enough of a shock for him to release his grip on Jake's wrist, but not enough for more than a second or two.

Jake was on his feet. So was Ra. Jake scrambled for the pipe, but Ra's boot suddenly connected with Jake in the ribs.

The air was knocked clean out of him and Jake reeled unsteadily.

Ra scooped up the pipe and reached into his coat for another dart.

That was Jake's cue to get out. Now!

He staggered for the door as fast as he could, bursting out of the room and into the maze of passageways that snaked through the Blue Hamam. He charged back through the misty depths of the building, up ancient stone stairs and along narrow, twisting corridors. He no longer noticed the sound of water dripping and trickling in unseen crannies and dark corners, nor the eerie wail of the distant chant mingling with the swirling steam. All he could hear now was the fast, heavy thud of Ra's boots on the stone floor behind him—

—and the high-pitched whistle of another dart flying through the air.

This time, there was no hope of dodging the shot. The corridor was too narrow and Jake's shoulders too broad, and before he had a chance to so much as duck, the needle-sharp point of the dart buried itself in his right shoulder blade.

Jake winced and turned, only to be met with another dart.

It thumped into his chest, piercing the skin in his left pectoral and drawing a trickle of blood.

Jake stared down in horror at the dart protruding from his chest, then shot an enraged glare at Ra. "You son of a bitch!" He snatched the dart from his body and it fell from his suddenly feeble grip.

Ra laughed.

Jake's head began spinning almost instantly. His shoulder sank into the wall beside him, his legs went weak.

At that moment, a shaft of light fell upon him. It was sunlight, bright and blinding. He could hear the noisy sounds of the busy Cairo streets filter in with the light.

As Jake's vision began to quickly blur, he made out the shape of an old man carrying a bundle of towels, entering the bathhouse from a side door that evidently led outside. Before his legs gave way completely, Jake pushed past the old man and staggered out through the open door, out into the stark afternoon light.

He took one step, then another, kicking up dust from the bustling alley he had stumbled into. He could barely see at all now, his vision nothing but dizzying smears of saturated colors. He heard voices echoing all around him, laughing.

He realized—vaguely—that he was still naked. But he didn't care. He was having trouble breathing, and even more trouble standing on his feet. Suddenly his large muscled legs buckled and Jake dropped to his knees. Everything in his view swirled, and in the next second he was flat on the ground, his limp torso twisted in a naked, barely conscious heap in the busy alley.

Before he slipped into complete darkness, Jake heard the deep, resonant laughter of his enemy once more. Ra had followed him out into the light and was standing over him now, as the street vendors and passersby gathered and laughed and pointed at what they thought was another drunk American tourist passed out on the ground.

"Don't worry," Ra muttered, indifferent to whether Jake could hear him now. "The darts are not fatal. This is a warning: you are being watched. Every step. Every move. Every mile. Just find the pyramid. It's worth Sam's life, and the life of anyone else who stands between you and Imhotep's lost treasure."

And with that, he turned and walked away, leaving Jake lying naked and unconscious in the dust beneath the hot Egyptian sun.

VIII

Paris, France

THE PROFESSOR LISTENED TO EACH IMPATIENT STEP AS Sam paced back and forth with his arms crossed and his fingers drumming anxiously against his young, still growing biceps. "I could've gone with them, you know. I could've gone to Brazil, or Egypt for that matter!"

The Professor was standing at the window of the hotel suite as though he was looking out. "Yes," he nodded. "You could have. And as the poison made its way through your veins toward your heart, you would have slowed them down, hindering their every effort to find the pyramid, obtain the antidote from Monsieur Perron, and save your life."

The Professor turned and made his way toward Sam, his face composed of wisdom, frankness, and a good dose of sarcasm. "Yes, young Samuel. What a fool I was not allowing you to tag along."

"Don't call me that," Sam grunted. "My name's Sam. Just Sam."

Frustrated, he took the Professor's place at the window, staring at the traffic outside. At that moment, the door opened and Elsa barreled in, her arms filled with parcels of pastries, both savory and sweet. She seemed flustered. Her cheeks were pink and her ample bosom heaved breathlessly.

"*Gott in Himmel!*" she panted, shaking her head and flopping her parcels on the coffee table. "The streets of Paris are *verrückt!* I nearly lost my strudels under a school bus! Too many cars! Big ones, little ones, fast ones, loud ones—"

"And black ones," Sam cut in, gazing out the window. "Long, black, evil-lookin' ones with tinted windows."

The Professor immediately picked up the hint of alarm in the young man's tone. "Sam? What can you see?"

"A big black limo just pulled up across the street and one nasty-lookin' chauffeur just got out. Jesus, he's one mean, ugly son of a bitch!"

"Mind your language!" Elsa barked, rushing over to the window. Then, in a monotone of dread, she uttered, "Oh, Professor, I think we have company."

Across the road, the hulking chauffeur in a tight-fitting suit was already opening the rear door of the black stretch limousine, allowing a stout Frenchman with a stout cigar in his chops to clamber his way out of the car. The fat little passenger grinned and waved at the window where Elsa and Sam stood gawking. Elsa saw instantly that half the man's index finger was missing.

"Oh, Professor," she gasped. "I think it's him."

"Him who?" Sam asked uneasily.

"If I'm not mistaken, that 'him' is Pierre Perron," the Professor answered.

Suddenly Sam's nervousness turned to anger. "That goddamn motherfu—" He didn't even finish before he spun from the window and bolted for the door.

"Samuel, no!"

But the Professor's words didn't stop him, nor could Elsa's reaching arm grab him in time. Sam was already out the door, racing down the stairs of the hotel, charging through the lobby and out through the hotel doors. He shot across the busy street to a symphony of screeching brakes and blasting horns.

He charged straight up to Perron, who was standing beside his black limousine, chortling and snorting through his cigar.

"Why, you bastard, I'm gonna kill you with my own two—"

As Sam lunged, Perron's big, ugly chauffeur seized him, twisting both his arms behind his back, threatening to break them with one powerful jerk.

Perron laughed even harder. "Forgive me for my derision, but you're going to kill me with your own two what?" He plucked the cigar out of his mouth and flicked it disdainfully at Sam. "Look at you! You want to be just like Jake, don't you. All brawn without the brains."

"Don't you talk about Jake, you oversized piece of shit!" Sam growled in pain as the chauffeur tightened his grip on the double armlock.

"I'd stop struggling if I were you. Mr. Goodwin here had to retire from boxing after killing a man in the ring. To say he still harbors a little rage over the incident would be an understatement. You've heard all that prattle about floating butterflies and stinging bees? Mr. Goodwin simply tears his enemies apart, limb from limb." At the mere mention of it, the colossal Mr. Goodwin made a low, guttural sound that was barely human. Sam turned his head to catch a glimpse of the man holding him captive. Mr. Goodwin's eyes were tiny angry beads, his nose looked like it had been broken a dozen times, and his jaw looked as though it was made of steel—in fact it was, after being pulverized in a fight four years earlier.

Just then, Elsa came rushing out of the Hotel Descartes, leading the Professor by the hand and calling out frantically. "Sam! Sam, come back!"

Perron watched, even more amused, as the large panicky German woman and the blind old Professor weaved precariously through the busy traffic to cross the street. "And to think, Jake was always so reluctant to do my bidding. Now look at the company he keeps. I suppose there's no accounting for taste."

"If you think you're so damn smart," Sam scowled, "how come you've only got nine and a half fingers, Stumpy?"

Perron's smug grin slowly sank into a hateful sneer. He reached calmly inside his jacket pocket and produced a small vial filled with a clear liquid.

At that point Elsa and the Professor reached the pavement. Elsa froze, knowing instantly what was inside the vial—as did Sam.

"I only have nine and a half fingers," Perron stated in a cold, clear voice, glaring in the Professor's direction, "because his men shot the missing half off before sending my Venetian mansion to the bottom of the Grand Canal." He turned back to Sam. "You see, my little friend, you're the innocent victim of other people's malevolent actions. If you're looking for someone to blame for what's happening to you, look no further than the self-righteous old man beside you."

"I ain't your little friend, so why don't you tell your apeman to let me go!"

Mr. Goodwin simply tightened his grip. Sam cried out in pain.

"Pierre, that's enough!" interjected the Professor. "My men are already searching for the Lost Pyramid."

"For the boy's sake I hope they find it," Perron smirked, then shook the tiny shimmering vial from side to side. "Tick-tock, tick-tock. Time is slipping away. Which is why

I'm here. I'd like you to join me at my villa in the south of France. You have the ailment, I have the remedy. Call it an intervention, if you will. Although, make no mistake, unless your men find the Lost Pyramid of Imhotep, my villa will be your final resting place."

"Swine!" Elsa breathed with sheer revulsion.

"Elsa, it's all right," the Professor said with an even tone.

Sam twisted his head to give the Professor a stunned glare. "You're not seriously gonna listen to this"—he struggled for the right insult, then nodded to Elsa as if asking for permission to use her word—"swine!"

"Samuel, think about it rationally. He has the antidote. If it comes to it, if seconds matter, we want that antidote as close at hand as possible."

"Are you crazy? He's kidnapping us! And we're letting him!"

"Not all of you," Perron interjected, then gave Elsa a sour look. "The goulash cook can stay. I've never had a taste for peasant food."

"I'll call the police!" she threatened.

The Professor shook his head. "Elsa, no. You'll only make matters worse. Stay here. Wait for us to return."

"But—!"

The Professor took her firmly by the arm. "Wait for us. *All* of us!"

Elsa listened to what he was saying, then clamped her mouth shut.

"We bid you adieu," Perron said, waving to Elsa, then nodded to Mr. Goodwin, who tossed Sam onto the back seat of the limousine. The Professor refused help, and willingly climbed in beside Sam. Mr. Goodwin slammed the door shut behind them before Perron joined his chauffeur in the front of the limousine.

The doors all locked. Sam tried to roll down the windows,

but they were sealed shut. The sleek black car pulled clear of the curb and sped away, leaving Elsa to watch helplessly from the pavement.

Elsa opened the door to the suite the moment she heard the knock. It was Luca, expecting a smile, maybe even a hug. But all he got was Elsa's frantic ramblings.

"Oh, Luca, thank God! The Professor's been taken. Eden's on his way to Brazil. Will, Jake, and Shane have gone in search of the Lost Pyramid in Egypt. And if they don't find it, he said he'd kill Sammy and the Professor!"

Luca gently sat Elsa in a chair. "Elsa, calm down! Who'll kill the Professor? Who's Sammy? You have to slow down and start from the beginning."

So she did. Elsa took a deep breath and told him everything. Luca listened carefully and calmly to every word, formulating plans in his head with each piece of information he gathered. At the end of it Elsa reached into the pocket of her apron and pulled out a watch. It was Luca's global tracking watch.

"This will take you to him. The Professor said it's accurate to within two hundred meters." She took his hand then, placed the watch in his palm, and said, "Make sure nothing happens to him. Promise me nothing will happen to him."

Luca nodded. "Stay here. Stay by the phone. I'll be back. We'll all be back. I promise."

IX

Cairo, Egypt

THE DOOR TO THE HOTEL ROOM FLEW OPEN AND SHANE and Will hurriedly carried a naked, unconscious Jake to the bed. They laid him out on his back as Daniel hastily shut the door behind them. None of the hotel staff had seen them move swiftly in through the back exit of the building, and now that they were safely inside, Shane closed the curtains too and fastened the lock on the door.

"What's going on?" Daniel asked. "Is he okay?"

"I dunno yet. But I think it's safe to say someone out there is after us."

"Ra," Jake breathed. His eyelids danced open and his eyeballs rolled wildly in his head.

Shane dropped down beside the bed. "Will, quick! Get a wet towel!"

"Ra!" Jake panted again. "He's the one! The one who shot Sammy!"

Will returned from the bathroom with the towel. "He's

got a puncture wound here on his chest," he observed, his fingers swiftly tracing their way over Jake's body. He rolled Jake's shoulders over. "And another one here."

"It's not... It's not deadly... I'll be fine..." Jake managed.

"How do you know?"

"He doesn't want to kill us. The pyramid... It's too important to them..."

Will dabbed at the wounds. "Then why the hell is he shooting you full of darts?"

"He's letting us know who's the boss," Jake said, wincing with giddy pain. He tried his hardest to sit up, but his head rolled around on his neck and he swooned, his strength completely drained.

"Easy, tiger!" Shane muttered, catching him before he hit the bed and easing his head back onto the pillow.

Will glanced at his watch. "The Curator's Ball starts in an hour. Moro's expecting three of us to stand in as waiters."

"I'll be...okay..." Jake uttered. "No time to lose..."

"Jake, there's no way you're up to it."

"I am," Daniel announced, standing guard near the door.

Will looked at Daniel, then at Shane, then shook his head. "No offense, dude, but we're on a very tight schedule here, our friend has just been shot with poison darts, and I don't know who the hell you are."

"I told you," Shane said. "His name is Daniel West. He's a—"

"Reporter. I know, I heard you the first time."

"You were the one who said we needed to rewrite history. Who better to help us than a goddamn writer!"

"Who's to say he doesn't work for Perron? How do we know his pen isn't filled with poison?"

"Actually, I prefer to use pencils," Daniel interjected matter-of-factly, adjusting his glasses. "And I work for the *London Town Crier*."

"I don't care if you work for the *New York Times*. It doesn't mean I trust you."

"Well, I do," Shane announced firmly.

Will stopped.

Silence fell over the room.

Jake was the first to break it. "We have to save Sammy..." was all he said.

Will took a deep breath. He bit his bottom lip and looked Daniel squarely in the eye. "If you slow us down, we leave you behind. If you screw up, you're on your own. We need to find this key, and we need to find that pyramid." He turned to Shane and asked, "Agreed?"

Shane nodded, a little reluctantly. Will was taking the hard line, but he was right. The handsome Texan looked at Daniel. "Are you sure you wanna do this?"

Daniel smiled and nodded at them both. "This is the story of a lifetime. If there's one thing you can be sure of, I won't be screwing up. And you won't be leaving me behind."

Midan Tahrir in central Cairo was choked with traffic and onlookers, and as the sun melted into the distant desert, the twilight over Egypt's bustling capital turned a hazy pink, the same color as the façade of the Museum of Egyptian Antiquities. Cavalcades of dignitaries and politicians arrived at the front entrance of the museum by limousine. Processions of local celebrities with press photographers in tow made their way across the cordoned-off street from the Nile Hilton Hotel.

Shane, Will, and Daniel avoided it all and met Moro's contact beside the loading dock at the rear of the museum, where the caterers were busy unloading dozens of crates and cartons for the party. People everywhere were shouting orders, lugging trolleys, directing deliveries, and jumping out of the way of reversing trucks. Amid the buzz and chaos, Moro's contact escorted them inside and led them into the staff changing rooms, where he handed them their waiter's uniforms and told them to change quickly.

"I'll say this quickly, so listen carefully," he whispered as the three men snapped off their shirts and jeans and pulled on their uniforms. "My name is Kamil. At precisely nine o'clock the guards change shifts, at which time the cleaner will steal a swipe card from the master control room. At five minutes past nine, I will walk through the main chamber and leave the key on a tray on the third side table on the west wall."

"The main chamber?" Will interrupted. "Isn't that where the party is?"

Kamil nodded. "There are security guards everywhere. If I hand you a key, we run the risk of being seen. If we meet someone out of the way, we run the risk of getting caught. But if you are picking up a tray of empty champagne glasses in the middle of the party, you are simply doing your job. Once you have the swipe card, take the stairs in the northwest corner leading down to the basement. The swipe card will get you into the storerooms downstairs. It will also trigger an intruder alarm."

Will nodded. "Moro mentioned that."

"All the Min artifacts are in Room 369. But you'll have to be quick."

Will nodded again. "Moro mentioned that too."

"Once you have the Min key, get out as fast as you can. Moro has arranged a boat. It will be waiting for you at the marina on Sharia Corniche El-Nil at the southern end of Old Cairo. Be there by midnight."

"Thank you," Will said, tying his bow tie as Shane buckled his belt and Daniel tied his shoelaces.

Kamil smiled. "Good luck, my friends. I hope you find what you're looking for."

In the main gallery of the museum, the walls were lined with one gold sarcophagus after another, while the showpiece of the main chamber was a recently unearthed clay goose, dating back to 2500 BC and miraculously intact. The plump life-sized statue nested proudly inside a glass case in the center of the room.

At one end of the chamber, a string quartet played. At the other end, an army of diligent waiters flowcd in and out of a preparation area that had been set up as the caterers' kitchen, carrying trays filled with champagne, canapés, and caviar for the four hundred guests of the Curator's Ball. Among the waiters were Will, Shane, and Daniel, serving the multitudes of partygoers silently and swiftly, avoiding any eye contact and conversation while glancing constantly at their watches, anxiously counting down the minutes.

At one minute to nine, Will saw Kamil vanish into the kitchen.

From somewhere near the center of the room, Shane noticed too. He shot Will a glance and saw a minute tilt of the head—a signal for the two of them to reposition themselves near the west wall of the chamber, ready for a rendezvous with Kamil and his tray.

Shane took a step in Will's direction when suddenly, from somewhere behind him, a man with a pompous English accent blasted, "Excuse me, waiter! Do you speak English?"

Shane grimaced and tried to ignore it. He took another step away from the berating voice.

"Waiter! I'm talking to you!"

Shane froze. Slowly he turned to see a stout, smug man in a jacket and cravat, waving a half-empty champagne glass in one hand and holding up a half-eaten hors d'oeuvre in the other. Several people in his tight little circle snickered. The man took it as encouragement to act even more arrogant. "I said, do you speak English?"

"Yes, sir," Shane muttered, trying hard to hide his Texan drawl.

"Then you'll understand my utter revulsion when I tell you this foie gras is tart." The man held the hors d'oeuvre up in disgust. "Do you even know what foie gras is, waiter?"

Shane desperately wanted to back out of the confrontation. He, Will, and Daniel were about to rob one the biggest museums in the world of one of its artifacts; the last thing he needed right know was an abusive asshole with too much Moët in him.

"Sir, I'll take it back to the kitchen immediately for you," Shane murmured apologetically.

He moved to take the hors d'oeuvre from the man, but before his fingers could grab it, the man smiled disdainfully and quite intentionally let it drop to the floor.

The foie gras landed with a soft splat. The man's friends laughed out loud as he groaned theatrically. "Oh, pick that up now, would you. The sight of it's making me sick!"

Shane quickly dropped to his knees.

Above him, the fat man in the cravat continued to talk down to him. "The curator will be most displeased with the muck you're serving us tonight. I daresay foie gras is on the menu in honor of his latest treasure, *The Fattened Goose*. But this tripe makes me want to spit up! It's put a foul taste in my mouth!" The man began laughing hysterically at his own pun, and his flock of friends quickly joined in. "Foul! Get it? Oh, I'm too clever for my own good!"

Shane began to scoop the foie gras quickly onto his tray. He discreetly checked his watch. It was three minutes past nine.

Across the room, Will had lost sight of Shane. Desperately he checked his watch and started to move toward the west wall when suddenly he heard—

"William?"

He knew that voice!

Will spun around, startled and feeling suddenly nauseous to see a handsome, distinguished, well-dressed gentleman with silver hair staring at him with the same surprised look as Will. The similarity between the two was striking—and undeniable.

"Dad!" Will gulped. His voice was high, his tone nervous, and suddenly he felt seven years old again.

As Charles Hunter, diplomatic advisor to the U.S. Consulate in Cairo, frowned at his son in utter confusion, Will's mission—the swipe card, the room full of Min artifacts, the quest to find the Lost Pyramid of Imhotep—left his thoughts completely, and the only thing remaining inside his head was: *I'm in trouble...again!*

Meanwhile, at the center of the room, the drunk, arrogant drivel continued while Shane knelt, frantically cleaning the foie gras off the floor. The fat man was determined to show off his superiority. "Did you know, waiter, the ancient Egyptians invented foie gras almost five thousand years ago?"

Shane said nothing, knowing the seconds—and his patience—were quickly slipping away.

"Indeed," the fat man slurred, "the ancient Egyptians were the first to force-feed their ducks and geese to engorge their livers, ramming grains and maize down their stupid little throats until they died. Obviously today we do it with machines. Lots of tubes, I imagine. It's all in the name of good taste and fine food. The very thought of it makes my mouth water. Can you imagine how plump and juicy their livers get? Can you imagine that, waiter?"

Shane gritted his teeth and muttered, "No, sir."

"Perhaps you should try some. Perhaps while you're down there, you should lick some up off the floor."

The laughter from above made Shane's blood boil. He clenched his jaw and swallowed back his rage, kneeling motionless for a moment over the foie gras smeared on the floor. "No, thank you, sir," was his only reply.

"Of course not," came the disdainful sneer from above.

"Even bad foie gras splattered on the floor is too good for you."

Taking a long, deep breath, Shane slowly stood to his full height, and for the first time he leveled his stern gaze straight at the man in the cravat.

The laughter abruptly stopped and suddenly the smug Englishman appeared less certain of himself.

A dozen apt responses ran through Shane's head, most of them involving his clenched fist. But he knew the seconds were ticking away—he knew their window of opportunity to find the key of Min was getting smaller by the minute—and so, with all the discipline and strength he could muster, Shane turned his back on the man in the cravat and began to walk away.

Unfortunately, the man in the cravat took this as a show of defeat.

"Go on, then," came that smug voice once more, again filled with overconfidence for the amusement of his giggling friends. "Go back to your kitchen and kill me another fat goose. God knows, the last one died for nothing!"

Shane halted in midstep. He turned, looked the man dead in the eye, and snarled, "No, sir. With all due respect, the only fat goose here tonight is you!"

The wave of shock could be heard throughout the chamber, but William and Charles Hunter were themselves in a state of shock and far too preoccupied to notice anything else.

"Dad? What are you doing here?"

Charles overstated the obvious. "Son, I work for the U.S. Consulate! I was posted here eighteen months ago, you know that!"

Yes, Will did know that. But the day he received his father's letter was a day he had tried hard to forget. Right now, the young man's head was dizzy with disbelief, but Charles was already badgering him.

"And what's this?" he was staring in shock at Will's uniform. "You're working as a waiter now? In Cairo? What's the matter with you, son! Is this what you do with my money? Throw it away on overseas jaunts, picking up good-for-nothing jobs here and there, working as paid help in Egypt—does this amuse you? You're not some working-class, backpacking, drug-smoking freeloader, are you, William? I won't stand for it! What about your college education?"

Out of the corner of his eye, Will caught sight of Kamil passing through the crowd and stopping at the third side table on the west wall. He set down a tray and walked away, and suddenly Will's purpose came flooding back to him.

"Dad, I know this looks weird, but I'll explain later."

Quickly he turned to leave, but his father's hand shot out and seized him firmly by the forearm.

"No, young man! You'll explain yourself right now!"

At the center of the room, the fat man in the cravat and his friends stood aghast, not sure what to do or say as their furious waiter stormed toward the smug Englishman, who was now beginning to cower.

"I'm a personal friend of the curator," the fat man blathered feebly, trying to stand his ground despite his quivering voice. "I won't just have you fired. Take one step closer and I'll have you arrested."

"And if you say one more word, the next thing that lands on the floor will be you!"

The fat man gasped. "Is that a threat?"

Shane couldn't help but smile as he pulled back his fist. "No. But this is."

By the west wall, Will tried to pull himself free from his father. He saw a security guard across the room spy the tray on the side table. He saw the guard's eyes land on the swipe card sitting among the empty glasses on the tray.

Suddenly Will panicked. "Dad, you have to let me go!"

Charles hissed back, his voice hushed and angry. "No! Enough of this foolishness! I'm here with dignitaries from all over the world, and my son is here in a waiter's uniform!" He glanced sideways to a large man in a suit who was watching him with concern, though keeping his distance. The man was obviously some sort of bodyguard. Charles glared at Will sternly. "You're about to embarrass me on an international level, do you understand that?"

"Dad, trust me. This isn't about you!"

"It will be if you don't get out of that ridiculous outfit and get the hell out of here. You think I work my ass off so you can jet around the world goofing off? You need a reality check, William. I've got a good mind to send you to military academy, young man. Don't think I can't arrange it!"

"Dad! I'm nineteen!"

"Well, you're acting like you did when you were twelve!"

"How would you know? You weren't even around when I was twelve. Felix raised me!"

Charles scoffed. "Get out of here! You're embarrassing yourself!"

"Then let go of my arm!"

Charles didn't even realize he was still holding on.

"That's the way it's always been with you, isn't it, Dad! You never want anything to do with me, yet I'm forever in your grip. Why don't you let me go?"

Across the room, Daniel saw Will struggling to get out of the grip of an angry, distinguished man in a dinner jacket.

He saw the tray on the side table and the guard heading directly for it.

And then he heard a loud *thwack!*—

—followed by gasps and screams.

He turned and saw the follow-through of a punch thrown by Shane directly into the face of a shocked fat man in a cravat who was now reeling backward, teetering on trembling, unsteady legs and stumbling directly into the glass case containing *The Fattened Goose*.

The glass smashed under the weight of the fat, flailing Englishman, who fell straight into the casing and knocked the ancient clay goose off its perch.

A deafening, whirring alarm sounded on impact.

Women squealed in panic.

Champagne glasses hit the floor and exploded.

The goose plunged to the ground and shattered into a hundred pieces.

Security guards pulled their weapons as people everywhere began to rush and scream and shout in fear. Civility disintegrated into utter chaos.

Daniel was already charging through the pushing, frenzied mob, scrambling for the swipe card on the tray.

Charles Hunter turned in a panic and was swooped upon by the nearby bodyguard, who hauled him away. "Sir, we need to get you out of here now! Back door!" He hauled Charles away, pushing forcefully through the screaming crowd. But Charles still had a lock on Will's arm.

"Dad! Let me go!" Will tried to pull himself free as hard as he could.

In the center of the room, the fat man flapped and floundered on the stand that once held *The Fattened Goose*, squealing helplessly as three security guards pounced on him.

At the same time, one of the fat man's friends shouted, "It was him!"

Shane saw a finger point at him through the panicked crowd, and two more security guards lunged at him. He nailed one square in the stomach with a right hook and knocked the other clear off his feet with a high kick to the chest.

He looked around wildly, trying to spot the others through the pandemonium. He caught sight of Daniel racing for the tray on the side table.

Daniel's hand seized the swipe card.

"Stay there!" Shane shouted to him through the crowd.

Daniel heard him. He looked over the throng to see Shane start to push his way toward him, then suddenly all he saw was a fist coming straight at him.

Pow!

The security guard who had spotted the swipe card earlier now appeared directly in front of Daniel and delivered a blow straight into Daniel's face.

He dropped the key and reeled backward.

The security guard dealt him another blow, this time to Daniel's stomach. The British reporter doubled over.

At the same time, the security guard pulled his weapon and took a step back to steady his aim.

Suddenly a leg came from nowhere, snapping upward through the air, kicking the gun clean out of the guard's hand.

Through his blurred, spinning vision, Daniel caught sight of Shane just as the cowboy threw a knockout punch directly into the guard's jaw.

As the guard slammed against the floor, unconscious, Shane scooped up the swipe card in one hand and Daniel in the other. "Come on!"

He looked desperately for Will and saw him being dragged away with the current of panicked partygoers, heading toward the back of the chamber. Behind Shane, half a dozen more security guards were closing in. He tracked Will's head bobbing through the crowd and shouted at the top of his lungs, "Will!"

Will heard Shane's voice and cocked his head.

"Will! Go long!"

Shane held up the swipe card, then hurled it long and far, high above the heads of the panic-stricken crowd.

Will locked onto the small object flying through the room and kept his eye on the ball. Then, with one final jerk, the young quarterback pulled himself free of his father's hold and scrambled through the crowd to intercept the swipe card.

It soared over everyone's heads, then began its descent into the throng a few feet away from him.

Will launched himself as high as he could. His hand shot out. His fingers locked onto the swipe card. He clenched it in his fist, then came crashing down into the crowd, taking out two men and a plump lady in a tiara. More people screamed.

Will jumped to his feet and helped the lady up, with a quick apology. He straightened the tiara on her head and vanished into the crowd, heading straight for the stairs in the northwest corner of the building—the stairs leading down to the basement.

Across the main chamber, Shane grabbed Daniel's hand and pulled him in the opposite direction, away from the charging security guards.

"Where are we going?" Daniel shouted over the chaos.

"Not downstairs. Will can find the key on his own. You and me—we're bait."

Shane didn't see the wide-eyed look on Daniel's face—he was too busy shoving against the madding multitudes to get to the stairs that headed up to the second floor, squeezing Daniel's hand tight and towing him behind.

While Shane and Daniel headed upward, Will bounded down the stairs to the basement, leaping four or five steps at a time. He heard nobody behind him and assumed Shane had set himself up as a decoy to lead the guards in a different direction. He was grateful—it was a smart move that bought him time. A little, at least. But the thought of finding the key of Min among hundreds of thousands of relics—while the entire Egyptian Museum descended into chaos—was a daunting one. Fortunately it was a thought he didn't have time to linger on.

He reached the door to the basement.

He swiped the key, and the small light on the lock turned from red to green.

The door opened and Will charged into a long and winding passageway lined with storerooms on either side, each with a number above the doorway.

"Room 369," he said to himself, remembering Kamil's instructions.

He looked at the number above the first door. It was labeled *Room 1*.

Suddenly a second alarm sounded. The door behind Will snapped locked.

The alarm rang loudly throughout the entire museum. It was not the same sound that was triggered when the glass casing around *The Fattened Goose* was shattered. This was a howling intruder alarm.

In the main chamber it competed with the screaming masses as people tripped over one another to get out, women slipping in their high heels and trampling on each other. They poured out onto Midan Tahrir, crying and panting with fear. The words "terrorist," "bomb," and "man with a gun" ricocheted through the fear-filled crowd.

Charles Hunter's bodyguard did much of the pushing, plowing through the crowd and evacuating his employer from the premises as swiftly and as safely as possible before hurrying him down the side of the building, away from the chaos.

Charles was looking back, angry and startled by the entire event. "My son! Where's that damn boy gone!"

"Sir, stay here," the bodyguard ordered. "I've called the car."

But there was no immediate sign of the vehicle.

"Sir, remain here." With that firm command, the bodyguard ran back to the corner to signal the two headlights that sped around the turn, ready to whisk the U.S. diplomatic advisor away. The bodyguard was only gone thirty seconds.

But thirty seconds was all it took for a poison dart to shoot through the night and slam into the side of Charles Hunter's neck, and for his hand to smack the dart against his neck as though it was a mosquito, before his eyes rolled back in his head. Out of the shadows, a large man swept in and caught the U.S. advisor before he hit the pavement, unconscious.

By the time the bodyguard and the speeding headlights arrived, Charles Hunter had simply vanished.

Inside the museum, Shane and Daniel raced up the staircase to the second story. Over the shrill sound of the security alarm they could hear the thunder of heavy boots echoing up the stairs behind them. There were perhaps a dozen security guards on their tails now, maybe more.

Shane and Daniel hit the top of the stairs and Shane tightened his grip on Daniel's hand. "This way."

They charged past glass cabinets exhibiting splintered vases, ancient dented jewelry, and small golden idols. They sprinted past one sealed sarcophagus after another, scanning the room for the nearest escape route. The pounding footsteps grew louder and louder as the guards neared the top of the stairs.

Shane and Daniel dashed by a life-sized display of ancient Egypt. Daniel caught it out of the corner of his eye. It was a snapshot of life on the Nile, with several naked wax Egyptians fishing at the edge of a shallow pool, unaware of a nearby crocodile—the pride of the taxidermy department—about to strike.

Daniel suddenly pulled Shane up with a sharp snap on his arm.

"Take off your clothes," he said above the screaming alarm.

"What!" Shane exclaimed.

Down in the basement, the corridor twisted and turned like a maze. Will ran as fast as he could, counting the numbers above the doors, trying to make sense of a numerical order which seemed to start and stop and spin off in different directions. He lost track of the sequence three times before he found it:

Room 369.

He wiped the sweat from his brow, swiped the card in the lock, and pushed the door open.

For a moment he simply stood there, panting breathlessly and staring wide-eyed at the room before him.

It was small, with a low ceiling, four blinking fluorescent lights, and virtually no room to move on account of all the Mins. There were hundreds of them. Crammed into every corner, filling every last gap. Large Mins, small Mins, gold Mins, marble Mins, Mins of all shapes and sizes, but all fitting the one description of the god of fertility: a tall man with his right arm raised and holding a flail and his left hand gripping his long, erect penis. It was a pose to show his dominance, to assert his masculinity, to prove himself as a giver of life and a god of power.

Standing there, awed and overwhelmed, Will simply whispered, "Holy Min."

Upstairs, Shane was already half naked before he even managed to ask, "What the hell are we doing?"

His abs rippled as he frantically pulled off his trousers. He paused at his underwear, but Daniel said, "Those too. And the watch!"

Daniel himself was already naked, bundling his and Shane's discarded waiter's clothes together and stashing them behind a fake bush in the Nile display. He plucked off his glasses and hid them on the branch of a fake tree along with Shane's watch.

There was yelling and stomping at the top of the stairs at the far end of the gallery. Shane's underwear was still on.

"Hurry!" Daniel pestered, reaching down and yanking Shane's underwear off for him.

Evidently the thrill of the chase and Daniel's sudden take-charge attitude were something of a turn-on for the cowboy. Shane's meaty semihard cock bounced abundantly as his underwear was stripped away.

"Shane, it's not exactly the time for that," Daniel whispered harshly.

"I can't help it! I'm naked...and you're naked...and you're..." Shane's hands were waving up and down Daniel's buff, naked body, trying to speak for him, until the words just blurted out. "Look at you, you're beautiful."

The sounds of trampling, angry guards came echoing through the gallery.

"We're going to be dead, soon! Now come on!"

"What the hell are we doing?"

"I think studying mime at drama school is finally about to pay off."

Daniel dragged Shane to the back of the Nile display and positioned himself and the naked Texan among the wax fishermen.

"Breathe through your mouth. Keep it slow and steady. Don't think of your lungs inflating and deflating, think of the air simply moving through you. Focus your eyes on a point on the floor. Lock your legs into place, and—"

Suddenly the guards arrived, waving their guns and shouting over the alarm.

"—freeze," Daniel finished in a whisper.

As the guards entered the room, Shane and Daniel froze like statues. With the exception of one uncontrollable part of Shane's anatomy.

Downstairs, Will began his desperate search to find the key of Min. He had no clues. No hint of any identifiable markings. No idea of precisely what he was looking for. The only thing he knew for certain was that the key of Min looked exactly like everything else in this room—like Min himself.

In the corridor outside, the distant sound of guards yelling and boots clomping reverberated down the twisting tunnels of the basement. Shane's decoy plan had bought Will a little time, but with alarms sounding all through the building and the Curator's Ball descending into sheer chaos above, the museum was heading into total lockdown.

Will closed the door to Room 369, shutting himself in. But he knew the clock was ticking. The only question was, could Will find the key of Min before the guards found *him*.

Desperately, he began looking and searching and *feeling* his way through the multitude of Mins. His fingers quickly probed the many gold limbs and stone torsos and carved abs and protruding penises—some only millimeters in length, others two or three feet long—trying to find any signs of etchings or markings that could turn one of these idols into a key that would unlock the biggest secret in Egypt's history.

But he could feel nothing—could see nothing—that looked out of the ordinary. Nothing that made him think, *This is it! This is the one!*

In the corridor outside, he heard doors banging open and closed. The guards were checking the rooms, one by one, getting closer and closer.

Will turned for the door, trying to decide whether he had time to keep searching for something he might never find, or he should get the hell out of there while he still could—*if* he still could!

That was when he caught a glimpse of it out of the corner of his eye.

The one statuette—as small as it was, hidden there among the many layers of Mins—that stood out from the others.

Only there wasn't just one of them.

There were two!

Two tiny identical Mins, slightly different from every other Min in the room.

Suddenly the door handle turned.

Upstairs, in the second-story gallery, a single bead of sweat raced down Shane's temple as he stood frozen to the spot alongside Daniel and half a dozen lifeless wax dummies. At that moment, a nearby guard scanning the area turned his gun toward the display.

The alarm was still squealing.

The museum's night lights were dim.

The guard flicked on his flashlight and shone it on the display, then stepped forward for a closer look. Something had caught his eye; something seemed odd, yet he couldn't quite put his finger on it.

As he stepped closer, the other guards in the gallery spread out into adjoining rooms, leaving him alone to inspect the display.

Shane felt another shimmering ball of sweat work its way down his forehead.

He was trying to let the air move through him, just as Daniel had told him, but it wasn't working. He was holding his breath and his lungs were burning.

Worst of all, he could feel his cock getting stiffer and stiffer by the second.

It was growing thicker and gaining altitude.

No matter what he tried to think of—a cold shower on a winter's night, nice old ladies crossing the street, puppies bounding through fields of flowers—it seemed nothing was going to stop that cock of his from reaching its peak.

The guard reached the edge of the display and crouched beside the stuffed, lurking crocodile, shining his flashlight up at the wax fishermen.

He had seen this display many times while walking the

halls at night, and although he had never actually stopped to count them, he could have sworn there used to only be six ancient Egyptians fishing at the edge of the Nile. He certainly didn't remember the one with the buff young body and the short black hair.

And then there was the muscular, tan-skinned blond. The guard shone his flashlight on the dummy's face. Its skin shimmered, as though it was sweating.

He moved the flashlight downward. Slowly the beam of light traced its way down the dummy's large chest, down its rigid abs, down to an astonishingly realistic thatch of blond pubic hair, and then—

The guard gasped as his eyes locked on the biggest, stiffest cock he'd ever seen. Startled, he dropped both the gun and the flashlight. He bent down and clutched the gun first, but when he looked up again, all he saw was the clenched fist of the blond mannequin coming straight at him.

The blow knocked him clean off his feet. The guard landed smack on his back. The gun went off with a random shot.

Shane ducked. The bullet cleared him by an inch and slammed into the wall, but the blast rang out loud enough to alert every other guard in the building.

As the startled guard floundered on his back, clutching at his bleeding nose, Shane grabbed Daniel's wrist. "Time to go!"

"My glasses! Our clothes!" Daniel snatched his glasses and Shane's watch from the fake tree branch, but Shane towed him away before he could grab their clothes.

Naked and moving at lightning speed, the two vanished from the gallery just as the room filled with the swarming guards. Voices shouted and fingers pointed in all directions, but Shane and Daniel were now long gone.

Downstairs, the door to Room 369 swung open.

A lone young security guard stepped inside the room, gun drawn. He saw nothing but countless figures of Min filling the space before him, then, suddenly, the door closed behind him and someone tapped him on the shoulder.

The guard spun around, startled.

The gold and marble Mins watched indifferently as Will's knuckles slammed into the guard's face. The man's legs crumpled. Will caught him, and lowered the unconscious young man to the ground.

"Sorry, pal," he whispered, then quickly began undressing.

The guard's uniform was snug around Will's chest, but it would pass. As he left Room 369, Will Hunter kept his head low and his pace steady. He walked straight past three other guards and straight out the basement exit without raising a single eyebrow. When he reached the street, Midan Tahrir was a circus of police lights and frightened guests being interviewed by the authorities.

Will kept walking. Discreetly he placed his hand over the gun holster on his belt to hide the fact that his weapon was missing. He had left it in Room 369, not by accident but on purpose. He needed the holster to smuggle out his secret cargo—the two small, gold statuettes of Min, each of them no more than five inches high.

Each Min holding a flail in its left hand and an erect penis in its right.

Jake woke with a start as the door to the hotel room burst open. He sat bolt upright, naked and giddy, as two men stormed into the room, each wearing nothing but a shenti, the loincloth of ancient Egyptians.

Jake's vision was blurred, his skull was aching. He couldn't focus; all he could see was the two men rush toward him. He grabbed the lamp on the bedside table and moved to strike. One of the men seized his unsteady arm.

"Whoa! Whoa! Whoa!" came a familiar voice.

"Shane?" Jake squinted, trying to focus. His bleary eyes

looked up and down the Texan's body and settled on the loincloth. "What the hell are you wearing?"

"Courtesy of the museum's costume display. It was on our way out the door. Which is exactly what we need to do right now."

Daniel had already found a pair of jeans and was slipping Jake's legs into them. He grabbed the backpacks off the floor while Shane put one of Jake's arms over his shoulders and helped him to his feet.

"Where are we going?"

"There's a boat waiting for us on the Nile, but we don't have much time."

"Where's Will? Did he get the key?"

"I sure as hell hope so. You know what he's like. Where there's a Will, there's a way."

Even this late in the evening, the side streets and coffee houses of Old Cairo were brimming with life and noise and overflowing with the scent of bubbling shishas. Before heading for the marina on Sharia Corniche El-Nil, Will felt compelled to make a quick detour to the house of Professor Henry Chamberlain.

He could still make it to the boat on time, if he hurried, but first he wanted to show Henry the statuettes. He wanted to share his find. He wanted Henry to know that he was one step closer to discovering the Lost Pyramid.

But when Henry's trusted companion Mikal answered the door, Will knew immediately something was wrong. He could see that Mikal had been crying.

Inside the lavish house, Mikal led Will upstairs to Henry Chamberlain's bedroom. There Will stood for a moment, silent and respectful, staring at the still, peaceful body of Henry Chamberlain lying on the bed.

"What happened?" Will asked.

Mikal sniffed and his chin crumpled, but he managed to

hold his emotions in. "He wouldn't take his oxygen. He said he didn't want it anymore. He didn't need it. He said he was finally free. He said his life's quest was about to be fulfilled, and now he could die happy."

Will took a step closer. Indeed, Henry Chamberlain had a gentle smile on his face.

"He has faith in you," Mikal whispered to Will. "He puts his hope in you." Then the emotion overwhelmed the grieving servant and he burst into tears.

Will hugged him and comforted him till the tears subsided.

Shane, Daniel, and Jake were already aboard the twenty-four-foot cruiser when Will arrived, still dressed in his guard's uniform. Shane and Daniel had changed into cargo shorts and T-shirts now. Jake was asleep below deck in the small sleeping quarters of the cruiser, his body struggling to recover from Ra's poison darts.

"Are you okay?" Shane said, rushing up to Will as he stepped aboard.

"I'm okay," Will said, but his voice was flat and distant.

"What's the matter? Is it the key? Did you find it?"

Will nodded, then pulled the two gold statuettes from his holster. He glanced up at the night sky, and smiled at the diamond stars shimmering in the desert night. "Someone's watching over us now. I have hope."

Shane started the boat's engine. It idled quietly as a young marina attendant untied the lines. "Moro wishes you luck," he said, smiling. "We all do. Get as far down the river as you can before dawn. By day your journey will be much slower—you'll have to avoid the feluccas and merchant barges. You should reach Koptos by midnight tomorrow. Moro has already arranged your transport into the desert to the Temple of Min."

"Thank you," Will said.

The cruiser pulled away from the dock. Will watched the lights of Cairo disappear behind them. He thought about Henry. He thought about Ahnu and his enraged father, Imhotep. And he thought about his own father, and how close he himself had once come to taking that final step, the same desperate measure Ahnu had taken.

All for a father's love.

X

Manaus, Brazil

THE TIGHT URBAN NEST THAT WAS MANAUS HAD LEARNED
to coexist with the endless sprawl of wilderness all around
it. It was a city buried deep in the thick, green rain forests
of northern Brazil, where the continent's two major river
systems—the Amazon and the Rio Negro—converged to
form one river near the city's southern ports; where the
heart of the Amazon beat hard and heavy like the pounding
of nearby jungle drums.

Eden arrived at his hotel to find that a large box had
been delivered to his room. It was black and tied with a
white ribbon, with a card tucked under the bow. Eden slid
the card out and opened it, one eyebrow raised in suspicion.
He read it aloud to himself.

> Dear Mr. Santiago,
> Before you get lost in the rain forest, lose yourself
> in something more civilized. Puccini is playing at
> the Teatro Amazonas tonight at 7 P.M. I would be

honored if you would attend as my guest.

Yours sincerely, Alexander Thorne III

Eden put the card down, untied the ribbon, and cautiously lifted the lid on the box. Inside was a brand-new tuxedo. He held up the jacket. It was tailor-made and looked like a perfect fit.

It seemed that even in the jungle, word traveled fast. He had been in the city for less than an hour, and already Alexander Thorne had tracked him down. They hadn't even met, and already Thorne was exerting his courteous and controlling authority over Eden. Eden checked his watch. It was 5:30 P.M.

He unbuttoned his shirt and slipped off his boots, and dressed only in his khakis, he opened the balcony doors to his room. He stepped out, half naked, into the sultry afternoon air, and spotted the gold-tiled dome of the Teatro Amazonas a few short blocks away. A short distance beyond that, he could see the edge of the small city. It was the line where man and jungle met. Beyond that, there was nothing but the vast, green expanse of the Amazon.

While the sun was setting and the wildlife in the rain forest turned up the volume to signal the end of another day in their dangerous paradise, in the center of Manaus different creatures emerged: dressed in diamond tiaras, silken evening gowns, and perfectly fitting tuxedoes. All were drawn to the pink-hued, golden-domed Teatro Amazonas.

Eden arrived at the box office and was about to tell the smiling female attendant he was a guest of Alexander Thorne III when a smooth voice spoke just behind him.

"Dr. Santiago?"

Eden turned to see an exquisitely handsome young Brazilian man standing in a tuxedo, smiling at him. "Alexander Thorne?" Eden asked quizzically.

The young man smiled. "No. I'm his assistant, Gael Zagallo." He offered Eden his hand, then a glass of champagne. "Please follow me. Mr. Thorne is waiting upstairs in his private box."

Eden followed Gael through the crowd gathered in the vestibule of the opera house—the rich, the beautiful, the sophisticated, all drinking from crystal flutes while discussing opera and politics.

Thorne's private box, adorned with plush red velvet chairs and gold-leaf columns, overlooked the stage. As Gael showed him inside, Eden noticed a man in his mid-forties standing alone at the banister looking down at the spectators below milling into the theater to fill their seats. He was tall and handsome, with a light tan, distinguished gray hair, and deep lines around the corners of his mouth—too many charming, smiling conversations at too many wealthy dinner parties. He turned as Eden entered, and smiled that charming smile.

"Ah, Dr. Santiago, I presume. I'm happy to see the jacket fits." Thorne had his own glass of champagne and raised it now in honor of his guest's arrival. "You're just in time for the performance. Please." He gestured to the chairs and all three men sat—Thorne and Gael on either side of Eden—as the lights dimmed and the crowd below hushed.

"I suppose I should thank you for your generous hospitality," Eden whispered, "but you'll forgive me if I enjoy it with a grain of caution."

Thorne grinned playfully. "From all accounts, I don't believe caution is one of your strongest suits."

"I know when to tread carefully, Mr. Thorne."

"Please, call me Alexander."

The strains of violins and cellos began to drift upward from the orchestra pit, the chaotic and untidy warm-up before the real show began.

"Have you seen *Madame Butterfly* before, Dr. Santiago?"

"Once, in Vienna."

"It's the most beautiful opera ever written. There's something awe-inspiring about an Italian opera set in Japan being performed in the middle of the Amazon, don't you think?"

"It's not the only reason you invited me here," Eden probed.

Thorne smiled. "No. But I wanted to show you some civility in the midst of such savagery. Puccini in the jungle. Everyone should experience this...before they die."

At that moment the musicians rehearsing in the pit all fell silent for a moment before uniting in one beautiful chord. The curtain rose to reveal Lieutenant Pinkerton of the United States Navy, standing on a small hillside beneath a snowfall of cherry blossoms. The tenor began to sing.

Thorne continued talking, his voice now hushed. His charming smile was gone. "There is a single Deldah-sha orchid known to exist in captivity, and it's currently in my possession. If you think you're here to change that situation, I should inform you that other arrangements have already been made for you. Dr. Santiago, for fear of sounding— how shall I put it—operatic, your decision to come here has sealed your fate."

"I make my own plans," Eden replied flatly.

"If you think you can save the boy by getting your hands on the orchid, you're sadly mistaken, Dr. Santiago."

As Butterfly entered the stage and the beautiful soprano began to sing, Eden turned to Thorne. "Perron," he breathed, quickly putting two and two together at Thorne's mention of the boy. "You've already made a deal with Perron."

Thorne's smile returned, this time bringing with it a sinister glint to his eye. "Monsieur Perron has made me an offer I cannot refuse. Your life for a briefcase full of cash. It's very simple."

At that moment, Eden felt a sharp pain in his side. He

glanced down to see Gael Zagallo was pushing the point of a seven-inch switchblade into his ribs.

Thorne raised his eyebrows. "I'd like to invite you to dinner, Dr. Santiago. Please, do me the courtesy of accepting."

"I don't respond kindly to threats," Eden stated sternly, his jaw locked in anger.

"Then perhaps you'll respond to the sedatives in your champagne."

As Eden stared in horror at the near-empty glass in his hand, Butterfly's exquisite voice suddenly lifted to the domed ceiling and lingered there for a moment that seemed to stop time itself.

Thorne closed his eyes and caught his breath, suspended in the moment. Then, as the soprano's voice descended slowly from the heavens, he looked back to see the champagne flute slip from Eden's limp hand.

As Butterfly slid into her famous aria, "Un bel di," Thorne's hand began sweeping back and forth, as though he was conducting the opera. He looked down at the woman in the kimono, her voice filled with hope but her eyes flooded with despair.

"Soon she'll pick up the sword and take her own life. Does she die needlessly, or honorably?" Thorne smiled at Eden as the young Brazilian's eyes rolled back and his chin sank against his chest, before answering his own question, "It depends entirely on your point of view."

XI

The Village of La Molière, France

THE LIBRARY OF THE VILLA PERRON WAS ONE LARGE, square room. Its walls were completely lined with shelves filled with books—volumes of encyclopedias, reference books, books of maps and drawings, photographs and letters, old diaries, rare anthologies, hand-stitched manuscripts, ancient scrolls preserved inside leather-bound albums.

There were no windows in the library, only a long reading table in the middle of the room, with four chairs and four individual reading lamps. The door was locked from the outside.

"Where the hell are we, anyway?" Sam asked. He'd been banging on the door with his fist for the last hour, to no avail.

Behind him, the blind Professor stood, facing a wall of book spines he could not read, flinching at every thump against the heavy wooden door. "Seventeenth century," he muttered eventually, almost to himself.

Sam stopped and turned around. "What did you say?"

"The door. By the sound of your relentless pounding, I'd say it was seventeenth century, perhaps earlier. That, and the sound of your protesting voice echoing off the limestone walls as Mr. Goodwin led us in here, draw me toward the possibility that we're in some kind of old millhouse or cathedral, or possibly a monastery. And from the time it took to get here, I'd say we're somewhere near La Molière, in the south of France."

Sam stared at the Professor, his expression skeptical. "How the hell do you know all that?"

"The same way I know that if you keep thumping mindlessly on that door, I'm going to take a book off the shelf and hit you over the head with it!" The Professor gave a saccharine-sweet smile. "Call it intuition."

"I'm sorry to annoy the hell out of you, but I don't get much sleep. I guess my temper's kinda short." Sam lifted his arm to bang his fist at the door once again, and Ernest Hemingway's *Islands in the Stream* struck him directly in the back of the head.

Sam screeched and fell against the door, where he hit his head again and tumbled to the floor. "What the fu—?"

The Professor seized *The Old Man and the Sea* off the shelf and warned, "Hemingway solved his problems using his fists. I'll go one better and solve my problems using Hemingway!"

Sam looked up, his face twisted in pain and anger. "Are you crazy?"

"No, but I guess my temper's kind of short too. Now stop kicking, stop complaining, and stop cursing!"

Absolute silence suddenly filled the library, as neither Sam nor the Professor moved or said a word. Then, as quietly as he could, Sam climbed slowly to his feet and took a seat.

He sat rubbing the fast-growing bump on his head as the Professor took a deep breath and returned his book-weapon to the shelf. "Well, then, since it could be some time before we find an opportunity to escape or help arrives—"

"Help?" Sam griped. "What help? You think Fräulein Elsa's gonna come flying through the window wearing a cape?"

The Professor took another deep breath and chose to ignore Sam's cynicism. "As I was saying, since we could be here for some time, I daresay this is an excellent opportunity for you and me to get acquainted. It certainly seems to me our relationship could do with a little...quality time. Shall we chat?"

"About what?"

"About you," the Professor said, shrugging.

Sam shrugged back. "Ain't nothin' to tell."

"Why do you have trouble sleeping?"

"What?"

"You said before, you don't get much sleep. Why not?"

"I live on the street. You tend to sleep with one eye open."

"I thought you lived with Jake."

"Sometimes yes, sometimes no."

"Sometimes he doesn't want you there?"

"Sometimes I don't wanna be there."

"Why not?"

"Because sometimes he don't understand me." Sam stood and returned to the door, feeling trapped by all the questions. "Is this why you're a professor? You some kinda shrink?"

"I'm a professor, not a doctor."

"And I'm not a patient, so we got somethin' in common. Happy?"

Sam went silent. The Professor took a moment, then changed the subject. "You know, I used to have a library like this. That is, until my house burned down. I wouldn't be here today, but Jake saved both Elsa and me."

Sam smiled, almost proudly, almost jealously. "So that's what he gets up to."

The Professor listened to the tone in Sam's voice. "You miss him when he's not there, don't you."

"Enough with the damn chitchat!" Sam stormed back to the door. "And enough with this goddamn fuckin' library! I want out! Now!"

At that moment, the lock mechanism inside the seventeenth-century door rotated with a loud *clack!* Sam jumped back. The door swung open and a smug Pierre Perron waltzed merrily into the room, accompanied by the enormous Mr. Goodwin.

"If I asked you to sit down, would you oblige?" Perron said, waving a smoking cigar through the air and gesturing from Sam to the table with the stump of his missing finger.

"I'd rather stand," Sam said, frowning defiantly.

Perron grinned his wicked grin. "What if it were Mr. Goodwin asking the question?"

Sam looked at Mr. Goodwin, and the gorilla in the tight suit snarled.

"Samuel, please sit," the Professor advised calmly.

Sam did as the Professor asked.

Mr. Goodwin was the only one who remained standing, positioning himself behind Sam's chair, discouraging any and all attempts to escape or rebel.

"Don't he have anything better to do?" Sam rolled his eyes behind him to indicate Goodwin. "Like go beat up his tailor or something?"

Perron smirked, ever so slightly amused. "Mr. Goodwin is simply doing his job, and a good job at that." He turned his attention to the Professor. "Much like my other employee… in Cairo."

"You have a man in Egypt?" the Professor asked, concerned for his men but not surprised.

Perron nodded. "Ra is his name. He's one of a kind.

An old-fashioned assassin, obsessed with poisons and treasures—fascinating dinner-table conversation. I met him in Paris, at an exhibition of ancient weaponry. Blow darts are his specialty. Exotic, deadly, to the point—much like the man himself. Although I daresay you know that already."

At that point, he winked at Sam, who tried to jump out of his chair and lunge at Perron. Mr. Goodwin held him down hard.

Perron snickered. "Believe it or not, young man, you and Ra have quite a bit in common. He grew up in the ghettos too, lived like a street rat in the gutters of Algeria, then, when he was old enough, he made his way to Paris. As a boy he quickly learned that survival is a simple game of trade. Cigarettes for food, opium for guns, life for a few shiny coins. Everything has a set value, and every man has his price. Ra's is gold and silver. Once your men find the Riddle of the Sands, I've promised Ra half of what's inside. All he has to do is follow your boys to the Lost Pyramid, then make sure they never leave."

"This is bullshit!" Sam snapped. "You're nothin' but a fucking low-rent liar!"

"Bullshit, is it?" Perron snapped back sharply. "Liar, am I?" Suddenly enraged, he reached into his jacket pocket and pulled out the antidote vial. He held it up and sneered, "If you think this is bullshit, you won't mind me doing this!"

Without a moment's hesitation, the angry Frenchman threw the glass vial against the hard wooden floor. The tiny fragile cylinder shattered. Minuscule shards of glass and drops of clear liquid exploded across the floor.

Sam gasped and tried to dive for the precious fluid as it quickly drained between the floorboards, but Mr. Goodwin seized him by one arm and hoisted him clear out of his chair, twisting Sam's arm behind his back and forcing the boy to his knees in one swift move.

Sam screamed in agony as the colossal henchman jerked his arm upward to within an inch of the breaking point.

The Professor had dropped to the floor at the sound of exploding glass. "Pierre, what have you done!" he cried in horror.

Before the Professor's probing hands could reach the liquid, Perron kicked the old man squarely in the ribs.

The Professor groaned and collapsed on his side.

"I'm taking revenge, that's what I'm doing!" Perron circled the helpless Professor like a predator, enjoying the sound of glass crunching beneath his shoes. He kicked the old man again, this time in the kidneys.

"Professor!" Sam shouted, but Mr. Goodwin silenced him by twisting his arm with one hand and squeezing his shoulder with the other, pushing on the shoulder blade till it popped out of place. Sam screamed again, even louder.

"Pierre, enough!" the Professor shouted, still clutching his ribs, struggling to breathe.

"No!" Perron panted, exhausted from the strain of kicking the old man. "It's not enough! Not until your men find me that pyramid. Not until I drag your miserable old bones down there and show you the treasure that will be mine!"

Perron laughed maniacally at the thought of it.

Mr. Goodwin laughed too, then savagely pushed back on Sam's shoulder and popped the bone back in place. Sam cried in pain, his eyes rolled back into his head. Mr. Goodwin let go of the boy's arm as he fainted, watching with amusement as Sam's body folded to the floor.

He lay there unconscious, and Perron smiled. While the Frenchman realized that a dislocated shoulder would cause many to faint, he knew there was much more happening inside Sam's body.

"At last, the poison's beginning to work." He glanced at the floor, at the last tiny rivulets disappearing between the floorboards. "And the antidote's all but gone. How wonderfully ironic!"

He pulled up a chair and leaned over the Professor. "Your boys think they can save Sam's life… What a shame there's nothing they can do now. If only they knew."

Perron leaned closer still, and whispered in the old man's ear. "You're all going to die in the desert, and unlike the Lost Pyramid, nobody will ever find you. One riddle solved, another one lost to the sands forever."

Luca pulled the rented Audi over to the side of the quiet, tree-lined lane on the outskirts of La Molière. He looked at his watch, not for the time, but for the red flashing dot on the GPS grid. It was accurate to within two hundred meters, Elsa had told him.

If that was the case, then this was the place.

Luca looked out the window of the car.

To the left of the lane was a row of trees that framed a field covered in wildflowers, interrupted here and there by a pair of rabbit's ears sticking up like stalks.

To the right of the lane was a high stone wall, covered in moss and, by the looks of it, built centuries ago.

Luca got out of the car now and found a nearby tree, one whose branches reached higher than the wall itself. He had no intention of jumping the wall; he simply wanted to see over it, to size up his challenge.

Hand over hand, limb over limb, Luca made his way up the tree with the dexterity of an eight-year-old.

From a high, secure branch, he peered over the wall to see a rolling green hill upon which sat an ancient stone monastery, complete with turrets and an old working watermill. It would have looked straight out of the seventeenth century but for the long driveway lined with two dozen security guards and the Bell 430 nine-seater helicopter resting on the flattened lawn by the main building.

Impenetrable by any standard.

But as every good art historian knows, seventeenth-century France was a bloody place. No church or convent or monastery was built without a tunnel system. Everyone had an escape plan up their sleeve. And a secret passage out meant a secret passage in!

XII

The Nile Valley, Egypt

BY NIGHT, THE STARS FLICKERED LIKE A THOUSAND floating candles, shimmering on the still, black water of the Nile. As the cruiser motored along the river at a steady twenty knots, they slipped past countless small villages and the larger town of El Minya. At dawn, they cruised by the town of Asyut, watched by the fishermen who draped nets over the sides of their tiny fishing boats, ready for the morning's catch.

"How do you feel?" Will asked Jake as he stirred from his deep, drug-induced slumber. Will was crouching beside the small bunk in the cruiser's tight sleeping quarters, where he'd been keeping an eye on Jake. In his hands were the two gold statuettes of Min. He had been toying with them gently, wondering how on earth these two stolen treasures could possibly unlock the Lost Pyramid.

"Is that the key?" Jake asked.

Will nodded. "I'd bet my life on it."

"What makes you so sure?"

Will held the two identical figures up for Jake to see clearly. Jake squinted and tried to focus, then shrugged. "What am I looking at?"

"Every depiction of Min throughout Egyptian history has him standing with his flail in his right hand and his erect penis in his left. Not these two. They're the other way around. Flail in his left hand. Cock in his right."

"A mistake," Jake said, shrugging again.

Will shook his head. "He was the god of fertility. The Egyptians respected Min way too much to make a mistake like that. No, this is the work of someone who wanted to piss Min off. Someone who no longer gave a damn about fertility or religion or society's preachings. This is an act of rebellion. This is a son saying to his all-powerful father, *Fuck your laws and fuck you*! This is the work of Ahnu."

"Forgive me if I sound a little hazy, but what the hell are you talking about?"

Will helped a groggy-headed Jake sit up. "Come on, let's get you some air. You'll feel better. I'll fill you in on everything."

The sun broke over the lush green banks of the Nile as Jake and Will emerged from below deck.

"Look who the cat dragged in!" Shane exclaimed, relieved to see Jake on his feet and looking much better.

Jake scratched his head. "Where the hell are we?"

As if to answer his question, the crack and whoosh of sails unfurling filled the warm morning air. Jake looked all around him to see half a dozen tall white felucca sails shoot up into the blue sky, then flap and snap and billow as they caught the wind.

Shane smiled and replied, "We're somewhere between Cairo and Koptos. Welcome to the Nile, my friend."

He steered the cruiser skillfully through the flock of feluccas that had suddenly appeared, the sailboats flowing gracefully down the river like tall white swans, just as they had done for thousands of years.

As the day passed, Will told Jake the story of Ahnu. The heady melodies of neys and Mizmar flutes dancing on the breeze signaled village after village of mud-brick houses. Shane maneuvered the cruiser between the sailboats and ferries as local women watched, weaving baskets of reed and river grass, and children waved from the shore.

They passed Sohag, and, as the sun began to set, they reached the larger settlement of Qena. All around them, the pillow-white sails of the feluccas turned pink with the dusk, then one by one the sailboats began to disappear.

As night fell, the river was theirs once more. Shane steered the cruiser around numerous small islands, until eventually the lights of Koptos appeared along the bank.

Jake looked at his watch, more anxious than ever now. They had thirty-seven hours left to save Sammy's life. They still had to find the Temple of Min and somehow access its secret chamber. And then what? What if there was no map to the Lost Pyramid inside? And if there was a map, would they be able to read it or follow the directions, even with Will's knowledge of Egyptology and Shane's cartography skills? And what proof was there that the Lost Pyramid even existed at all?

Jake pressed another button on his watch, the global tracking system, hoping that checking Sammy and the Professor's location would comfort him. It did the opposite.

"Hey guys." Will, Shane, and Daniel turned and saw the concerned look on Jake's face. "The Professor's not in Paris anymore."

"The south of France," Shane said, checking his watch too. "What the hell's he doing there?"

"Perron has a villa in the south of France," Jake told them.

Will saw the frustration and anger on Jake's face. "We'll

get the map," he assured him with a soft squeeze on the shoulder. "We'll find the pyramid. I promise you."

As they neared Koptos, Daniel suddenly announced, "Over there!" He was pointing to a flashlight signaling to them from a remote pier. It was Moro's contact.

Shane steered the cruiser toward the blinking light and the men moored the boat to the pier, greeted by a slender, soft-spoken young man in an oversized caftan. "I have camels for you," he explained. "And a compass. Head north of the town, then, when you reach the last lit road, take a course due east. You'll reach the Temple of Min by sunrise."

The young man handed Will the compass and nodded politely. "I'll be waiting here for your return."

"Thank you."

The four men found their camels waiting at the foot of the pier.

"Oh, joy," murmured Shane, taking a deep breath of courage. "Don't be fooled, boys. They bite!"

The grinning, dribbling animals groaned and spat as their riders attempted to untie the reins and mount them.

Will jumped back as a thick, slimy rope of camel drool slapped him in the face. "Jesus! Ugh! Holy crap!" He disgustedly wiped his pretty face. "Goddamn it, Shane. Is there any graceful way to handle these dudes?"

"In my experience," Shane offered, awkwardly grabbing at his camel's hump and pulling himself up, "absolutely none."

Somehow Jake hauled himself up onto his animal without incident.

Daniel managed to climb up onto his hump and stop himself from sliding all the way down the other side.

Will's slippery, saliva-covered hands had trouble gripping, but with a little encouragement from his camel—which tried to take a chunk out of Will as he considered the ascent—he swiftly pulled himself up onto the beast.

"I never met a hump I didn't like," the young quarter-back said, frowning. "Until today."

Shane grinned and called, "Yiddy-up!" and at once the four camels jerked into motion.

Will, Jake, Shane, and Daniel held on tight, swaying and rolling and pitching with the rhythm of the camels' long-legged strides.

They journeyed north of the town, just as they had been told, then, when they reached the last lit road, they turned due east and began their trek into the dark of the desert.

For the most part, they traveled in silence, except for the sound of sand shifting beneath hooves, and the occasional snort or fart from a camel. The desert was still, quiet, vast.

When dawn broke, and Will saw the outline of a grand stone temple etched against the pale blue and pink sky, he said nothing. He simply pointed.

At that moment, the sun spilled upon the horizon behind the temple, and the desert dunes were suddenly drenched in a sweeping flood of golden light.

None of them spoke until they reached the entrance to the temple.

It was an awesome sight, an enormous ancient structure with its entryway flanked by crumbling, sun-baked columns, each rising up to a carved cornice depicting farmers and slaves tending to crops along the banks of the Nile. And in the middle of the cornice stood Min, three times taller than any other figure in the carving, his flail in his right hand and his cock in his left.

"Welcome to the Temple of Min," Will breathed softly.

The men dismounted and even the camels seemed to stand silent and still, in awe of the temple.

Slowly Will walked up the steps of the entryway and into a cavernous antechamber.

Jake followed, as did Shane and Daniel.

Already the temperature of the day was rising as beams of sunlight spilled into the antechamber through the enormous entryway, as well as through countless openings in the ceiling, designed to cast light upon the giant two-story-high stone statue of Min standing in the middle of the antechamber.

He cut a formidable figure, tall and ominous.

In his right hand, his flail looked ready to whip anyone who dared enter his domain.

In his left hand, his giant cock stood hard and erect, measuring at least six feet long.

"That's enough to give any man penis envy," Shane murmured.

"He's holding his cock in his left hand," Jake observed.

"This temple was built by Imhotep, not Ahnu," Will said. "Imhotep built this statue in the traditional image of Min. Ahnu made his gold statuettes a mirror image. The exact opposite."

"What's this mean?" Daniel asked. He was pointing to a large, square grid set into the floor in front of the huge Min statue. It was divided evenly into nine large, flat stone squares, three rows across and three rows down. Each stone square was about three feet by three feet, each with a different ancient symbol carved into its face.

A burning sun.

A crescent moon.

A river bird.

A coiled earthworm.

A netted fish.

A scarab beetle.

A flying arrow.

A vulture.

An open-jawed crocodile.

Will looked at the grid in the floor and answered, "I don't know."

Jake knelt and lightly dusted the desert sand away from

one of the stones. "Maybe the keys fit one of the symbols?"

Will shook his head. "Ahnu made the keys. This place was built by Imhotep after Ahnu and the Pyramid and the City of the Impure were consumed by the desert. Imhotep built it to house the map to the City. And to challenge anyone who dared to look for it."

Will's eyes were scanning the ceiling and walls now. He felt the sweat trickle down his forehead and the back of his neck. He watched the dust particles drift in the bright beams of hot sunlight, and noticed how they swirled and danced near the base of the wall behind the statue of Min.

"That's not a wall," he announced confidently, making a beeline for it. "It's a doorway. There's air on the other side of it."

All four made their way to the wall. Will knelt and ran his fingers along the base of it. He blew sand and dust away to reveal a thin crack, then held the back of his hand against it and felt a draft. He looked up the length of the wall. "It goes up. We just have to figure out how."

"The symbols in the floor," Shane said. "Could they somehow open it?"

Will stood back and looked from the wall to the symbols, and thought about the possibility for a moment. But it seemed too obvious.

"Every map has a cipher, a legend," he said, shaking his head. "I don't think the symbols are the way in."

"Then what?" Jake asked. "What are we looking for?"

Will started scanning the antechamber, the walls, the ceiling, the statue. "Some sort of mechanism," he replied. "A handle or a switch or a—" He stopped in midsentence, his eyes suddenly fixed on the huge protruding phallus of Min.

"Or a what?" Shane asked.

Will grinned. "Or a lever." He turned quickly to Shane and Jake. "I need a leg up."

The men hurried to the foot of the statue and Will kicked off his boots. Shane bent low so that Will could step up onto his back. From there, the young man climbed onto Jake's shoulders. "Keep it steady, Jake."

"I'm trying," Jake grunted. "But for a kid, you're a lot heavier than you look."

Will hoisted himself up into a kneeling position, then a standing position, his bare feet digging into Jake's shoulders, his toes wriggling, trying to find a grip.

Jake wavered unsteadily for a moment before Will managed to grab the thick stone erection—now at eye level in front of him—and stabilized his balance.

"For decades, Egyptologists have tried in vain to access this temple's secrets, but Chamberlain himself told me how conservative they all are. I bet my sweet ass none of them ever dared touch Min's cock."

Will fidgeted excitedly while Jake continued to grimace, gripping the bare feet on his shoulders to try to keep them still. "It may be sweet, but if that ass of yours doesn't quit wrigglin' around it's gonna end up on the floor!"

Will ignored him, lost in the thrill of the moment. "Don't you see? Imhotep and the pharaohs worshipped Min for his masculinity, his ability to sow his seed, to fertilize civilization. His cock was the very key to existence."

With that, Will placed two hands under that heavy giant cock. He felt the warm stone beneath his fingers and was surprised at the detail that had survived the ages: the thread of capillaries carved into the rock; the ripples of stone skin; the thick shaft of a main vein. Then he dug his feet into Jake's shoulders, and with all his strength he lifted Min's erect cock upward.

A cascade of built-up sand fell away from the statue's pubic region and showered down into Jake's eyes and hair. He shook it off, spreading his own legs wider to steady himself.

Will grunted, straining as he lifted the cock.

His biceps bulged.

He squinted and blinked away the sweat that trickled into his eyes.

Then, with a loud groan and the sharp grinding sound of stone scraping against stone, the cock of the Egyptian god began to rise. The erection tilted upward—five, ten, twenty inches—as though Min had just emerged from a long, deep slumber into a heightened state of pleasure. When it pointed diagonally up at the ceiling, the cock stopped moving and something else began to rise.

With a deafening hiss and a rumble so deep and resonant it sent a tremor through the entire chamber, the stone wall behind Min started to ascend.

The floor shook. The statue trembled. The stone columns in the entryway to the antechamber grumbled and swayed.

Will jumped from Jake's shoulders and landed on the floor like a cat, watching the wall lift to reveal an empty chamber beyond. As the wall slid into the ceiling with a loud thump, all four men stood wide-eyed and silent, staring into a chamber that no human had laid eyes on for more than four thousand years.

"What is it?" Jake breathed, not moving a muscle.

"I don't see any map," added Shane, his voice also hushed as though they had all just sneaked into someone's house. "It's just an empty room."

"I don't think it's a room," Will said. "I think it's part of a—" As if to finish his sentence for him, the far wall at the end of the secret chamber began to move, this time from right to left. "—a passageway."

Again the temple shook all the way to its foundations. Every particle of sand resting on every surface jumped and jittered.

As the wall rolled away, it revealed another empty section of the passageway. Then, as soon as the second wall had opened, a third wall—the farthest wall—began to move. This time, it descended from the ceiling and disappeared slowly into the floor.

Will stood up on his toes, desperate to see what secrets were behind it.

As it lowered itself, the wall revealed one last room, one that was not part of a passageway, but rather an entire chamber unto itself.

The wall slotted neatly into the stone floor and disappeared from sight.

Will, Jake, Shane, and Daniel peered all the way down the passageway to see something set into the floor of the far chamber.

Will was the first to say it. "That's our map, boys!"

"The walls!" Daniel suddenly breathed. "They're moving back into place!"

He was right. No sooner had the rumbling stopped than the three walls simultaneously began to slide back into place.

The far wall began to rise from the floor.

The middle wall began to slide from left to right.

The near wall began to descend.

Barefoot and sweating, and without a second's hesitation, Will launched into a sprint down the passageway to the far secret chamber.

Jake bolted after him, his boots kicking up sand.

Shane and Daniel were hot on their trail. They had to duck their heads to clear the quickly descending first wall, but after a few steps, Daniel hesitated and stopped.

"It's a puzzle," he whispered to himself.

In the haste of their mad dash, surrounded by grinding stones and rumbling walls, Shane didn't notice that Daniel was no longer beside him.

Ahead, Will easily made it past the second wall and sprinted for the third, which was rising fast. He could see he was going to have to jump and climb to get over to the other side. The young athlete put on an extra burst of speed.

As Jake raced past the second wall, Will launched himself onto the top of the third, ascending wall. His fingers hooked the top of the wall. His bare toes found cracks and crevices in the stone and pushed him upward. He clambered to the top and swung one leg over, then glanced over the other side into what he hoped was some sort of map room.

He saw nine empty squares making up a grid in the floor.

He glanced quickly around the chamber. On the walls were nine square stone tablets, three on each wall, each with a symbol on it.

Far behind him, Daniel had already begun to backtrack, racing back into the antechamber, recalling Will's words, *I don't think the symbols are the way in.*

Atop the rising wall, staring down at the empty grid on the floor of the map room, Will made the same realization at the same time. "They're the way *out*!"

The wall was rising fast. In a panic, Will lurched toward the map room. He moved too fast. He lost his balance. One leg flew over the other and he fell off the ascending wall awkwardly. Badly.

His head was the first thing to hit the stone floor of the map room.

Shane cleared the second door before realizing Daniel was no longer beside him. He spun around quickly, then crouched low and craned his neck to see that Daniel was all the way back in the antechamber, standing in front of the statue of Min and staring at the floor. "Daniel!"

Shane saw Daniel look up and make a breakneck bolt for the first wall. He dropped into a slide and glided through the sand beneath the wall, inches before it sealed shut. But no matter how fast he ran now, there was no way Daniel was going to make it to the second wall in time.

Shane had already turned back. He raced for the second sliding wall and was trying to hold it back for Daniel, but it was no use. He pulled his fingers free just before he lost them, and caught one last glimpse of Daniel before he was completely sealed inside the first section of the passageway, trapped between the first and second walls.

"Dammit!" Shane quickly turned back and saw Jake jump for the ascending wall.

He clambered swiftly to the top of it.

The ceiling was fast approaching.

Jake glanced over the wall into the map room and saw Will lying motionless on the stone floor, unconscious in a pool of blood.

Atop the wall, Jake lowered himself as the ceiling threatened to crush him and shot a glance back at Shane.

"Shane! Will's hurt!"

And with that, Jake slipped out of sight over the other side of the wall.

There was no time for Shane to even attempt the ascending wall.

With a loud, echoing *thunk*, it slammed into the ceiling and sealed shut.

Shane was trapped alone in the second chamber of the passageway, between the second and third walls.

In the first sealed chamber, Daniel had dropped to his knees, drawing quick symbols in the sand with his finger, his brain frantically ticking over.

In the third chamber—the map room—Jake landed beside Will. He lifted the young man's unconscious head gently in his hands and looked beneath the long, blood-matted blond locks.

The blow was superficial. Nothing but a cut, but enough to knock him out.

"You'll be okay, kid," Jake muttered. "So long as we can find a way outta here."

At that moment, a dull thud pounded through the wall next to Jake's head.

It was Shane on the other side, hammering his fist against the stone.

"Jake! Jake, can you hear me?" came Shane's muted voice.

"Yeah—just barely!"

In the second chamber, Shane stood back from the wall. If Jake could just barely hear him, then so could Daniel. Shane raced to the other end of his chamber and slammed his fist against that wall. "Daniel?"

Daniel was still kneeling in the sand. He had drawn a grid of nine squares with his finger and had started filling in the blanks. A sun, top left. An earthworm beneath it. A netted fish next to that. And in the bottom right corner, an open-jawed crocodile—like a signature, a warning of impending doom.

Faintly, behind him, hollering through the thick stone wall, he heard Shane's voice. "Daniel? Daniel, can you hear me?"

"Yes!" he shouted as loud as he could, still concentrating on his sand drawing. "Where are the others? What can they see?"

Shane ran back to the far end of his chamber. "Jake! Is Will okay?"

Jake had already cupped his hand against Will's wound and had managed to stop the bleeding. He scooped the unconscious young man up in his arms and laid him down in the middle of the map room, next to the empty grid on the floor. Jake took off his shirt and rolled it up to use as a pillow under Will's head.

"He'll be okay," Jake called.

He looked around him then and noticed the square stone tablets on three walls of the chamber. He noticed that the symbols on the stones were the same symbols as the ones on the floor of the antechamber.

"What can you see?" Shane's voice was barely audible through the wall. "Jake, what's in there?"

Jake made his way back to the wall. He shouted into the stone. "A grid on the floor. Symbols on the walls. The same symbols that we saw before."

Shane raced to the other end of the chamber and relayed this information through the wall to Daniel. "There's a grid on the floor. Stone symbols on the walls. The same symbols as before."

"Just like the antechamber," Daniel said, smiling. "Shane, listen to me. It's a puzzle. Like a game of memory. We have to rebuild the grid. Put the pieces in place."

"What if we put them in the wrong order?" Shane asked warily.

"Where's Will?" was Daniel's only answer. "He'll know what to do."

Shane charged back to the opposite wall. "Jake!"

Within seconds, Jake had straddled Will's unconscious body and was trying to shake him awake. "Come on, kid! We need you right now!"

He took Will's jaw in his hand and shook it back and forth gently. Will opened one eyelid and uttered, deliriously, "Dad?" Then nothing.

"Shit!" Jake cursed. "I got nothin'," he shouted back through the wall. "The poor kid's off with the fairies."

Shane slammed against the wall at the far end of his cell. "Will's down for the count," he told Daniel. "We're on our own."

Managing to replicate most of the symbols in the sand, Daniel adjusted the glasses on the bridge of his nose and pressed himself against the wall. "Tell Jake to start with the sun," he shouted, as clearly as possible. "Top row, first square, tell him it's the symbol of the sun. He needs to take the stone symbol of the sun off the wall and place it in the first square, top row."

Shane stepped away from the wall, whispering over and over again to himself, "Top row, first square, sun. Top row, first square, sun." He reached the far wall and his whisper turned to a shout. "Jake, find the sun. Put the symbol of the sun in the top row, first square in the grid on the floor!"

Jake stood leaning against the wall, his palms pressed against the stone. At the sound of Shane's muffled voice he turned and scanned the symbols on the adjacent walls. "Sun," he said to himself, spotting the stone. Then dubiously he shouted back, "Are you sure about this?"

"No" was Shane's honest reply. "Do you have a better idea?"

"No" was the soft reply Jake gave himself. He let out a nervous sigh and promptly made his way over to the left wall. He stopped in front of the stone tablet bearing the symbol of the sun. He wasn't even sure if it was going to release itself from the wall, but he took it in both hands nonetheless, tightened his grip on it, and gave it a good, hard yank.

The stone budged a little.

He tried again, and it budged a lot.

Jake stumbled backward as the heavy stone tablet completely gave way and came loose in his hands. "Whaddaya know," he muttered with a grin.

But the grin was short-lived.

A second after the stone tablet came free, things began to move in the chamber. It was the sound of things sliding, things grinding, things groaning, that made Jake step back in alarm.

At first he had no idea what was moving, or where!

Then his eyes caught sight of them: four piercing iron spikes emerged from the stone surfaces of the chamber.

One from behind the stone tablet he had just removed.

One from the wall opposite.

One coming down from the ceiling.

One rising up from the floor.

They moved at a slow, steady pace, determined to drive a hole through anything in their path, getting longer and longer and longer.

"Oh, shit," Jake whispered, stepping out of the way and watching as the slow-moving needles protruded into the map room.

"Oh, shit," Shane breathed. In the second chamber, four identical spikes appeared from the left wall, the right wall, the ceiling, the floor. He hurried around them, dodging them easily to get to the far wall. "Daniel?"

"There are spikes in here!" Daniel shouted back.

"My God, this place is a deathtrap," Shane uttered to himself. He raced to the other end of the chamber, avoiding the four spikes again. "Jake?"

But Jake was already positioning the sun stone carefully into the first slot in the grid on the floor. The tablet fell into place with a hefty *foomp!*

And as soon as it was in place—

—the spikes ceased moving.

In the map room.

In the second chamber.

And in the first chamber.

The long, deadly needles froze in place, ready to prick or slice or puncture anything that scraped by them.

Daniel let out an anxious breath.

Shane wiped the sweat from his brow. His shirt was already drenched and heavy with perspiration. He peeled it off and let it smack to the floor, giving his gleaming, heaving torso a little relief.

In the map room, Jake heard Shane's voice faintly through the wall. "Jake! You okay?"

"Yeah. But I don't know if I like where this is going.

If that piece of the puzzle was right, I'd hate to see what happens when we get a piece wrong."

"Me too," said a hushed Shane.

He made his way to the other end of the chamber and called to Daniel. "I think this is gonna get sticky."

"Me too." This time it was Daniel who whispered it to himself. He called back, "Next to the sun is the crescent moon. He needs to place the crescent moon in the next square. Then the river bird. And tell him he's going to have to move. Once he pulls a stone off the wall he needs to move as fast as he can."

"I think he's already figured that out." Shane ran to the opposite end of the chamber. "Next is the moon. Then the bird."

Jake listened to the muffled instructions through the wall and looked around the room. "And be quick!" he heard Shane add.

"Don't rush me," Jake said. His eyes darted from one symbol to the next. He saw a moon. He saw a vulture. He stepped up to the moon and shook his arms, flexing his muscles, wiping his sweaty hands on the seat of his cargoes, terrified of what might happen if one of the tablets should slip from his grip and smash on the floor.

He took the stone firmly in his hands.

He positioned one leg forward, one leg back, ready to swing into action.

He plucked the stone off the wall. It was heavy, and his muscles rippled.

He stepped back as a spike materialized from the wall where the tablet had been, as though the stone had been put there to plug a hole. The spike moved toward him in a straight line, traveling faster than the previous spikes.

Clutching the stone, Jake raced toward the grid in the middle of the room.

He saw three more moving spikes—again randomly

appearing from the opposite wall, the ceiling, the floor. Several of them began to crisscross each other as they protruded further and further into the room. It didn't take a genius to figure out that the more symbols he removed from the walls, the harder it was going to be to make his way around the map room.

Jake dropped into a kneeling position as one of the spikes traveled steadily over his head. He ducked under it and reached the grid. He locked the tablet in place.

The moving spikes cranked to a halt, suspended in space.

In the second chamber, Shane sized up the four new spikes that had just pierced their way into his section of the passageway. "Jake? You good?"

"All good," Jake called back. He was already standing in front of the symbol of the vulture. He wrapped his fingers tightly around the sides of the stone tablet and tightened his grip.

In the first chamber, Daniel navigated his way around all eight spikes, careful to avoid their needle-sharp ends. He was beginning to sweat profusely now himself. The air in the chamber was stifling. He pulled off his sweat-soaked shirt and used it to mop his neck and torso. "The river bird next," he said to himself, adjusting his steamed-up glasses as he gazed intently at his sand drawing on the floor. Suddenly it dawned on him that the vulture he had drawn in the bottom row looked very much like the river bird in the first row. How easily the two could be confused...

Daniel bolted for the wall. "Shane! Make sure Jake doesn't choose the—"

Jake yanked the vulture off the wall, and the spike behind it didn't just slide out at a steady, determined pace. It *flew* out!

Jake stumbled back, not letting go of the stone tablet. He crashed onto his back. The heavy stone tablet thudded against his chest, punching the air out of his lungs. Above him he saw the blurred streak of the spike as it shot across the chamber like a spear.

But it wasn't the only one.

With a deadly whistling sound, three other spikes shot across the room.

Ffppttt!

One flew out of an arbitrary place on the opposite wall.

Ffppttt!

One shot from the ceiling into the floor like an iron bar.

Jake suddenly rolled onto his stomach and glanced across the floor, panicked by the sheer randomness of the spikes, panicked by the fact that Will was still lying in the middle of the room.

Ffppttt!

The fourth spike rocketed out of the floor, right beside Will's bicep. The point of it grazed his shirt, slicing through the material and drawing blood.

The spike shot up into the ceiling.

Will still did not move, but a red stain seeped through his shirt.

"Will!" Jake uttered, leaping up off the floor.

In the second chamber, Shane managed to get halfway across the passage before a puff of dust and sand burst from a small opening in the wall beside him. He instinctively dropped to the floor, lying flat on his stomach as a spike torpedoed out of the wall and pierced the air where he had been standing.

It slammed into the opposite wall, the span of it reaching the entire width of the chamber from one wall to the other.

He stayed low, hands covering his head as he heard three more spikes cut the air and slam into the floor, the ceiling, the wall nearest him.

In the first chamber, the surprise attack of the first spike firing out of the wall like a missile and missing Daniel's head by mere inches was enough to knock the young reporter flat on his back. His legs simply folded beneath him as the *whoosh* of the flying spike filled his ears.

He counted three more spears shoot through the air before Daniel even entertained the thought of getting up.

In the second chamber, Shane was shouting left and right, scrambling to his feet. "Jake! What the hell happened! Daniel! You okay?"

From the wall leading to the first chamber, he heard Daniel's panicked shouting. "It was the wrong stone. It was supposed to be the river bird. Not the vulture, the river bird! It was the wrong stone!"

Daniel's words were suddenly confirmed by a new sound.

A lurch and groan from above.

The temple gave another thunderous growl, even deeper than before, only now the rumbling was accompanied by something *crumbling.*

Shane looked up.

The ceiling cornices were giving way. Small stones snapped and broke into dust, raining down into the chamber.

The ceiling was coming down!

Slowly.

Steadily.

And nothing was going to get in its way.

"Oh, shit," whispered Shane.

"Oh, no," said Daniel in the first chamber, staring up at his own slowly descending ceiling.

"No, no, no!" Jake breathed. He had already placed the vulture stone to one side and was crouching over Will, hurriedly peeling the kid's shirt off his shoulders and tearing it into shreds to wrap around the wound on Will's bicep. He froze when the ceiling began to rumble. "Sorry, kid. But I think things just got a whole lot worse." Jake threw the shredded shirt away and bolted for the wall. "Shane! Talk to me!"

Shane was already at the far wall. "Daniel, talk to me!"

Daniel had already raced to his sand drawing, memorized the next few symbols, then charged back to the wall. "The river bird! The river bird is next! Then in the next row, from left to right, start with the worm wrapped like a coil, then the fish in the net, then the scarab beetle. Got it?"

Shane's lips were desperately mouthing each symbol in order, over and over. He looked up at the slowly descending stone ceiling as he ran and unwittingly caught his bare side on one the spikes protruding from the wall. Its razor-sharp point cut a gash half an inch deep through his torso. He winced and reeled to the right, where another spike, jutting at him from the opposite direction, nearly punctured his shoulder. He steadied himself quickly, and with his eyes darting up, down, left, and right all at once, he navigated his way past the remainder of the deadly suspended spikes.

"Shane!" Jake was shouting.

"The river bird! The river bird is next! Can you remember this? You have to remember this! It's the river bird! Then on the next row it's the coiled worm, then the fish—can you remember this?"

"Shut up and keep calling them!"

"The worm, the fish, then the beetle!"

"The worm, the fish, the beetle," Jake rattled off. Suddenly the ceiling gave a deafening groan as it scraped against an uneven surface of the wall. Jake turned quickly at the sound and watched as the unstoppable ceiling simply pulverized the protrusion, shaving three inches of stone completely off the wall before continuing its descent.

The hardened New Yorker gulped and his mind suddenly went blank. "What was first?" he yelled anxiously back through the wall.

"The river bird!"

Jake charged for the river bird. He jerked it off the wall with all his might.

A spike rumbled out from behind it, churning slowly into space.

Jake let out a sigh of relief. "Right stone." But there was certainly no time to relax. More and more spikes were filling up the room, turning the entire space into a deadly obstacle course.

As Jake raced to the middle of the room, he kept his eyes trained on the accompanying three spikes emerging from the opposite wall and floor, even the moving ceiling. He slotted the river bird into the grid and scanned the walls for the earthworm.

In the second chamber, Shane looked up and guessed that the ceiling was now about eight feet from the floor, and getting closer by the second. "Hurry, Jake! We're running outta time!"

In the map room, the earthworm stone fell into place.

Jake was six feet tall. The rumbling of the ceiling was loud in his ears now and only a foot and a half away. He ran quickly to the symbol of the netted fish, gripped it tightly in his hands, then glanced back at the grid, ready to bolt. That's when he saw it.

"Will!"

Amid the chaos, Jake hadn't noticed that one of the spikes descending from the ceiling was heading straight for Will, only ten or so inches away from boring straight into the unconscious young man's chest.

Jake left the stone symbol on the wall and ran, at the same time ducking, bending, jumping, and stretching around the three-dimensional network of spikes.

The sharp tip drilled toward Will, three inches from his left pectoral—

Two inches—

One—

Headed straight for his heart.

Jake dived over one last pointed rod and hit the ground.

The tip of the spike pressed into Will's chest, making an impression in the muscle. It drew blood.

Jake reached out, seized Will's arm, then yanked with all his might.

The kid slid across the sand.

The spike drew a line of blood across Will's chest as his body was pulled out from underneath the sharp, pointed tip—out of harm's way.

Jake let out a sigh of relief, stunned, wide-eyed, then heard Shane's muffled voice over the ever-deafening rumble. "Jake! The ceiling!"

Shane was bending now. The ceiling was below the six-foot mark. He only had time for one last trip to Daniel's end of the chamber and back again before—

"Ahh!" Another spike jabbed him in the arm, puncturing the skin and drawing blood.

Shane wasted no more time. He lifted one leg, arched his back, turned his bare chest left, then dipped low and raised himself high, avoiding spikes coming in from every direction, moving like a contorted dancer as quickly as he could.

In the first chamber, Daniel was making his final journey back from the wall, bending lower and lower as the ceiling grumbled and sank. He twisted through the moving maze, sidestepping and snaking his way in one direction before realizing his path was now blocked by spikes. He backtracked quickly.

In the map room, Jake cradled the fish stone to his chest, keeping one eye on the spikes and one eye on Will. Moving swiftly. Straining. Curling. Winding. Weaving.

He reached the grid. He dropped the stone in place.

The ceiling was only five feet from the ground now, and he still had four pieces to put in place before the puzzle was complete.

"Tell him to take all the stones at once!" Daniel shouted

through the wall of the first chamber to Shane. "We don't have time. So long as he gets the order right! The beetle's next. Then the final row. The arrow, the vulture, and last—" the ceiling groaned even closer now, and Daniel's head sank with it, lower and lower and lower "—and last, the crocodile."

Shane was already on his way back to Jake's end of the chamber, curving and coiling through the spikes as fast as he could.

The ceiling was grinding lower and lower.

Time was measured in inches now.

"Jake! All at once! Pull the other stones off the wall in order, then carry them to the grid in one trip." Shane began to sound off the remaining symbols.

"Are you crazy?" Jake said to himself. "I can't carry them all at once."

The ceiling, however, begged to differ. It pressed down on Jake's already tilted head and he knew he had no choice but to try.

He folded his body quickly through the tapestry of spikes.

"Beetle," he said to himself, jerking the stone off the wall. "Arrow." He stacked it on top of the beetle stone, feeling the weight. "Vulture," he said, adding it to the pile and juggling the stone tablets like a waiter juggling plates.

In the first chamber, one spike after another after another penetrated the air. Daniel tried to look for the safest place in the room, but there was none.

In the second chamber, Shane was being outmaneuvered by the relentless onward march of spikes from all directions, forcing him left, right, and against a wall while the ceiling pressed him lower and lower toward the floor.

In the map room, Jake swung right and stretched as far as he could, holding the stones to his chest with one hand while reaching for the crocodile on the wall. Sweat streaked down his torso and face. He blinked it out of his eyes. His hands were slippery. His biceps burned under the burden of the stacked stones. His legs trembled.

"One more," he uttered determinedly through clenched teeth.

Out of the corner of his eye he caught sight of Will near the middle of the room, unconscious and helpless. There were three more spikes coming for him now, homing in as though they could smell his blood.

In the first chamber, Daniel felt a prick in his right side. He jerked left and let out a pained cry as a spike on that side buried itself into his flesh.

In the second chamber, Shane sank into a crouching position, then a sitting position, and flattened his back against the wall. A spike was headed for his throat, another for his shoulder, but the one making him sweat the most was the spike headed straight for his crotch. He spread his legs wide and tried to push himself back against the wall as far as possible, but he couldn't give another inch. The spike zeroed in on his balls. "Come on, Jake. Hurry!"

Jake's fingers grabbed hold of the crocodile stone and yanked it from the wall just before the descending ceiling had a chance to crush it, and suddenly the entire stack of stones began to teeter in his arms. They swayed left. Jake tried to catch them and overcompensated to the right. He felt a spike jab him in the back. He snapped forward, veered left, tilted right, and somehow regained balance of the tower of tablets.

That's when the ceiling began to grind down on the tablet at the top of the pile.

Jake dropped into a crouching position, his biceps about to burst, every vein bulging, his thighs screaming out in agony. His feet dug deep into the sand, pushing him forward, over and around the spikes.

The ceiling rumbled below the four-foot mark.

Jake flattened himself as much as he could without dropping the stones.

He saw the insatiable spikes approaching Will's young, tasty flesh.

In the first chamber, Daniel managed to rotate his body, buying himself a few more inches. The spikes coming at him from either side were now on course for his lower back and stomach.

In the second chamber, Shane tried to press himself further against the wall, but the spike pressed mercilessly into the crotch of his cargoes, pushing unrelentingly into his balls.

In the map room, Jake reached the grid. He stretched under and around the spikes, still juggling the stack of stones, and slid each tablet into the grid in order.

The scarab beetle. Locked in!

He shoved the arrow stone into place.

The vulture made a loud thud as it fell into place.

There was only the crocodile left.

Jake stretched as far as he could, but the spikes were stopping him from reaching the square and the stone tablet fell well short of its mark.

He twisted around quickly and tried to kick the stone across the floor. It inched bit by bit toward the last spot on the grid, but teetered on the edge of falling into place.

Across the chamber, a spike pressed into Will's thigh. Another into his side.

In the first chamber Daniel breathed in, trying to make himself as thin as possible, but felt a hot tip pierce his stomach.

In the second chamber Shane squeezed his eyes shut tight as the spike punctured the material of his cargoes and pushed into his ball sack, about to impale his manhood.

In the map room Jake kicked his leg out as far as he could.

He managed to give the crocodile stone a tap.

Then a nudge.

Then, with the very last flick of his toe—

Ffmmp!

The crocodile stone fell into place.

Jake held his breath and felt the rough stone surface of the ceiling press down against the back of his neck. Then, suddenly—

Everything stopped moving.

The rumbling ceased.

The grinding stopped.

Daniel gasped.

Shane opened his eyes.

Jake breathed, "Imhotep, you son of a bitch. Admit it, we beat you!"

And so it seemed the temple knew the rules of the game too. Suddenly, as if conceding defeat, the ceiling reversed direction and began to ascend. All the spikes retreated and the walls between the three chambers rolled away.

Daniel clutched at his bleeding stomach, shocked and relieved to find the wound only half an inch deep.

Shane swiftly unbuckled his cargoes and took his precious manhood in his hands. There was a tiny pinprick in his left testicle, but his balls were otherwise unscathed. "Thankyou, thankyou, thankyou!" he gasped.

He looked toward the wall sliding open to reveal the first chamber. "Daniel? You okay?"

Daniel nodded and staggered toward him.

"You're bleeding," Shane said, catching Daniel as he ran into his arms.

"It's only shallow. I'm fine."

The two raced into the map room as the wall retracted down into the floor, opening the secret chamber.

Inside, Jake was already checking Will's wounds, nursing the kid's head in his lap. "He's a little cut up, but he'll mend," Jake told Shane.

"Thank God," Shane breathed.

But the temple had one last surprise in store.

With a groan and a crunch, each of the stone tablets within the grid suddenly flipped over, revealing an underside covered in contours and etched markings.

Daniel and Shane both stepped back. Jake stared in wonder.

As all the stones overturned, it became apparent that the underside markings on each of them connected to one another. The grid suddenly transformed itself into—

"The map! It's the map!" Shane muttered. He circled the grid quickly, sizing up the markings. "Look, it's the Nile," he said, pointing to a long, distinct furrow running the length of the joining stones. "This is us, here."

Jake stood and shook his head. "How can you be sure? The Lower Nile doesn't look like that."

"Cartography's my thing, remember? The river's flooded now, but this is exactly how it would have looked before the Aswan Dam was built." He pointed to several small clusters of square-shaped mounds. "And these. These must be the cities of ancient Egypt. Cairo. Koptos. We're here, at the Temple of Min. And down here is Aswan. Which means"—Shane pointed to a small, obscure cluster seemingly in the middle of nowhere—"it means this city here in the empty desert north of Aswan must be—"

Jake and Shane looked at each other and both finished the sentence together.

"The City of the Impure."

It was a day Will thought he had pushed from his mind forever; it was a word he had managed to forget.

Impure.

But since arriving in Egypt, since seeing his father for the first time in a long time, the memory of that day, that word, came flooding back.

It was an official letter on government stationery—a letter from his father in response to a nervous phone call Will had made to his dad shortly after his eighteenth birthday, telling Charles he was gay—that led to the accident. It was even the reason why Will had so easily forgotten about his father's posting in Cairo. The young man had simply blocked all of it out.

Now it was back.

At the top of the letter was the crest of the U.S. Embassy in Cairo, and beneath it was printed: *From the office of Charles Hunter*. Charles had always been a succinct man. His words—and emotions—were always precisely chosen and to the point. The letter was brief.

> Dear Will,
> Thank you for your phone call regarding certain issues you feel the need to raise with me. As I mentioned on the phone, I am unsure why you believe it necessary to burden me with such nonsense. If you insist on experiencing these absurd adolescent growing pains, let me assure you that I pay Felix more than enough to deal with these matters. If you want me to leave you with any fatherly advice at all, it is this: any inclination toward homosexual tendencies is unnatural, self-indulgent, attention-seeking, and impure. I would greatly appreciate it if you would refrain from raising such matters with me ever again.
> Yours sincerely,
> Charles Hunter

To say that Will was enraged would have been an understatement. Through splintered, tear-filled vision he ripped the letter into a dozen, two dozen, a thousand pieces. He threw the confetti of hate onto the floor of his bedroom and stormed out of the house, rushing past Felix, who stood over a simmering saucepan in the kitchen, asking in a suddenly concerned tone, "Master Will? Are you all right?"

Felix charged after him, but as he reached the front door the Ducati roared to life and Will squealed up the driveway before Felix could stop him.

He wasn't wearing his jacket or helmet, but Will didn't care. At that moment, he didn't give a damn about anything. Not even himself.

Least of all himself.

With a roar of the engine, Will opened the throttle and screamed along the coast road at twice the legal speed. He tore around the bends, hugging low to the ground, driving with sheer reckless abandon as though he wanted to kill himself. Looking back, there was no denying that somewhere deep inside him—in some dark, angry corner of his heart—that's exactly what he was trying to do.

He overtook two cars, then swerved to miss an oncoming van, then attempted to pass a truck around a hairpin curve, and—in a flash and a wild blur—caught the yellow glimpse of a school bus coming the other way. Coming straight at him.

And in that split second, he felt the gravity of it all. The danger he had just put himself in. But not just himself. Every driver on that road, every passenger in every car, and every kid on that bus.

Will jerked the handlebars of the Ducati.

He dropped the bike flat to the ground.

He came off it, missing the bus and sliding clear under the truck, its heavy wheels bouncing and braking all around him until he shot out from under the other side, sailing for the edge of the coastal cliff, gliding along the road in a clean, straight line at a hundred miles an hour—so fast his body barely touched the ground.

The bike was in front of him, on its side now, shooting sparks into the air until it smashed through the guardrail and launched itself off the cliff and disappeared into the unknown.

And then Will himself was flying.

Through the broken guardrail.

Straight off the edge of the hairpin curve.

Straight out into the air.

Into the—

"*Water!*"

Will sat bolt upright, gasping for air. "Water! The water saved my life! I came flying off the cliff and landed in the ocean. I could have been dead, I could have killed myself, I… I…"

But Jake had him now, his large, safe hands holding him firmly by the shoulders. "Shh, shh, shh! Kid! You're okay, there's no ocean. You were having a bad dream, but you're okay now. I got you."

Will looked around, disoriented. Quickly he sized up his surroundings and realized he was in the small sleeping quarters of the cruiser. He could feel the hum of the engines. They were back on the Nile. "The temple! The map?" he blurted desperately.

"We found it," Jake replied with a wink. "Piece of cake. Just take it easy."

Will suddenly realized his chest felt tight and restricted. He looked down and saw a bandage wrapped tightly around him. He peeled back the sheet and saw another bandage wrapped around one thigh as well as a piece of blood-stained gauze taped to his side.

Suddenly he felt the freight-train headache tear through his head. Instinctively his fingers probed under his matted hair and felt the butterfly clips holding his scalp together.

"What happened?"

"Don't worry," Jake assured him. "You'll heal. You

didn't miss a thing, I promise. Just rest up." He eased Will back down and pulled the sheet over him, then turned to leave.

"But what about the city?" Will asked desperately, despite his pain. "The City of the Impure? Where is it?"

"What is it?" Charles huffed.

Not that he was at all interested. All he cared about was squirming his way out of the ropes. At last he felt the knots begin to give a little, and for the first time since leaving Cairo he could move his wrists, if only slightly.

Ra was in front of him, crouching with his back to Charles, staring in wonder at the map on the floor of the chamber. Charles couldn't see the grin of excitement on Ra's face, but he could hear it in his voice.

"It's a map. They found it. They actually found it."

Charles felt the ropes behind his back loosen even more. His heart gave a little leap of hope. He tried to keep Ra distracted with more questions as he managed to wriggle one thumb free. "A map of what? Who found it?"

"A map to the City of the Impure," Ra replied, studying the markings and contours on the floor. "And it was your clever son and his friends who found it, just as we hoped they would."

"My son!" Charles exclaimed, yanking his other thumb loose. "William may be errant in his ways, but I assure you my son has nothing to do with any of this nonsense!"

"Perhaps you don't know your son as well as you think you might."

"Perhaps I don't care to. Not until he grows up and starts acting a little more—"

Charles suddenly let slip a gasp as the ropes fell from his wrists.

Ra heard it and spun around.

Astonished that he had actually managed to free himself,

Charles stared at his hands, then stared at Ra, and then, not knowing what else to do, he turned and ran as fast as he could, sprinting upright and awkward in his now dusty and disheveled dinner jacket, heading back toward the antechamber of the temple.

Behind him, Ra began to laugh, genuinely amused and feeling truly empowered over his crusty bureaucratic captive. In no desperate rush, Ra reached inside the pocket of his long coat and pulled out his blowpipe.

He selected his poison. The knockout drug.

The dart smacked into the back of Charles's neck and he toppled instantly to the floor of the temple, falling into the middle of the drawing that Daniel had made in the sand only a few hours earlier, his face landing beside the finger-etching of the coiled worm.

The poison in the dart worked quickly.

Charles's vision blurred. His eyes rolled wildly in their sockets.

Before he lost consciousness completely, he heard Ra's footsteps approach. He heard that deep, sinister laugh, then saw the large man standing over him.

"You won't get away with this," Charles slurred, before sinking into the black, murky depths of another drug-induced slumber.

Ra smiled. "Oh, yes, I will. Soon you and your son and the others, even Monsieur Perron, will all be dead. And I'll be richer than any man on earth. I'll get away with anything I like."

His laughter echoed throughout the Temple of Min as he pulled his cell phone out of his coat and dialed. "Monsieur Perron. I believe it's time to pack your things. Our treasure awaits."

XIII

Villa Perron, La Molière, France

SAM THREW UP IN A CORNER OF THE LIBRARY. HE WAS giddy and nauseous and had trouble getting back on his feet. The Professor helped him up and held a hand against the boy's forehead. His skin was on fire. The Professor felt for a chair and eased the boy into it. "Here, sit down. Take slow, deep breaths."

"I'm sorry," Sam whispered breathlessly. "I don't feel so good anymore."

"It's okay. Deep breaths."

"I'm sorry about the door, too. I kept bangin' when you told me not to. I guess I was just—"

"Pissed off?" The Professor winked. "Don't tell Elsa I swore."

The comment made Sam smile, despite his obvious suffering. "You ain't so bad for an old man. I feel like you and me, we kinda—"

"Understand each other?"

Sam nodded feebly. "Somethin' like that. Yeah. Too late now, I guess."

"It's never too late," the Professor assured him, stroking the boy's dark, sweat-slicked hair. "We'll find you a cure. I promise."

"How?" The brusque remark came not from Sam, but someone standing in the doorway. Perron was back. He stood smirking at them, with his bully Mr. Goodwin looming large behind him. "The antidote's gone and it's time to leave."

The Professor and a very pale-looking Sam both turned to Perron. "We're not going anywhere," the Professor snapped. "The boy's ill."

"I know that!" Perron snapped back. "I'm the one who made him that way. And you call yourself a professor?" Perron clicked his fat fingers and Mr. Goodwin swooped into the room and roughly seized Sam.

"I said he's sick!" the Professor shouted as Sam was pulled from his grasp and dragged out of the library.

"Yes," Perron sniffed sourly. "I can smell it! And if the stinking little street rat vomits in my helicopter I'll throw him out of it!"

"Helicopter?"

"You heard me. We're on our way to the single greatest discovery in Egypt's long and distinguished history. Thanks to me!"

Suddenly a guard came rushing up to the door. "Monsieur Perron! There's been a security breach in the northwest corner of the estate."

Instantly Perron looked accusingly at Professor Fathom, then turned to Mr. Goodwin. "If it's one of *his* boys, invite him along for the ride. We'll be waiting in the chopper for you."

Luca found the entrance to the tunnel in the northwest corner of the estate, hidden in a thicket of tangled trees and bushes. Many years ago, monks had fled their besieged monastery by torchlight in the dead of night. Today, this secret passageway was little more than a stinking sewer.

Luca laid his hand against the rocky limestone wall. When he pulled his hand away, his palm was covered in strings of glistening green slimc. He wiped them off on the seat of his pants, then peered once more into the long, black tunnel, listening to the distant dripping of algae-filled water and the panicked scurry of rodents' feet echo through the darkness. He took one step into the sludgy shallows of the tunnel and his boot squelched and filled with murky brown fluid. He took another step, then another, then his footing began to slip in the slime. He tried to steady himself by grabbing the wall, but what he grabbed had hair.

It was a rat.

It let out an ear-piercing squeal.

Luca's fingers snapped open like a spring-lock mechanism, releasing the wretched little creature just before it had a chance to sink its diseased fangs into the back of his hand. It plopped into the foul, muck-filled water and swam away shrieking.

Luca's eyes could make out the ripples caused by several rats now swimming away in panic. Hc steered well clear of them. When he was halfway down the tunnel he heard a strange thump and gush ahead of him. For a moment he wondered what it was, then realized the gush was the sound of thrashing water, and the thump was the sound of the mill wheel, turning over and over above the tunnel.

Thump-splash! Thump-splash! Thump-splash!

The sound of the churning wheel of the water mill grew louder and louder above the tunnel until Luca realized he was standing directly beneath it. On the wall beside him he saw several slimy green stones jutting out at regular intervals, like rungs in a ladder. They were leading up to a wooden hatch in the ceiling of the tunnel. It was a fair guess that the hatch opened up into the water mill.

Thump-splash! Thump-splash! Thump-splash!

The muffled rhythm of the waterwheel.

Tightly gripping each of the handholds, Luca climbed the rudimentary ladder and pushed gently on the hatch. It was unlocked. Luca opened it an inch and peered ahead of him.

The water mill was a small rickety old building with water spraying and splashing everywhere as the huge wheel spun around and around at a rapid, unstoppable pace scooping up the dark pond water. Belting. Churning. Booming like thunder. Luca sized up the rest of the mill quickly. There was a closed door, a grimy old window holding back the light of day, and a few garden tools hanging by chains on the wall.

From where he stood, Luca saw no sign of life. The mill looked abandoned. Cautiously he lifted the hatch, climbed out of the underground tunnel, then spun around quickly at the sound of a gruff, deep voice behind him.

"I'm gonna tear you limb from limb!"

The hulking form of Mr. Goodwin stood large and menacing on the other side of the hatch. Without a moment's hesitation, the little Italian shot a glance left and right in search of a weapon, then swiftly sprang toward one of the walls and grabbed the rusted hoe hanging there. It felt weak and brittle and Luca instantly tossed it to the floor, reaching for a better option: the chain that was suspending the hoe.

He wrapped it quickly around his wrist, securing his grasp, leaving a length dangling at the end, making a weapon of it.

Mr. Goodwin smiled and charged at Luca, undaunted. He made a powerful swipe with one giant fist.

Luca jumped out of the way.

Mr. Goodwin lunged again.

Luca swung the chain at his attacker. It whistled through the air. Mr. Goodwin caught it with his right hand, then struck Luca across the face as hard as he could with his left fist. Luca staggered back, then was snapped forward with a yank. The chain was still wrapped around his wrist. Mr. Goodwin had him on the end of it like a dog on a leash.

The killer boxer reeled Luca in and pulled him near, then dealt him another hefty blow to the head. Blood splashed from Luca's lips.

Mr. Goodwin yanked him closer still, but before he could strike again, Luca threw a high kick at Mr. Goodwin's right hand—the hand holding the chain.

Fingers cracked.

The chain flew out of Mr. Goodwin's grip.

It looped through the air—

—and coiled itself up in the spinning spokes of the water-wheel.

"Oh, shit," Luca breathed, frantically trying to unwrap the other end of the chain from his wrist.

Too late.

The chain caught in the wheel and snapped tight.

It jerked Luca off his feet and dragged him swiftly across the floor toward the thrashing wheel.

Thump-splash! Thump-splash! Thump-splash!

Suddenly Mr. Goodwin leapt forward and seized Luca's ankle. He wasn't about to let the waterwheel finish his fight for him; he was having far too much fun beating Luca to a pulp to let him go now.

The chain snapped taut.

Mr. Goodwin pulled in the opposite direction.

Luca's body stretched and left the ground, suddenly becoming the rope in a tug-of-war between Mr. Goodwin and the waterwheel. The young Italian cried out in pain, trying frantically to unravel the chain now cutting into his wrist.

The wheel groaned and strained, trying to chew up the resisting chain.

Mr. Goodwin growled, not at Luca, but at the wheel that was trying to ring the bell to end the round early.

Luca jerked his wrist, trying desperately to pull the chain free. Suddenly one of the coils unlooped. His body jolted and the tension gave a little. The wheel quickly picked up the slack, but then another loop unraveled.

Then another.

Then another.

Then—

—the chain slid from Luca's wrist and was gobbled up by the wheel.

Luca fell toward the floor, his ankle still in Mr. Goodwin's grip. Before he could hit the ground, Mr. Goodwin had hurled him across the room.

The young Italian flew through the spray-filled air, hit the grimy window on the far wall, and crashed straight through it. Shattered glass exploded everywhere as Luca burst into the bright daylight and hit the ground with a grunt and a thud. He opened his eyes to the blinding sky. He heard the churning of the waterwheel somewhere behind him now. And in front of him, he heard shouting.

He heard the boots of security guards trampling down the hill toward him.

And he heard a mechanical whir. The whir of rotor blades.

He sat up quickly, and suddenly Mr. Goodwin was in front of him once more, his bunched-up fist flying through the air. Luca caught one last glimpse of Mr. Goodwin's knuckles, then everything turned black.

With an unconscious Luca draped over one shoulder, Mr. Goodwin made his way up the grassy slope to the luxurious Bell chopper, as it was about to lift off.

As the blades of the chopper whirred impatiently, Mr. Goodwin dumped the unconscious body of Luca on the helicopter's floor.

"Now you have two of them to nurse," Perron said, grinning at the Professor, who, with the help of a pale Sam, tried to lift Luca into one of the seats and strap him in.

"No good can come of this," the Professor warned Perron in a flat, almost regretful tone.

Perron simply laughed. "I'm not asking for *good*. What I want is the *gold*!"

The Professor said nothing more. He checked Luca's pulse, then made sure both Luca and Sam were strapped in tight.

Mr. Goodwin sealed the cabin, then stepped into the cockpit and buckled himself into the pilot's seat. He put on his earphones. He checked the navigation sequence he'd logged into the chopper's guidance system. A loud sonic whine filled the countryside, and with a gentle list, the helicopter lifted off over the trees of La Molière before cutting a straight line south.

Heading directly for the Mediterranean.

And beyond that—

Egypt.

XIV

Manaus, Brazil

THE THORNE MANSION WAS BUILT ON THE EDGE OF Manaus, on the edge of civilization itself. It was a luxurious heritage house constructed during Manaus's economic boom of the 1920s. Thorne had always considered it sufficient. Livable. An adequate venue for parties or dinner with guests—

—the ones he didn't want dead.

The house was three floors of many rooms, including a ballroom, an indoor swimming pool, and a library dedicated to botany and horticulture. There was also a cellar. An ancient dungeon filled with rare and priceless bottles of champagne. A dark, isolated, subterranean refuge. A place filled with sparkling sophistication—and startling savagery.

It was here in this cellar that Eden awoke—his head pounding and his body racked with pain—to find himself suspended by chains.

His hands were shackled and hoisted high above his head. He was completely naked, his body awash with sweat and seeping blood. Through one red, swollen eye he saw the handsome Gael Zagallo grinning at him, his own shirtless torso gleaming with sweat, his wet lips twisted in a satisfied grin. Then he saw the young man's fist, swinging toward him at an astonishing, merciless speed.

Gael's fist slammed into the right side of Eden's face.

Eden's giddy head rocked to one side on impact, his cheekbone throbbing in pain.

A moment later, he felt Gael's face brush past his, he felt the young man's breath against his bruised cheek and felt his soft lips kiss and caress the flesh he'd just beaten to a pulp.

"Is he tender yet?" came the voice of Alexander Thorne somewhere beyond the shadows.

Gael turned to the voice in the darkness and shook his head.

An amused chuckle echoed through the cellar, and Thorne emerged from the shadows, champagne flute in hand. "I don't care how tough he thinks he is. Soften him up!"

Eden heard a sudden whoosh and felt a piercing pain as something cut across his chest. He winced sharply, then opened his eyes to see the weapon in Gael's hand: the switchblade. It had cut a thin, shallow line across Eden's flesh, enough to draw blood.

Gael raised the knife high and sliced the air with it once more, slashing Eden's stomach, leaving a bloody gash from one side of his tortured torso to the other. His body jolted, his thick muscles tensed, his heavy cock swayed from thigh to thigh with his spasm of pain. Gael followed through with another punch, this time to the left side of Eden's battered jaw.

Eden panted and huffed, and tasted the blood between his clenched teeth. "Dinner," he spluttered. "I thought I was supposed to be your damn dinner guest."

"Indeed you are." Thorne began to laugh, then drained his champagne. "Gael! Pull him down and tie his hands with rope. It's time we showed Dr. Santiago the greenhouse."

The ride was rough and rugged, and every dip and bump on the remote trail sent a wave of pain through Eden's bloody, still naked body. He sat in the back of Thorne's jeep with his hands tied together, Gael Zagallo's revolver trained on his head.

Twelve miles into the rain forest was Alexander Thorne III's crowning achievement. His secret opus. The living, thriving showpiece of his life's work.

Shining through the trees, distant at first, then getting brighter and brighter until it glittered in the reflection of Eden's eyes.

The greenhouse was a massive, multifaceted glass sphere.

A giant orb glowing in the night.

The jeep slid to a halt. Thorne marched proudly up to his gleaming temple. Gael—revolver in hand—hauled Eden's bruised body out of the vehicle. Despite his pain—despite the swelling and the bleeding—Eden couldn't help but stare in astonishment and breathe, "My God."

Standing in front of him, Thorne turned, with an egomaniacal grin on his face. "Why, thank you."

The greenhouse, he explained, was one hundred feet high and a hundred feet in diameter, with three levels of steel gangplanks twisting and winding through thirteen separately controlled weather systems.

Thorne proceeded to lead them into the giant orb and along a raised gangplank, past fans of gigantic leaves and clusters of petite flowers, through archways of prehistoric ferns, over wetlands covered in a blanket of mist. As they walked—Thorne in front, Gael bringing up the rear—their reflection bounced off every octagonal facet of the glass walls, almost as though they were walking through a lush, green hall of mirrors.

"Welcome to the greatest single achievement in botanical science. Jungles, rain forests, desert plains, native bush—every floral landscape this Earth has to offer, painstakingly reconstructed and assembled together in a single, artificially sustained environment." Thorne smiled at Eden with more than a glint of self-importance in his eye. "You talk about God? You're looking at him."

"At what cost?"

"Oh, I assure you, Dr. Santiago. No expense has been spared."

"I don't mean the monetary kind."

"Sshh!" Thorne hissed. He held up one hand to silence Eden, then with the other he reached into his pocket and pulled out a remote control. He clicked a button, and suddenly the sound of opera—Madame Butterfly herself—filled the entire chamber. "That's better. Now, what was it you were saying?"

"You're not a god, Thorne. You're a plunderer. You've raped the planet for your own private collection, your own amusement."

"I've built an ark, Dr. Santiago. A living wonder. A scientific marvel!"

"All you've built is an ego, one that can't possibly sustain itself."

Thorne huffed. "What a pity. As you are a scientist, I had hoped you might cherish this opportunity. Surely, as a man of knowledge, as a creature of curiosity, you can appreciate the phenomenon around you—a complete collection of every single living plant species known to mankind. And one species that mankind didn't even know existed."

"What are you talking about?"

Thorne didn't answer. He simply turned and began

storming along the gangplank, ordering at the top of his voice, "Gael! Bring our dinner guest!"

Gael shoved Eden forward with the snub end of his revolver. "Move it!"

Eden was pushed forcibly along, keeping up with Thorne until he stepped out along a short gangplank that seemed to go nowhere.

Eden's mind was racing. This was some kind of viewing platform, but to view what? Thorne answered the question by reaching for Eden, seizing his roped hands and pulling him toward the edge of the gangplank. Gael flicked open his switchblade and handed it to Thorne, who proceeded to cut a deep gash across the palm of Eden's left hand.

A river of blood flowed freely from the open cut and poured over the edge of the gangplank.

Shining red drops fell six feet, and then, with a monstrous growl and a loud, wet snap, a giant plant below the gangplank leapt to life—two massive crimson petals, with razor-sharp spines along their edges—lapping and gulping at the trail of blood.

Horrified, Eden tried to jump back from the edge, but Thorne held him there, forcing him to watch as the giant plant lurched and grumbled and swallowed ravenously.

"Behold," Thorne brimmed with pride. "*Carna-Venus amazonas.*"

"I think they're hungry," Gael observed with a sinister smile.

"They?" Eden's eyes scanned the moving landscape below the gangplank and saw that there was not just one, but a dozen of the bloodthirsty plants, all moving now, swaying back and forth, opening their jaws wide like monstrous baby birds in a pungent, mossy nest, just begging to be fed.

"Explorers and adventurers have reported seeing these plants for centuries," lectured Thorne. "And yet people still believe they are a myth. A story to frighten children, which, incidentally, happen to be their favorite food! In order to keep my precious plants fed, Gael and I are single-handedly ridding Manaus of its wretched street kids."

"You what?" Eden stood, staring, appalled at Thorne's murderous confession.

Thorne simply smiled. "You heard me. It's quite a marvel to behold. The digestion process of the Carna-Venus is fascinating. The chemical makeup of the plant's saliva acts like acid. Needless to say, consumption is quite thorough and surprisingly fast, depending on the portion sizes. They enjoy their meals in pieces. Limbs. The odd severed appendage."

Thorne took the knife and held it against Eden's hung cock. Eden refused to flinch, feeling the sharp blade against his shaft. His defiance made Thorne laugh. "Of course, a single Carna-Venus is more than capable of devouring a man whole, but it does take several days for the flesh to break down, and the larger meals tend to repeat on them. Quite a stench, you can imagine."

"You can't get away this, you son of a bitch—!"

Gael cocked the trigger on his gun.

Thorne snatched the blade away from Eden's cock and laughed even louder. "From plunderer to son of a bitch. I'm not entirely sure whether I've gone up or down the social ladder. Perhaps I can restore my status to gentleman by offering you dinner before you die. It's a courtesy I extend to all my greenhouse guests, a last meal before mealtime."

Thorne pushed Eden back into Gael's grip, then turned in an entirely new direction. "Come."

Butterfly's aria continued to resonate through the sphere as Thorne led them to a steel-grate platform raised high above a trickling waterway covered in floating lilies.

In the middle of the platform was a table set for three. At each place was a steaming silver bowl with a lid on top, a silver soup spoon on the side, and a sparkling crystal champagne flute. As a centerpiece for the table—like flowers in a vase—was a small cryogenic cylinder containing a single, delicate, moonlight-blue-petaled orchid: the Deldah-sha.

Thorne gestured for Eden to take a seat at the table. Gael promptly sat Eden's naked ass into a chair, then flicked open a folded cloth napkin and draped it slowly across Eden's lap like a waiter.

"By the way," Thorne remarked, "I thought I might do you the honor of letting you know what you're worth." He reached down beside him and set a metal briefcase on the table. He flicked the locks and opened the lid. "Half a million in U.S. dollars, courtesy of Monsieur Pierre Perron. A man can buy a lot of champagne with that kind of money, Dr. Santiago."

On cue, Gael popped the cork on a vintage bottle of champagne and filled their glasses, Thorne first.

Thorne sipped the bubbles and closed his eyes, capturing a moment of sheer pleasure. "Ah! Dom Pérignon! Puccini! I mentioned before how enchanting this place is. Such civility. Such savagery. Can you think of anywhere else in the world you'd rather die?"

"I don't know," Eden replied flatly. "But I think you're about to find out."

Thorne laughed back the bubbles of his champagne. "At last! A sense of humor." Across the table, he eyed Eden's naked body up and down. "You really are the perfect package, Dr. Santiago. It seems a shame to kill you. But business is business, and dinner is served! I hope the ropes don't hinder you too much."

Gael appeared beside Eden then, and with his revolver in one hand and a napkin in the other, he lifted the silver lid on Eden's bowl. A plume of steam billowed into the air, then evaporated to reveal a simmering broth.

"Alligator tacaca," Thorne announced. "A delicacy of the region. The trick is to beat the meat till it's soft. Succulent. Tender. Much like yourself."

Gael began to snicker.

"Be careful not to burn yourself, Dr. Santiago," Thorne said, smirking. "It's quite hot."

Eden leveled his gaze. "I'm Brazilian. The hotter the better!"

That was his cue. In a single lightning-fast move, Eden snatched the base of his steaming hot bowl in his bound hands and launched it up into the air, straight into the laughing face of Gael Zagallo.

As the scorching soup splashed his face, Gael's cackle of glee turned to a scream of pain that echoed throughout the entire sphere.

He let go of the gun and clutched at his burning eyes.

He staggered backward, collapsing to the steel-grate platform, shrieking.

The revolver clattered and bounced across the grate.

Eden pushed himself out of his chair and lunged for the gun.

Thorne got to it first.

Eden reeled back and grabbed the metal briefcase off the table. Thorne snapped up the gun and fired off a random shot in Eden's direction. Eden held up the briefcase and used it as a shield. Sparks flew off the case. The bullet ricocheted into a panel of glass in the ceiling, and shattered shards rained down on all three of them.

Thorne dropped the gun as he crouched and covered his head.

The gun rattled across the grid platform—

—straight into the waiting, wide-open palm of a furious-faced Gael Zagallo.

Half blinded and full of rage, Gael pumped a shot straight at Eden.

The bullet left a dent in the metal case and knocked Eden off his feet.

Thorne looked around desperately for the nearest escape route, but before vanishing he seized his one and only bargaining chip off the table.

As Gael fired off two more shots, Eden jumped to his feet and sprinted down the nearest gangplank, disappearing in the dense foliage. Gael staggered to his feet and hissed, "You're mine!" He reached into his pocket and pulled out his knife, flicking open its seven-inch blade. With the gun in one hand and the knife in the other, he vanished down the gangplank after Eden.

Naked, unarmed, and bound at the wrists, Eden raced as fast as he could through the greenhouse, turning left, weaving right, hooking back through the intersecting interlevel maze of gangplanks. He pushed past leaves and branches and slippery tendrils. Behind him, closing in fast, were the running footsteps of Gael Zagallo, stomping relentlessly down the gangplanks.

"You can't hide, Dr. Santiago," called the killer tauntingly.

At that point, Eden decided to take his chances in the vegetation.

He jumped off the side of the walkway and into a wilderness of fern leaves, staying low and quiet. Somewhere above, through a thatch of trees, he heard his pursuer's bounding steps.

And then—

—nothing.

Eden stopped still.

He heard a rustle in the bushes a short distance away and realized Gael Zagallo had had the same idea.

The hunt was on in the thick of Thorne's greenhouse jungle.

Eden moved fast, crouching low, making his way swiftly

through thickets, under canopies, past fully grown palms. Although it provided him a shield, the heavy metal briefcase was weighing him down. He stashed it in a thatch of ferns and kept moving. He knew he had to take care of Gael, somehow, then get to the Deldah-sha. But his hands were still tied and he had no knife, no gun, no weapon at all.

Gael, on the other hand, had every advantage.

He was also, suddenly, standing straight in front of Eden, popping out of nowhere.

Eden and Gael saw each other at precisely the same moment.

They both stopped dead, facing one another, standing ten, perhaps twelve feet apart.

Eden gasped. There was no escape.

Gael laughed and raised his revolver.

He aimed straight at Eden's head and pulled the trigger.

The bullet ripped through the air and slammed straight into Eden's forehead—

—in an explosion of shattered glass.

Gael watched, confused, as his target smashed into shards and crashed to the ground.

At the same moment, Eden watched his killer break apart in splinters.

Both men realized at the same time that they had been looking at each other's reflection in an octagonal panel of the glass wall.

Gael quickly looked left.

Eden glanced right.

The two men were but four feet apart, side by side, separated only by a cluster of black bamboo.

Gael swung his pistol around.

Eden lunged forward and seized a bamboo stalk. He pulled it back as far as it would go, then released it.

Gael's finger squeezed the trigger.

The bamboo whipped through the air and smashed into the bridge of his nose.

He fired a shot.

Another octagonal panel of glass shattered.

Eden kicked high, connecting with Gael's knife hand.

The switchblade flew straight up into the air.

Eden caught it by the handle.

Gael aimed the gun again and pulled the trigger.

The barrel clicked.

The chamber was empty.

Eden threw the knife. It somersaulted through the air and thudded straight into the center of Gael's chest. The handsome young killer inhaled deeply and stared in shock at the knife handle protruding from his body. Then slowly his eyes rolled back into his head and his body fell backward.

He landed with a soft thud in a bed of luminous night mushrooms, staring lifelessly up into the tapestry of branches above.

Eden stepped forward, pulled the knife from Gael's chest, then twisted it in his hands and severed the ropes around his wrists. He backtracked through the captive jungle and retrieved the briefcase, then looked up, trying to figure out the quickest way back up to the network of gangplanks.

"Gael?" Thorne called uncertainly, now standing on the edge of the gangplank above the hungry, lurching Carna-Venus. "Gael! Can you hear me?"

"Gael's dead," Eden announced, stepping through a veil of hanging vines at the far end of the walkway. He moved defiantly up to the edge of the gangplank, only a few feet from Thorne.

"Don't take another step," Thorne warned in an angry, panicky voice. The botanist suddenly produced the cryogenic cylinder containing the Deldah-sha from behind his back and held it over the growling man-eating plants below.

Eden made a countermove.

He thrust his arm out over the edge of the gangplank, holding the briefcase over the hungry Carna-Venus. Clutching the handle of it tight in his fist, he took Gael's switchblade and cut open his own hand—the hand holding the briefcase. His blood splashed down his wrist, down his forearm, down the sides of the metal case, soaking it in blood. Below, the plant-beasts thrashed and growled at the scent of flesh blood. But they wanted more. Much more.

An anxious bead of sweat trickled down Thorne's brow. "Don't be foolish! Put the case down and step back or I'll drop the Deldah-sha!"

But Eden stood his ground. "I came for the orchid, and I'll leave with the orchid."

As Eden and Thorne squared off, Butterfly's heart-wrenching aria soared to its crescendo, filling the sphere.

Thorne smiled thinly. "You don't reasonably expect to come out of this alive, Dr. Santiago. The only question left to ask is, will you die honorably—or needlessly."

"The only answer is—not at all."

Suddenly Eden hurled the briefcase, not over the gangplank, but directly at Thorne.

The orchid hunter saw it coming and gasped in horror. "My money!" His hands flew forward, letting go of the orchid cylinder to try to catch the flying briefcase.

The cylinder hit the gangplank and scuttled toward the edge.

Eden dived for it. He thudded against the gangplank, his arm shooting out as far as he could reach, his finger-tips snatching the cylinder tight just as it bounced over the edge.

At the same time, the heavy briefcase thumped into Thorne's chest.

The lid snapped open.

The money exploded into the air.

Thorne stumbled backward with the force of the blow, tumbling over the edge, his arms flailing through the air, trying in vain to catch his fluttering bills.

The metal briefcase fell onto the steel gangplank and clanged like a dinner bell.

The jaws of the Carna-Venus opened wide, wet and quivering.

Thorne plummeted through the air and landed directly in the mouth of the beast, its jaws clamming shut around him, sealing him in, smothering a bloodcurdling scream that would last several hours. Several agonizing, flesh-eating hours. Until, eventually, there would be nothing left of Alexander Thorne III.

No sound.

No skin.

Not even a skeleton.

Eden climbed to his feet, the cryogenic cylinder clutched tightly in his fist. He glanced over the edge of the gangplank at the hideous sight of Thorne's body—or more accurately, the shape of it—writhing inside the locked jaws of the plant, then quickly looked away. The plants had turned on their captor. The rain forest would soon reclaim this entire place. It was inevitable that nature would win in the end.

As money continued to rain down all around him, Eden bent down and picked a wad of cash up off the gangplank. If he wanted to get the Deldah-sha orchid out of the country he was going to have to buy his way through customs.

Quickly, he checked his wristwatch for Professor Fathom's location. The small dot on the global grid was moving, heading toward the Mediterranean on a trajectory that would take it somewhere within the vicinity of—

"Aswan," Eden said out loud. "Time's running out."

XV

The Desert North of Aswan, Egypt

UNDER COVER OF DUSK THEY MOORED THE CRUISER IN THE tall reeds on the bank of the Nile, and as the moon rose behind them, they made their way west into the desert. Will carried the two small statuettes of Min in his pocket. Shane led the way. His acute cartography skills and his instinctive feeling for distances and spatial dimensions provided him with a built-in compass, one that was yet to fail him. The miniature shapes and contours of the map they had uncovered in the Temple of Min were now life-sized, rising and falling all around them as they trekked along dry rocky ridges, traversed isolated canyons, and entered the vast, empty desert, striding steadily toward the City of the Impure.

In the light of the moon, the entire landscape was a duotone of blue and black.

Suddenly, Shane stopped in his tracks.

The others came to a halt beside him.

For a moment, all four of them stood in complete silence,

wondering if there was such a thing as a night mirage.

But within moments, Will broke the silence and dispelled their doubts. "Trees. Palm trees. It's the oasis. The oasis where Ahnu built his city. Come on!"

He started to run, his boots sinking in the sand and his backpack swaying awkwardly from side to side. But it wasn't enough to slow him down. In fact, the young football player had broken into a sprint, a triumphant dash, a breakneck pace the others were determined to match.

The four of them bolted through the desert, kicking up sand in a furious wake.

Their hearts pounded, their lungs burned, their legs ached, but they didn't slow down until they reached the point where the sand turned to a rocky stretch, sloping down toward a bed of wild grass and shrubs.

And beyond that, date palms and thickets and sprawling ferns.

And beyond that—

—a grove of palm trees bursting into the sky, surrounding a glittering desert lake.

"It's beautiful," Daniel panted.

"We found it!" Will didn't even stop to catch his breath. He raced down the slope into the thick of the oasis, unable to contain his sheer joy.

"Will, wait up!" Jake bolted after him, followed by Shane and Daniel.

Giddy rapture overwhelmed the young history student as he leapt and bounded his way through the ferns and trees, calling to the others, "Come on! We're so close now!" He burst out of the lush forest and stopped at the shore of the small, shining lake. At the far end was a large cluster of boulders, smooth and pale in the moonlight. On the surface, the moon's reflection danced and sparkled as though Isis herself had filled the lake with stars. The very sight of it dazzled him.

He shot a glance at the night sky. "Oh, Henry. I hope you're seeing what I'm seeing." But he knew the real wonder was yet to come.

Jake, Shane, and Daniel suddenly rushed out from the bushes behind him.

Will slipped off his backpack and laid it on the ground. He couldn't take his eyes off the lake, the swaying palms, the clusters of ferns and rocks all around. "This is the place. The pyramid is here somewhere, I know it is. We just have to find it now."

Shane shook his head. "I still don't get it. How do you hide somethin' that big? It's a goddamn pyramid."

"For the ancient Egyptians, discovery was a process. A journey. You reach your destination one step at a time. To find the pyramid, we shouldn't be looking for a pyramid." Will slipped his hand in his pocket and pulled out the two golden statuettes. "We should be looking for something to unlock."

"It'll be dawn soon," Jake said, his voice tight and concerned. He looked at his watch. "Sam's only got a few hours left. In the meantime, finding a tiny keyhole in this forest, in the dark, ain't gonna be easy. There's no time to waste."

Shane nodded, "Let's split up. Jake, Will, you guys cover the shoreline. Daniel and I will head into the forest and see what we can find."

They all agreed. Will reached into his backpack and pulled out a pair of flashlights. He gave one to Shane.

"Good luck," the cowboy said to Will and Jake. He and Daniel turned and swiftly vanished among the palms.

Will snapped on his flashlight, then turned to face the lake. "Henry Chamberlain said to me, water is life."

"Are you saying you think the lock to those keys is somewhere in the lake?" Jake asked.

Will answered, "Do you feel like a swim?"

Jake looked at him for an uncertain moment, then remembered what he himself had said a minute ago. There was no time to waste.

Quickly he pulled off his shirt. "Is that flashlight waterproof?"

Their fingers traced the surface of every rock, the circumference of every tree trunk, feeling for the slightest crevice or hole, anything that felt or looked as though it could have been carved out with human hands.

Shane shone the flashlight beam on the trunks of palms. He traced the fronds of ferns down to their roots. Daniel ran his fingers around the rim of a rock ledge—

—then realized it wasn't a rock ledge at all.

"Shane?"

"What is it?"

Shane raced over to where Daniel was squatting. "I don't know. But I think it's a...I think it's a roof."

The beam of the flashlight bounced off what looked like a cracked brown dome concealed beneath a thatch of ferns and half buried in the earth. Shane stood and shone the light through the forest. "Not just one roof," he said.

Daniel stood too. In the beam of the flashlight, they caught glimpses of not one, not two, but dozens and dozens of clay hemispheres sunk into the sand and overgrown with vegetation.

"The City of the Impure," Shane whispered. "This is where they lived while they built Ahnu's pyramid. Imagine how many more there must be, buried beneath the ground."

Daniel was already pushing aside the underbrush covering what appeared to be the top lip of an entryway to one of the huts. It was a gap ten inches high. He lay flat on his belly and scraped away sand and earth, trying to peer inside. "Shane, bring the flashlight. If this is where one of the workers lived, there may be a clue inside."

But Shane was already standing over him, shining the light on the roof of the clay hut, just above the entrance where Daniel was digging.

"I'm not so sure this house belonged to one of the workers."

Daniel picked himself up. "What do you mean? Who else would it belong to?" Then he stood and saw the symbol in the light of Shane's flashlight.

Carved into the clay above the entryway was a large depiction of Min.

But not the traditional portrait of the god.

This image was the same as the statuettes. It was the reverse of Min. Left hand raised with the flail, right holding his phallus.

This was the Anti-Min.

A symbol that now appeared to be synonymous with Ahnu.

Shane looked at Daniel. "I think this house...was *his* house."

The flashlight was indeed waterproof and the beam cut through the clear water, shimmering through the reeds, which were undisturbed except for the currents created by Will and Jake as they swam through the depths. They kicked hard, pushing themselves deeper and deeper as the beam of their flashlight bounced off the rocks on the bottom of the lake.

Occasionally they broke the surface for air.

"Did you see anything?" Jake asked, gasping, filling his lungs again.

Will shook his head. "But there's gotta be something in this lake."

Suddenly, *something* appeared—

—a twelve-foot crocodile, fat and silent and perfectly still.

As Jake and Will treaded water, the monster reptile

simply floated to the surface between them, completely motionless.

Jake's eyes turned to saucers.

Will froze in the water.

The croc's left eye blinked and looked at Jake.

Its right eye blinked and took in how tasty Will looked.

For a moment, all three of them floated stock-still in the water, the men rendered motionless by absolute fear, the crocodile simply sizing up his meal.

And then—

"*Fuck!*" Jake jerked backward with an awkward kick and a splash.

The croc thrashed to life, its giant, open-jawed head and massive tail both curling toward Jake, lunging straight for him.

Jake smashed the prehistoric creature with a right hook, clouting it on the side of the head as hard as he damn well could.

The animal snapped back in the opposite direction, head and tail now lashing at Will.

As the gaping jaws swung at the college kid in a torrent of splashing water, Will whacked it with the flashlight, dislodging a fang that rattled down the croc's throat.

Will bounced off the blow and swam away as fast as he could, but the beast rolled into a frenzy, causing a storm in the water, churning up the currents and sucking Jake down into the swirling depths.

He tried kicking against the pull of the water, but as the croc's giant jaws lunged at his feet, he realized he was better off kicking at something else.

His foot connected with the snout of the croc.

The beast twisted out of its roll and whipped around for another try.

Jake fought his way to the surface, arms stretching, hands clutching.

A rock appeared out of nowhere.

His hands snagged it.

He launched himself up onto its jagged surface, getting his arms out of the water fast, pulling his chest up onto the rock, lifting one knee, then one leg up, then the other. He got to his feet. Then, suddenly—

—the rock sprang to life.

Its prehistoric head lifted out of the water, then smacked back down.

Its tail cracked back and forth.

And suddenly Jake realized he wasn't standing on a rock at all, but the back of a second crocodile, even bigger than the first.

It writhed and arched and snapped back and forth, trying to throw him off.

Jake tried to ride the angry monster, suddenly realizing that more and more of the man-eaters were cutting their way across the surface toward him. All hungry. All of them wanting a piece of the action.

Precariously, Jake teetered on the back of the thrashing croc.

It tipped him left.

He leaned right.

It began to roll.

Jake had no choice but to jump. He leapt clear off the back of the croc and landed the only place he could—

—straight onto the back of another crocodile.

The next reptile bucked and spun around.

Jake pitched to one side, swayed dangerously backward, then jumped again, leapfrogging over the open jaws of the croc and onto the back of a fourth crocodile.

Snap!

Then a fifth.

Clamp!

Then a sixth.

Chomp!

Until suddenly Jake landed on a real rock.

He was so ready to lurch and list and launch himself off what he thought was going to be another angry, rollicking reptile that he completely overbalanced, reeling forward. He hit his head on a second huge boulder and staggered backward, dazed, losing his balance entirely.

He felt himself stumbling back toward the water—

Back to the insatiable, snapping jaws of the crocodiles—

When suddenly a hand grabbed him and pulled him forward.

"Quit foolin' around! I found something!" It was Will, grinning excitedly.

Jake shook his dizzy head. "There's crocodiles!" he screeched in horror.

"Of course there's crocodiles. We're in Egypt."

Jake stared incredulously at Will. "You knew that! You knew that and yet you thought it was a good idea to go swimming!"

"They're bigger than I thought they'd be," Will conceded, then grinned excitedly and said, "But trust me, it was worth it! I found a cave!" He pointed the flashlight to a small stream trickling away down a narrow crevice between two boulders. Without waiting for Jake, Will squeezed through the gap.

For a moment, Jake stood where he was, mouth agape in shock. As the beam of Will's flashlight rapidly disappeared into the blackness of the crevice, Jake figured the way ahead was a better option than what lay behind him.

He inhaled deeply, sucking himself in, and squeezed through the narrow crevice between the boulders.

Apart from the bounce of the flashlight beam ahead of him, Jake couldn't see a thing. He followed as best he could, descending farther and farther into the cave, listening to the stream trickle and splash along the rocks beneath his feet. The temperature dropped. The sound of the trickling water turned into an echo, becoming more and more hollow, as though the sound had farther to carry. Then the jerking beam ahead of him stopped.

Jake hurried and caught up with Will. "What is it?"

The answer came in the slow arc of the flashlight beam taking in a gigantic underground cavern, the size of a football field.

At first, Jake thought it was a naturally formed chamber. But then the light caught what looked like a giant stone wheel.

Then another, interlocking with the first.

Then another.

"They look like—"

"Giant gearwheels," Will finished.

Dozens of them.

Some were lying flat and horizontal, others stood upright and vertical. All of them were connected with huge cogs. All carved out of stone, and covered in moss and cobwebs, as though they hadn't moved in a very long time.

There were walls at either end of the chamber too, high and straight, reaching all the way to the ceiling.

"Look," Will breathed at that moment. "The ceiling."

"Holy shit. Is that what I think it is?"

"Yep," nodded Will. "A pyramid. Only it's—"

"Upside down!"

The ceiling was indeed just that. A mammoth pyramid pointing down toward the center of the giant cavern. Its four walls sloped downward and inward to a pointed tip that almost reached the floor of the chamber. Each wall had diagonal channels down the sides, like the winding grooves in a screw.

"Henry was right," Will whispered. "It's a drill. This is the bottom half that drives the other half up to the surface. It winds its way up, then bores its way back down. That's how it disappears. But how do we make it *reappear*?"

Jake took the flashlight from Will and shone it on the biggest gearwheel of them all, lying flat directly beneath the upside-down pyramid. Then he turned the light on the wall closest to them and saw that its surface was gleaming, the rock extremely porous. "Hydraulics," he answered. "The lake is on the other side of that wall. We open the wall, the water from the lake comes flooding in and fills the chamber. The force of it turns the gearwheels, one by one, building energy and momentum—"

"And motion. The wheels put everything in motion—"

"Activating whatever mechanism rotates the pyramid to the surface."

Will pulled the two statuettes from his pocket. "They don't unlock the pyramid," he said. "They open the flood-gate."

Jake started scanning the edges of the wall with the beam of light, searching for anything that looked remotely like a keyhole, until—

"There!" Will saw it first.

A small groove. It was positioned four feet off the ground on a side panel next to the wall, little more than a hole cut into the wall in a particular shape.

Will and Jake both rushed toward it.

Will looked at the two statuettes, one in each hand, not knowing which of them would fit the lock.

He picked one at random and both men held their breath, knowing all too well the consequences of making a wrong decision in situations such as this. Will pushed the small gold Min into the lock, headfirst.

But the statuette wouldn't fit.

It clunked around in the groove, the arms, the flail, the cock of Min all jamming in places and catching in the hole.

"Careful," Jake whispered anxiously, feeling the sweat building on his brow.

"Ssshh! You're making me nervous."

Will pulled it out and turned it the other way, pushing it in feet first. But this seemed even more of a mismatch. He yanked the Min out of the hole and took the second statuette. It too jiggled around uselessly in the hole, scraping and catching and getting stuck in all the wrong places.

"Maybe it's not the right key," Will said, his teeth clenched in frustration.

"Or maybe..."

Jake took the two statuettes from Will. He held them up, facing one another, and then, quite simply, he joined them together.

They clicked.

Face to face.

Interlocking together.

Mouths connecting.

Penises touching.

Golden lips pressed against each other.

Jake smiled. "What Imhotep called impure—we call love. Love is the answer."

Will beamed. "They're not idols of Min at all. It's Ahnu and Khay."

Jake gave him back the two statuettes, now locked together as one key.

Will positioned it at the hole.

The key fitted snugly.

Suddenly Jake put his hand on Will's and stopped him. He gestured to the upside-down pyramid. "Wait a second. If this key really is the button that makes the elevator go up—what's the down button?"

Will didn't have an answer. "I guess we'll find out."

That was good enough for Jake. Time was running out, and they had come too far to let uncertainty stop them now.

Together, with Jake's hand resting on Will's, they pushed the key all the way into the hole.

187

It slid in easily, smoothly, perfectly.

For a moment nothing happened, as though the *open sesame* command was lost somewhere down the corridors of time.

Then something clicked deep inside the wall.

And suddenly, with an almighty groan, the wall began to rise.

With the first inch came a high-pressure jet of water, shooting across the floor.

The water covered the entire surface of the chamber in seconds.

The wall continued to ascend.

The inch-high jet of water turned into a foot-high jet of water.

Will and Jake began scrambling upward, away from the wall, heading for higher ground. They climbed up from ledge to ledge.

The rumbling of the ascending wall was joined by the roar of more and more water storming into the chamber like a flash flood.

The unstoppable deluge charged at the first gearwheel, and with a heavy groan it began to crank, turning counterclockwise. Its cogs connected with the next gearwheel, and in turn it too began to move. Rumbling like thunder. Turning slowly at first. But as more and more water charged through the ascending floodgate, the sheer weight of it forced the gearwheels to turn faster and faster.

There were three giant gearwheels turning now.

Four.

Five.

One of the upright wheels began to crank, like some ancient stone Ferris wheel.

The water was rising faster than Will and Jake could climb. They were running out of ledge space fast.

Will took the flashlight and shone it across to the narrow

crevice through which they had entered. It was flooding fast. If they were to get to it now, they were going to have to battle the current and swim for it—and pray that they didn't get sucked into one of the gearwheels.

"Come on!" Will shouted over the raging torrent to Jake. He took a deep breath, ready to dive headlong off the ledge into the water.

But just as he was about to jump, Jake grabbed his arm and pulled him back. "I wouldn't advise that."

He snatched the flashlight back from Will and shone it on the surface of the whitewater surge. In the churning flood, Will saw the swirling black shapes of dozens of thrashing, snapping, writhing crocodiles, caught in the flow.

"There's gotta be a way out! The Egyptians always built a way out!"

But the water was rising fast. It flooded over onto the ledge.

At that moment, a mean, confused croc suddenly washed up next to Jake. He jumped out of its way as fast as he could, not into the water, but over it, landing precariously on the flat surface of the nearest turning gearwheel.

The croc cracked its hungry jaws at Will, the next in line on the ledge.

"Jump!" Jake shouted, already spinning away on the turntable of the gearwheel.

Will didn't need to be told twice.

The croc lunged.

Will sprang.

He hit the edge of the gearwheel, grabbing onto a cog. He tried to pull himself up. The stone was wet and slippery. Out of the corner of his eye he saw that the wheel was about to connect with another, and when it did, he was going to be sandwiched between two interlocking cogs.

Suddenly Jake grabbed him.

He yanked him up onto the flat surface of the wheel.

The cogs crunched together, jetting water high into the air.

Will let out a terrified breath. "Thanks!"

As they rotated quickly on the flat, spinning wheel, Jake pulled Will to his feet. "This water's gonna keep getting higher. Which means we gotta do the same. Look, up there." He pointed, flashlight still in his hand. "There's a ledge up near the ceiling. We just gotta figure out how to get to it."

The second-to-last gearwheel was suddenly set in motion with a loud groan.

As its cogs turned, it connected to the final piece in the puzzle—the massive flat gearwheel sitting directly beneath the upside-down pyramid. It creaked slowly into motion, then, with a deafening blast of air, four hatches blew open on the flat surface of the wheel.

The explosion of air was enough to knock Jake and Will off their feet.

They landed on their backs on the wheel and stared wide-eyed at what emerged from the hatches—

Four enormous columns, rising into the air as the gearwheel turned.

The columns ascended higher and higher until, with an impact that sent a quake through the entire chamber, the top of each column connected with each of the four walls of the upside-down pyramid.

The giant gearwheel continued to turn.

The columns continued to turn and rise.

And so, as the entire chamber trembled and shook, the giant pyramid began to turn too.

Turn, and ascend.

Rotating its way up to the surface.

"My God" was all Will could say to himself.

Shane and Daniel had managed to dig out enough sand and dirt to squeeze through the top of the entrance into Ahnu's mud hut. They found themselves in a small, enclosed space, wedged between the ceiling of the hut and the layers of sand that had built up over thousands of years.

"There's an opening up ahead," Shane told Daniel.

He wriggled on his belly, moving like a snake through the sand in the dark, claustrophobic space, the back of his shirt scraping and tearing against the rough, dry-mud ceiling. Daniel followed close behind.

As Shane reached the small opening at the end of the tiny space, he saw the buildup of sand slope downward into a somewhat more protected room. He had to push some of the sand away, into the small room, before he could slide down the naturally formed dune on the other side.

He rolled onto his back and shone the flashlight around the room. It was bare. There was nothing here to indicate a rushed exit or a panicked departure. When Ahnu left this place, he was ready to go.

Suddenly Daniel squeezed through the entrance and rolled head over heels down the sandy slope, tumbling directly on top of Shane.

"Sorry," he whispered in the quiet space.

He was facedown on top of Shane. Shane was lying faceup. The two looked straight into each other's eyes.

"Don't be," Shane replied.

For a moment, they said nothing. Then, suddenly, their lips locked. Shane rolled them both over, quickly tipping Daniel on his back and taking the dominant position over him. He plunged his tongue into Daniel's wet, hungry mouth, probing deep. Daniel bit at Shane's lip gently, wanting more.

He laid his palms flat against the sand beneath him, pushing his hips upward, rubbing himself against Shane.

Then he stopped.

"Shane," he muttered, trying to pull out of the spontaneously passionate moment. "The earth's moving."

"It's moving for me too," Shane slurred through the kiss.

Daniel shook his head. "No, Shane. I'm serious. The earth really is moving."

Shane stopped kissing and raised his head, suddenly realizing Daniel wasn't joking.

In the glow of the flashlight, he saw tiny grains of sand jitter around, bouncing higher and higher and higher.

He heard a noise, a tremor, low and soft at first, then getting louder and louder.

He pressed his hand against the ground and felt the rumble. Building and building and—

"Hold on!" he cried and dropped himself on top of Daniel, shielding them both.

With a thunderous blast, a geyser of air exploded from the earth inches from their heads, rocketing up through the ceiling of the mud hut, smashing the dry-clay rooftop to smithereens and fountaining into the night.

Then, as quickly as the blast came, it died down, leaving a hole in the floor of the hut beside Daniel's head.

Shane stared at it, stunned.

He peered into the blackness of the hole that had just appeared.

With the release of pressure, a cold current of air blew gently on his face.

"What the hell is it?" Daniel swallowed, a little rattled.

"A tunnel," Shane replied.

"To where?"

"I dunno. But we're about to find out."

Shane grabbed the flashlight.

The turbulent water rushed over the top of the flat gear-wheel, washing three snapping crocodiles onto its spinning surface.

Jake had already leapt onto the next gearwheel, crossing as the cogs connected.

Will felt the water splash against the backs of his legs as a croc's jaws clapped shut inches behind him.

He jumped and landed next to Jake.

"I think we're outnumbered," Will panted.

"Just so long as we don't get outsmarted."

Jake and Will spun clockwise on one gearwheel, out of reach of the scrambling, dizzy crocs as they turned counterclockwise on another.

Jake looked at the network of wheels and cogs ahead of them.

"We go left. That one, that one, then onto the big Ferris wheel." He raised the flashlight and shone the beam to the upper ledge. At that moment, Shane and Daniel emerged from a small opening on the high ledge.

"Shane!" Jake shouted.

They saw the astonished look on Shane's and Daniel's face as they stopped short of slipping from the tiny ledge into the chamber of flooding water, churning wheels, and snapping crocodiles.

Shane spotted them and quickly shouted back, "Behind you!"

The water had washed higher again, and a giant snapper was lunging straight for them.

Jake jumped left.

Will stumbled right and leapt as far and fast as he could, landing on a completely different wheel from Jake.

Jake shone the flashlight. "Will!"

"I can make it over to you!" he shouted back, trying to figure a new path through the spinning wheels. But the water was rising fast, and the number of crocodiles was multiplying rapidly as the floodgate continued to rise.

"You have to jump back!" Jake shouted.

"But there's a crocodile there!"

Indeed, the giant reptile had positioned himself nicely on one side of the spinning turntable, ready to attack anything that stepped on his wheel.

"Time it so that you jump on the opposite side to him!"

Will knew Jake was right, it was the only way. He positioned himself on the edge of the wheel. He watched for the place to jump, where the water splashed up into the air every time the cogs connected.

The croc watched him hungrily, spinning near him, then spinning away.

Will readied himself to jump.

"Now!" Jake yelled.

But just then, a second croc washed up onto the wheel, right where Will was about to jump.

"Oh, shit!" He pulled back instead of jumping forward. "What do I do now?"

Jake looked around desperately. He didn't have an answer, and the water was now rising over the edge of his own gearwheel. Crocodiles were swirling around the edges in a thrashing torrent of teeth and tails.

"Through the middle!" Shane suddenly shouted from his bird's-eye view.

Will looked up. "What?"

"Run straight through the middle of the wheel, as fast as you can, between the two crocodiles, exactly when I say to."

Will stared at the turning wheel in front of him and breathed, "Is he crazy?"

Jake stared wide-eyed, sizing up Will's odds. "Is he crazy?"

"When I say," Shane shouted from above, watching the mechanics, his own head turning in time with the motion of the connecting wheels.

Will gulped hard and stepped up to the edge of a cog.

Jake positioned himself at the edge of his wheel, ready to catch Will.

Shane watched the wheels turn. "Not yet," he called.

Will bent his knees and dug his heels in, ready to launch himself.

"Not yet."

The two hungry crocs eyed him from opposite sides of the wheel, ready for dinner.

"Not yet."

Jake crouched low, ready for the catch.

The cogs connected.

"Now!" Shane shouted.

Will jumped, his legs like pistons.

He landed on the crocodile wheel and ran, as fast as he could, straight through the middle.

Ahead of him he saw Jake's wheel coming around. On both sides he saw the crocs come crashing toward him. One lunged. Will put on a burst of speed. The second croc snapped. Will jumped into the air. Both crocs missed him by an inch, then smashed headlong into each other, jaws smashing and tails thrashing. As the reptiles attacked each other in a frenzy of blood, Will hit the edge of the wheel and sprang into the air.

Jake caught him.

The two crashed onto the surface of Jake's wheel, just as three more crocs washed up around them.

The two men bounced to their feet.

They leapt from one wheel to the next, then grabbed on to the ascending cogs of the upright gearwheel.

The wheel lifted them out of the rising water, up and over toward the ledge where Shane and Daniel were now lying on their stomachs, arms reaching as far over the ledge as they could, ready to grab Will and Jake as the wheel carried them up and over.

All four knew they had one chance at this. One slip and the wheel would carry Will and Jake back down the other side, down into the flooded chamber of crocodiles below.

Shane's hand gripped Jake's.

Daniel's hand locked with Will's.

With all their strength, Shane and Daniel pulled Jake and Will up onto the ledge, gasping and heaving.

Will clambered onto his stomach and looked at Daniel, his face full of gratitude. "I'm glad you tagged along."

Daniel smiled back. "I'm glad I came."

The light of dawn had begun to seep in through Will and Jake's now submerged entry point, filtering down through the narrow crevice and sending shafts of light into the chamber, refracting through the turbulent water and illuminating the entire cavern.

"What the hell is this place?" Shane asked, staring in astonishment at everything in the massive chamber turning and churning.

"The key," Will panted. "It fits into a panel in the wall down there, which opens that floodgate, which in turn makes the pyramid rise." In the middle of the chamber, the ascending pyramid was almost out of view, its massive columns lifting it higher and higher. "So how the hell do we get out of here?"

"This way," Shane told them.

The four men raced up a passageway which was essentially one long spiral staircase carved out of stone, leading directly up to the room inside Ahnu's mud hut. It was the master engineer's access to his life's work.

Shane didn't bother squeezing out through the sand-filled entrance this time. Instead he lifted himself through the hole that had been blown through the roof of the hut. The others followed and hurried through the oasis forest.

The desert air was now filled with a loud, low rumbling. The entire world was shuddering. The ground beneath their feet shook and the ferns quivered violently. Dawn had arrived, and the first glimmer of light spilled through the trembling palm trees.

As the four men emerged on the outskirts of the oasis,

they stopped dead in their tracks, watching as Ahnu's almighty structure ascended from beneath the earth, as though a mountain was being born before their very eyes.

The giant pyramid rose in perfect time with the golden sun.

It was beautiful. Unharmed. Unscathed.

There was no sign of erosion, no evidence of damage or decay whatsoever. It was exactly the same pyramid Ahnu and his followers had built four and a half thousand years ago, unseen and untouched by a single human being in all that time.

As the almighty pyramid rumbled and rose to its full, magnificent height, pushing out huge dunes of sand around its base, Will noticed the entrance holes to a dozen or so small shafts, about three feet square, opening at various points in its walls.

"That's the down button," he whispered to himself.

And then, the pyramid came to a grand, grinding halt, the shifting sands sliding down the dunes it had formed leading up to its walls.

Will saw the entrance, one-third of the way up one wall, the sun shining upon it.

What he said next surprised all three of his companions.

"We're not going in."

Jake turned to him, stunned. "What do you mean, we're not going in! That's what we came here for!"

Will shook his head. "We came to find the pyramid. Not enter it. It's a tomb. It's Ahnu's burial site. We didn't come to raid it."

"I did," said a low, stern voice directly behind them.

Will, Jake, Shane, and Daniel all spun around, startled to see Ra behind them, grinning. Will was even more startled to see Ra's arm locked around his father's throat, as if one move would break Charles Hunter's neck.

"Dad!"

He went to make a move for his captive father, but Ra tightened his grip on Charles's neck. Pathetically Charles pawed at Ra's bulging bicep. "Will! What's g-g-going on here!" The words came out in a choked stutter.

"Let him go!" Will snapped at Ra.

But Ra only grinned at him, his teeth gleaming bright white. He began to laugh, then pulled his blowpipe from the inside pocket of his long, black coat. He propped the end of it against Charles's temple and said, "Take me inside. Show me the treasure. Or else your father dies, right here, right now."

Will swallowed hard.

Shane and Jake both looked from Will to Charles, struggling in Ra's grip.

"Will, it's okay," Shane said, seeing the torment on his young friend's face. "Do as he says. Take us inside."

Eden wiped the sweat from his brow and raced through Aswan International Airport, checking his watch. The red dot indicating the Professor's whereabouts was still on the move, heading toward a location just north of Aswan, in the middle of the desert.

Eden put his hand in his pocket, making sure the cryogenic cylinder was still there, still safe.

He reached the rental car desk and pulled out the last of Thorne's cash. It was all that was left after he had paid officials in both Manaus and Aswan to smuggle the orchid out of one country and into the next.

"I need a four-wheel-drive," he told the clerk behind the desk. "The fastest one you've got."

Each stone that made up the pyramid was almost as tall as a man.

The six men grabbed on to handholds wherever they

could, pulling themselves up, one after the other.

Ra pushed Charles ahead of him. The dinner-jacketed diplomat struggled with some of the larger stone blocks. Will looked back, wanting to help his father, but the threat of Ra's blowpipe was enough to ward him off.

Sweating and panting, they soon reached the entrance. It was a large opening with a cantilevered stone ceiling, leading down into a passageway that disappeared into the darkness. Will shone his flashlight inside.

The passageway sloped downward, stretching so far into the pyramid that at some distant point the darkness simply swallowed the beam of his flashlight.

Ra stared eagerly into the passage. "Show me what's inside."

Will hesitated.

Ra offered a little incentive by seizing Charles once more around the neck.

"It's not safe in there," Will warned.

Ra sneered, "Nor is it safe out here." He squeezed Charles's arm, tightening his grip on him. The man spluttered helplessly.

"Let him go!" Will demanded. "I'll take you inside by myself if you promise to let everyone go!"

Ra chuckled. "What's the matter? I thought you'd enjoy a little family reunion. Looks like you both need it."

"Leave my family out of it! Take me instead."

"No!" Ra snapped, his chuckle turning to a scowl. "We all go. Now take us inside!"

Suddenly the air filled with a distant *thump-thump-thump*. Ra looked toward the horizon. Everyone else followed his gaze. A speck appeared in the morning sky, far beyond the tall, swaying palms of the oasis.

Ra's head snapped back toward Will. "Quickly! I want to see it all before he arrives! I want it *all!*"

"He?" Will asked.

Jake's eyes were trained on the dot approaching from the desert horizon. "Perron," he answered. "Perron's on his way."

Jake smiled. He checked his watch, and sure enough, the red dot on the tracking grid was racing toward the desert north of Aswan. That meant Sam was on his way too. And the antidote. Perhaps for once, Pierre Perron intended to live up to his end of the bargain.

Maybe Sam had a chance after all.

Luca's eyes opened slowly, the sound of the chopper blades thudding in his already pounding head. At first all he saw was a blur of gold. He pulled his head off the helicopter's cabin window and focused.

He realized he was looking down at a sea of golden sand, stretching as far as the eye could see, all the way to the blinding yellow sun rising on the far horizon. The shadow of the low-flying Bell 430 rose and sank over the fast-moving dunes.

Luca turned his eyes sharply and saw the Professor sitting beside him. The old man was cradling Sam's head in his lap. The boy's skin was pale, almost gray. Sweat ran from every pore. His dehydrated lips were parted. He was fighting for every last minute of life.

The sight filled Luca with rage.

He turned again, and this time saw Pierre Perron sitting opposite him, a smirk on his face and a gun in his hand. It was pointed straight at Luca.

"Monsieur Perron!" called Mr. Goodwin suddenly from the pilot's seat.

Perron turned quickly. Through the cockpit window of the helicopter he caught a glimpse of it. A lush green oasis. What was left of a glistening lake.

And overlooking it, a giant pyramid rising up out of the desert.

A wide grin spread slowly across Perron's face. "They actually found it!"

Behind him he heard Luca's seat belt buckle unsnap. Perron turned, quicker than lightning, to shove the snout of his gun dead into Luca's chest.

"I'd sit back down if I were you, Mr. da Roma. You wouldn't want us to have an accident so close to the end of our journey. And believe me, for you and your friends, we are indeed very, very close to the end!"

The black four-wheel-drive Porsche Cayenne tore along the rim of the Aswan Dam.

Eden looked east, to the golden sun rising beyond the massive dam wall, then glanced at his watch. The red dot had stopped moving. Eden estimated the distance between himself and the dot. It was seventy miles north of him. Perhaps more.

He put his foot all the way to the floor and the rental car flew down the road, launching loose stones and sand into the air in its wake.

Ra hurried them down the slope of the entrance passage, pushing them deeper and deeper into the pyramid.

At the end of the descent the passage flattened out for twenty feet or so, then began to climb. The six men made their way upward, Charles struggling to keep up, Ra nudging him on.

"Let me help him," Will said, leading the way.

"Just find my treasure!" Ra demanded.

Shane suddenly stopped, shining his flashlight ahead of them all. "I think we just did."

The rise had led them to the entrance of a chamber, humble in appearance, with nothing inside it but a stone altar in the center of the room.

It was the burial chamber.

On the altar lay two ancient bodies. One was mummified, tightly bound from head to toe in tattered, frayed clothes. The other was nothing more than skeleton, its bony hand clutching the hand of the mummy.

Slowly, reverently, Will stepped up to the foot of the altar.

The two bodies before him were smaller than he was expecting. But if anything, they were the only things he had hoped to find here.

The remains of Ahnu and Khay.

Together.

There was nothing else in the chamber. No treasure. No gold. No silver. They had nothing else to take into the afterlife—

—but each other.

"It's them," Will said. "Together for all eternity."

"And my treasure?" Ra roared. He was staring at the sparse chamber in dismay, searching desperately for his idols and trophies and treasures. "Where is it? What's down there?" he demanded, pointing to three doorways leading away from the chamber, each on a separate wall.

"Death," Will told him, gesturing to the doorways on either side of them. To the left was a doorway with the symbol of a small coiled earthworm above a passage that sloped away into darkness. To the right was a doorway marked by the symbol of a snake. "All except this one," Will said, pointing to the last doorway. Above it was a hieroglyph of a snake, a horizontal semicircle, a horizontal rectangle, and a circle on top of a cross. Beyond that was a small passage that ascended toward the light. "Living forever," Will said to himself, instantly recognizing the hieroglyph as the one he had drawn on the blackboard in Nathan's office. "This is the path of eternal life. The passage for the entombed souls to ascend to the—"

Will stopped. Suddenly they were not alone. They heard

panting from the entrance passage. They heard footsteps rushing up the ramp.

Then they saw Perron's flush, greedy face. "Where is it?" he demanded, waving his gun at the gathering. Behind him, Mr. Goodwin appeared, dragging the Professor along by the back of the neck. And behind them came Luca, carrying a semiconscious Sam in his arms.

"Sammy!" Jake shouted, racing toward Luca, taking Sam out of the young Italian's arms.

"He's not well," Luca warned Jake.

"Where's the antidote?" Jake shouted at Perron. "You said if we found your pyramid, you'd give him the antidote!"

"I destroyed it! Now, where's my treasure?" Perron snapped back. "I don't see any treasure here!"

"What do you mean, you destroyed it!"

Perron smirked at Jake. "I smashed it! It's gone."

Jake stared at Perron in shock, mortified, furious.

"It's true," the Professor told Jake gravely.

"You goddamn bastard!" Jake let go of Sam and charged for Perron, but Mr. Goodwin intervened and slammed Jake with an uppercut to the chin.

Jake flew into the air and landed smack on his back on the floor of the chamber, stunned and winded and gasping for air.

Perron sneered at Jake, then turned to the others and in a cold, flat voice said, "The next person to piss me off dies. Now tell me where my treasure is!"

"There is none," Will announced, unafraid.

"What do you mean, there is none! All pyramids have treasures!"

"You want a treasure? That's your treasure right there!" Will shouted back, pointing to the mummified remains of Ahnu and Khay on the burial altar. "Proof that Ahnu existed! Proof that Ahnu and his lover were real! Proof that four and a half thousand years ago there was someone smarter, someone greater, someone with more courage and knowledge and logic and wisdom than Imhotep—his son! A son he rejected because of pride and intolerance. Because he couldn't accept who he really was."

"And who was that?" Charles asked somberly, defensively. All eyes turned to him now, including Will's.

"Just a kid. A kid who wanted his father's love."

Perron stormed up to Will and shoved the gun under his jaw. "You lie!"

Defiantly Will shook his head. "Go ahead. Look for yourself. But I'd hurry up, if I were you."

Perron pushed the gun higher into Will's jaw, forcing the boy to raise his head. "Why?" the Frenchman spat.

"Because this place is a ticking clock."

"Shut up! What would you know? You're just some young brat!"

"He's my son!" Charles piped up. "And given the cost of his education, he ought to know something!"

"Thanks, Dad," Will muttered out of the corner of his mouth, "I think."

"All of you shut up!" Perron shouted. He stepped away from Will and seized the sickly Sam—a decidedly easier, less defiant target—by the back of the neck, hoisting him to his feet.

Jake tried to make a move, but Perron cocked the trigger and pushed the nozzle of the gun into Sam's temple. "Find me my treasure now, or this boy will be the first to die."

"Listen to me," Will said, trying to reason with him. "The second the pyramid reached the surface, it began to fill up with sand. There are shafts on the outer walls. Some high, some not so high. The lower shafts near the base of the pyramid would have started filling with sand almost immediately. Don't you get it?"

"The down button," Jake muttered.

Will nodded. "If the pyramid needed the weight of the water to push it up, it needs the weight of the sand to pull it back down. Any second now, we're gonna start sinking. Turning and sinking. Slowly at first. Then faster and faster as the pyramid gets heavier and heavier, boring its way back underground."

The Professor asked in a serious tone, "Can we stop it?"

"We have to get back to the key and open the floodgate back up," Will explained. "It's simple. Water versus sand. Life versus death."

"Enough of your garbage!" Perron barked. "Stop talking and find me my treasure before I—"

Suddenly the entire pyramid began to quake.

With a jolt, everyone rocked to one side as it dawned on them all—

—they were moving.

The whole pyramid was moving.

It was turning.

And it was sinking.

Perron dropped his gun and fell over, his arms flailing like an upturned turtle. Everyone else crouched, staggered left, then right, then steadied their balance and ran.

Jake lumbered desperately across the floor for Sam. He scooped the kid up in his arms and bolted for the first passage he saw, dashing into the doorway of the snake. Pierre Perron watched him disappear, clambered to his feet, and like a frightened child raced after him, knowing his best chance of survival at this stage was with Jake Stone.

Ra shouted after the scurrying fat man. "Perron, you liar! Where's my gold?" Clutching his blowpipe in one hand and his bleeding shoulder in the other, he stormed down the passage after them.

At the same time, Charles lost his balance and began to slide. Will tried to hold him back. "Dad!" But he clutched the lapel of Charles's tattered dinner jacket just as Charles toppled backward, pulling Will with him down into the dark, sloping passage of the coiled earthworm.

The pyramid rocked and rumbled. Luca grabbed the Professor and Shane grabbed Daniel. They bolted for the doorway of eternal life. But they were not alone. Shane glanced back and saw the colossal bodyguard charge after them. "Go! Go!"

As the four of them rushed up the cramped, sloping passage toward light, the hulking Mr. Goodwin squeezed up the passage, his huge frame consuming every inch of the shaft as he pushed his way up the steep ascending tunnel.

The wipers slammed back and forth, throwing sand off the windshield until Eden saw it loom before him—the Lost Pyramid. He stared in astonishment as the mighty pyramid seemed to be shrinking, then realized—it's not shrinking, it's *sinking*!

In a churning skid, he swerved the Porsche to a halt beside the Bell 430 helicopter, which sat at the edge of a growing well of sand. The circumference of the well was expanding by the second as billions of tiny golden grains trickled down toward the turning, descending pyramid.

It was like a black hole, starting to suck the whole world into its sinking whirlpool.

Eden quickly realized that if he left the car at the edge of the growing pit, it wouldn't be here when he got back. He shoved the gearshift into reverse and pulled up a safe distance away, near the edge of the oasis. With the orchid cylinder clutched in his hand, he leapt from the four-wheel-drive and charged across the sand and down the slope toward the rotating pyramid.

His feet sank deep into the sliding sand as he took one giant bound after another, getting closer and closer to the moving structure. As he neared the stone walls—sinking faster than he realized—he slowed his downward journey and changed direction, running alongside the spinning pyramid as though he was about to jump onto a moving train, until he was so close that all he could do was leap—

—or be sucked underneath it.

Eden jumped.

With Sam dangling limp in his arms now, Jake bolted as fast as he could down the passageway of the snake. Behind him he could hear the breathless, terrified whimpers of Pierre Perron.

"Jake! Don't leave me! I beg you, wait for me!"

Jake didn't respond. Sam was getting heavier and heavier in his arms and he needed to save his breath.

"Jake! I don't want to die!"

Suddenly Jake heard a different sound. The whistle of a dart whizzing past his ear. *Dammit!* he thought. *Ra's coming!*

Perron's squeal echoed down the passageway.

The down ramp flattened out. Jake hit the level surface at top speed and his knees almost buckled, but he managed to stay on his feet and kept sprinting until he turned a corner and suddenly skidded to a halt.

From behind he could hear the endless, panicked cry of Perron, wailing like an ambulance siren, getting closer and closer till the fat little Frenchman rounded the corner.

Jake quickly put Sam down and held out one arm to stop Perron.

He caught him just before Perron went flying into the air. Flying into the long, massive pit of snakes, slithering and writhing before them.

Jake himself had managed to stop at the very edge of the pit.

Perron teetered, squealing even louder than before, his eyes saucers, staring at the enormous pit of serpents.

Sand and loose stones fell away from beneath his overhanging shoes.

Snakes hissed and stabbed at the falling debris.

Reluctantly, Jake pulled Perron back from the edge and the Frenchman instantly latched his arms around the tall American, digging his fingers deep into Jake's back with absolutely no intention of letting go anytime soon.

"Get off me!" Jake spat angrily, trying to peel Perron's tentacles away.

"Don't leave me!"

"I oughtta throw you down that pit right now, you piece of—" Jake went silent. He could hear the bounding steps of Ra tearing after them.

With some effort, Jake managed to pull Perron off him and push him aside, then quickly he sized up the pit before them.

It was at least fifty feet long and twenty feet deep.

From the stone ceiling above, more snakes slithered through tiny holes and dropped into the pit below, becoming one with the twisting, twirling, swirling mass of reptilian bodies below.

There were no ledges on the side walls, only a series of wide, round columns randomly spread along the length of the pit, spaced four or five feet apart, all of them moving—

Slowly descending—

Lowering themselves into the well of serpents.

The tops of the columns sank to the same level as the passageway, then continued to sink lower and lower into the pit.

"Stepping stones," Jake realized. He looked beyond the far end of the pit. At the end of the passage was a doorway leading toward a shaft of daylight. It was their way out. "We have to make it to the other side before the columns sink all the way."

"What?" Perron shrieked.

"One column at a time. We're going to have to jump from one to the next." Jake scooped Sam up into his arms. "Stay here if you want, but the way I see it, it's him"—he jerked his head back toward the echo of Ra's boots, getting closer and closer—"or them!" He nodded his head toward the snakes below.

With Sam held tightly in his arms, Jake launched himself into the air and landed with an unsteady thud on the top of the first sinking column.

Shane and Daniel raced toward light at the end of the small ascending passage. Luca and the Professor were close behind, but heaving and grunting behind them was Mr. Goodwin in hot pursuit.

"Keep going," Shane breathed, pushing Daniel ahead of him.

"What about the others?" Luca asked desperately, guiding the Professor toward the light.

"They'll be okay," Shane assured him. "So long as we get to the key."

"What key?"

"The key Will used to kick-start the pyramid. If we can get to it in time, maybe we can stop this thing from burying everyone alive!"

Charles rolled and grunted the entire way down the passage of the earthworm, banging his head, twisting his limbs, and tearing his already tattered dinner jacket the entire way down. When the ramp finally leveled out into a flat passageway, he tumbled to a stop, resting in an exhausted, gasping heap.

With a groan he pressed one palm against the stony passage floor, then the other, and pushed himself achingly to his feet.

The moment he was standing, Will came rolling at high

speed off the ramp, shouting "*Whhhoooooooaaaaa!*" until he slammed into the back of Charles's knees, knocking his father clean off his feet and sending the pair of them clattering and bouncing even further down the passage.

As soon as they rolled to a halt, Will shook his giddy head and pulled himself to his feet. "Come on, Dad. Look ahead, stairs!"

Indeed, at the end of the dark passage, no more than twenty feet ahead, was a set of stairs leading up to daylight. Will grabbed his father's elbow in an attempt to help him up, but Charles merely shook Will off his arm. He floundered to his feet unassisted and straightened his scuffed jacket furiously. "Don't *'come on, Dad'* me! I've had just about enough of your unruly ways, young man! You've ignored my perfectly sound advice and look what it's got you! Nothing but trouble!"

"Dad! We gotta go! Now! Save the damn lecture for later, okay?"

"And that language!" Charles spluttered, shocked. "What's Felix letting you get away with?"

"Felix is letting me get away with having fun! And being young! And being proud of who I am!" Will finally snapped. If there was one thing he couldn't bear, it was his father bullying poor old Felix. "He lets me live my life and he loves me for who I am, Dad! Just like my friends out there!"

"Your so-called friends out there are the ones who got us in this predicament in the first place!"

"Dad, shut up! You don't know them. You don't know *me*."

"On days like this, I don't want to know you. I'm nothing but ashamed of you. You have no idea how hard I worked so that you could make the right choices in life. The important choices. But look at you! The man you've become—the life you choose to live—it's unnatural—"

"Dad, being gay is not a choice—"

"It's self-indulgent—"

"Dad, shut up—"

"It's attention-seeking—"

Will clenched his teeth. "Dad, don't even say it—"

"It's—"

Will saw it coming and clamped his jaw.

"—*impure!*"

Suddenly the young college kid's hand balled up into a fist, but before he could throw it at his father, he stopped himself. No matter how much he wanted to hurt Charles at that moment—no matter how much Charles had hurt him—he knew all too well that causing any more pain was not going to bring them closer together. Instead, Will stood there, holding his breath in anger and glaring in silence.

Charles simply scoffed. "Just as I thought. Nothing to say. Because you know I'm right." He turned with a self-righteous shrug, took one step toward the stairs, then, suddenly—

—disappeared!

"Dad!"

Will watched as his father seemed to drop into the stone floor and vanish completely. Only it wasn't a stone floor at all. Charles had stepped into a massive pit. A pit filled with millions upon millions of wriggling, writhing, squirming—

"Worms!" Will gasped.

Jake swayed uncertainly, trying to balance himself with the unconscious weight of Sam, still dangling in his arms. He spread his feet wide in the center of the first sinking stepping stone and prepared himself to make the leap to the second.

He counted twelve columns between him and the far end of the pit. Some were placed to the right, some to the left. He'd have to zigzag his way from one to the next.

From the ceiling, a hissing asp suddenly dropped

onto his bare shoulder. Its scaly body looped and slunk against his skin, trying to cling to the ball of his shoulder muscle.

Jake quickly shook it off and it fell into the deadly, coiling mass below. He took a deep breath, then, gathering all his courage and focus, he jumped again. His feet slid a little as he landed on the top of the second column, but he managed to pull himself up and quickly steady his balance.

Behind him, Perron moaned as though he was in pain. "I can't do it! Come back and get me, Jake! I can't do it alone! I can't, I can't, I—"

Without warning, a deep, scornful laugh echoed through the chamber. Perron turned, then yelped at the sight of Ra, tall and mean, standing right behind him. "I can!" Perron shrieked, suddenly changing his tune. "I can! I can! I can!"

And with that, he began jumping as though someone had just rammed a firecracker down his pants. Precariously, he landed on the top of the first sinking column, then bounced straight onto the second.

The appearance of Ra and Perron's suddenly frenetic leaps and bounds forced Jake to step up the pace too.

He sprang into the air, then thumped onto the surface of the fourth column.

Behind him, Ra raised his blowpipe to his lips and paused a moment, deciding whether to shoot Perron first, for all his false promises, or finish the fight he had started with the American in the Blue Hamam.

With another screech, Perron launched himself into the air like a chicken trying to fly, landing in a fluster on the third step.

Jake also jumped again, a little too hastily, and crash-landed onto the fifth descending step. He dropped to his knees, but managed to keep Sam in his arms and keep from toppling over the edge at the same time.

Ra laughed even louder than before. This game amused

him greatly, as did the panic of its players. It was time to join in the fun, he decided.

With great care he replaced the blowpipe in the inside pocket of his coat. Then, with a long, confident leap, Ra flew threw the air and landed on top of the first sinking column. Snakes rained from the ceiling and he shook them off. His long, black coat fanned out behind him like a villain's cape as he soared through the air to the next step.

Perron glanced behind in horror. "He's coming for us!"

But Jake didn't look back. He only looked ahead, at the far wall of the pit, which was getting higher and higher as they sank lower and lower.

He tightened his grip on Sam and jumped again.

Daniel reached the opening of the shaft and climbed out onto the outer wall of the pyramid, followed quickly by Shane, who helped the Professor and Luca into the bright sunlight. As they stepped hurriedly out onto the terraced stone wall of the turning pyramid, Shane shielded his eyes to take in a slowly descending, rotating, three-hundred-and-sixty-degree view of the world.

"Come on!" he said, leading the way down the side of the pyramid.

Below them, the desert consumed the pyramid layer by layer, stone by stone. The sand swirled below and was itself swallowed up in the process, sucked into the deepening hole that the sinking pyramid was creating.

As the pyramid turned, and the oasis came into view, so too did Perron's Bell 430 chopper, now sitting on the edge of the ever-widening sand hole.

The four of them clambered down to the safest, lowest possible place on the wall. The pyramid rumbled. The sand was turning below them, rising fast.

"We're going to have to jump," Shane told them. "As far as you can. As soon as we hit the ground, we gotta climb like hell, otherwise the pyramid will suck us under."

Luca gripped the Professor's hand tight. "Whatever you do, don't let go!"

The far rim of the sand hole rose above them as they descended quickly toward the lowest point of the deepening pit. Then Shane shouted, "Jump! Now!"

The four of them leapt into the air as one and plunged deep into the sand.

With a loud gasp of air, Shane broke the surface first.

"Climb!"

The others emerged, gasping and choking. Under their feet, the sand was quickly pulled away, sucked into the pyramid's wake.

The Professor struggled to find a firm footing. Luca hauled him up the sliding slope. Daniel battled, his feet sinking deep into the sand. Shane grabbed Daniel and used his free hand to dig deep and pull himself up the sloping dune, almost in strokes, as though he was trying to swim through the sand.

His legs pumped hard.

He dragged Daniel higher, and higher, and higher still.

Luca pulled the Professor along behind him, gripping him tight.

Until at last they were far enough away from the drag of the pyramid for them to think they were safe—

—until they heard the groan of metal above them.

As the pyramid continued to sink behind them, Shane glanced up to the rim of the expanding sand hole and saw the edges of it sliding away. This in itself was not a concern. What made Shane's eyes widen in panic was the sight of the enormous Bell 430 helicopter teetering on the collapsing brink directly above them, until the edge of the sandbank it was resting on began to give way.

"Luca!" Shane shouted, not taking his eyes off the chopper. "Go wide!"

Luca shot a glance at Shane, then followed his gaze up the slope to see the teetering chopper.

"Professor, hold your breath," Luca warned.

The massive craft began to slide down the dune, heading straight for them.

Frantically, Luca started digging into the sand.

Above them, the chopper slid twenty feet down the dune before it picked up momentum and began to twist around like an out-of-control sled, then tilt sharply to one side, then topple. Its rotor blades broke and hurtled into the air. The body of the craft cartwheeled down the slope, flipping and twirling and breaking apart as it bounced down the dune, faster and faster and faster. Shards of metal snapped off and speared into the sand.

Shane and Daniel leapt clear as a chunk of the bird's tail spun and thumped into the sand beside them.

Luca kept digging, as fast as he could. He grabbed the Professor and unceremoniously planted him headfirst into the shallow hole, before throwing himself on top, as the runaway chopper headed straight for them.

With an almighty *crunch!*

An ear-shattering *crack!*

And an air-splitting *whir* and *thunk!*—

—the Bell 430 plowed into the sand inches above them, then bounced up in the air, whirled around in an acrobatic spin, somersaulted over them and crashed into the sand dune below.

Luca pulled himself out of the sand, heaving desperately—more out of shock than any need for air—then quickly hauled the Professor up.

Behind them, the chopper crunched and groaned as it became caught in the pyramid's wake. There it clattered and quaked, screws and bolts bursting through its metal seams. It shook and rocked in the throes of death before the fuel tank burst apart.

The metal sparked against the stone of the pyramid, and *KA-PHOOOM*!

The chopper erupted in a giant orange fireball that unfurled into the sky, leaving tendrils of smoke billowing from its charred skeletal remains.

Then, through the smoke, Luca saw something and seized the Professor's hand. Shane saw the same thing and was already pulling Daniel up the sand slope. "What is it?" Daniel panted. But before Shane could say a word, Daniel had already glanced back and answered his own question.

Mr. Goodwin had emerged from the pyramid's shaft and was now bounding down the stepped wall toward them.

Will dropped to his knees, his eyes swimming with horror at the sight of a pit full of a million worms. Worms as long as his arm. And not just worms—maggots too, the size of his thumb. Millions of them. Crawling and squirming and slithering and lurching as one throbbing ocean of glistening ooze.

And amid it all, no sign of his father.

"Dad!"

With a loud squelch, Will Hunter plunged both arms into the sticky, slippery pit. His hands slid through the moving mass, gliding left, groping right, until he caught what felt like the collar of Charles's jacket.

With all his might Will yanked, and up popped Charles, gasping and spluttering, spewing worms from his gaping mouth and snorting maggots from his flared nostrils. His glistening, gooey eyes stared at Will in horror as the younger Hunter hauled his father hastily from the pit.

"Oh, God!" Charles spat, coughing up a maggot the size of a cockroach. "What's that!"

"Worms. Maggots. To finish off the dead."

"Dead? Who's dead!"

"Us. Unless we find a way across this pit."

Wide-eyed in search of a plan, Will stared across the pit to the stairs on the other side. "Dad, did you feel anything at the bottom? Could you touch the bottom of the pit with your feet?"

Charles was grimacing and groaning, desperately shaking unwanted company out of his sleeves and the legs of his trousers. "What? Oh, God, they're down my shirt!"

Will took that as a no. "Take it off."

"What? My shirt?"

"And your jacket."

"What on earth for?" Charles asked, untucking the bottom of his shirt. Dozens more thrashing worms and maggots rained onto the stone floor. Charles screamed again before Will grabbed his jacket and started pulling it off his father's back.

"Because if we wanna get across that pit of worms, we're gonna have to act like worms. That's why. Now take off your shirt!"

Will was already snapping his own shirt off his back. He tied the sleeve of it to the sleeve of Charles's now slimy dinner jacket. He turned to his father and gestured for his shirt.

"I hope you know this shirt came from Rome and cost a fortune!"

"Dad, just give me the damn shirt!"

Charles pulled off his shirt and reluctantly handed it to Will, who tied it to the other sleeve of the jacket, forming what could only be described as a clothes rope. Stepping up to the edge of the pit, Will took one end of the clothes rope in one hand and swung the other end, once, twice, three times through the air before tossing it as far as it would reach across the pit. The shirts and jacket flew across the pit, then settled like a blanket over the wriggling mass of grubs, landing within a few feet of the opposite ledge.

Then Will got down on all fours.

"What on earth are you doing?" Charles asked, already horrified at what the response might be.

"It's all about weight distribution," Will answered, lowering himself to the edge of the pit and eyeing the clothes rope before him. "Just like the lost pyramid. Sand. Water. Up. Down… Across."

Charles gasped. "You don't expect me to—"

"What, Dad? I don't expect you to get a little dirty? Well, guess what. If your gay son can do it, so can you! We're not gonna get across this pit by walking, I think you already proved that. So if you want outta here, we're gonna have to wriggle our way across."

"Are you crazy? We'll sink! They'll eat us alive!"

"If we stay here, that's exactly what they'll do," Will warned. "We'll be sealed in. We'll starve. They won't! That's not gonna happen!" Slowly, gently, he extended himself belly-down over the surface of the writhing mass.

His arms were throbbing. His legs were burning. His knees almost caved again as he hit the surface of the sixth step. Jake gave a grunt, then bit back the pain. At the same time, snakes continued to rain down in long, slithering coils, falling into the writhing pit below, which was getting closer and closer by the second.

Jake stood and prepared to jump again, but suddenly he felt a heavy blow behind him. It came with a terrified squawk.

Perron's panic had propelled him from one step to the next to the next until he had caught up with Jake, crashing into him on top of the sixth column.

Jake lurched as the fat Frenchman slammed into his back.

Sam slipped out of his grip.

Jake struggled to regain his grasp on the boy, dropping to his knees and grabbing desperately at Sam before he toppled out of his arms and over the edge of the column.

Seeing an opportunity, Perron used Jake as a spring-board, jumping on his back and launching himself across to the next stepping stone to take the lead.

Jake grunted again, his hands pawing at Sammy, one locking onto the back of the kid's shirt, one onto a leg. He managed to haul him back onto the surface of the step.

Up ahead, Perron hurtled himself from one column to the next, bouncing his way to the far wall with surprising speed.

Then Jake once again heard that low, deep laugh from behind him. He turned and saw Ra glaring, just two steps behind.

Quickly, Jake realized he wasn't going to win a race to the far wall with Ra on his tail—not if he was carrying Sam in his arms. The only options he had were to abandon Sam—or fight. The way Jake saw it, it was an easy choice to make.

He laid Sam's limp, unconscious body safely in the middle of the descending sixth column. Then, before Ra had a chance to advance any further, Jake made the leap back to the fifth step, jumping away from the far end of the pit, back toward Ra to block him from getting to Sam.

He dug his heels into the sinking surface of the column, ready to leap at his assailant. He clenched his fists, ready to fight.

Ra smiled, his large teeth gleaming, then opened up his coat to reach for his blowpipe.

Before Ra could draw his weapon, Jake launched himself into the air with all the force he could muster—

—jumping straight toward his enemy.

"Don't let go of my shoulder," Luca told the Professor as they followed closely behind Daniel and Shane, down the spiral stone staircase leading from Ahnu's hut to the under-ground cavern.

Shane raced out onto the ledge first and saw the giant gearwheels all turning in reverse now. The lower half of the pyramid was descending back into the cavern. Below them, the tide had turned and the water, still swirling with savage crocodiles, was being channeled out of the chamber by the spinning wheels.

Shane glanced at the floodgate. It had sealed itself shut again as the water was transferred back into the oasis lake via a network of underground conduits and canals. But while the level of the water was slowly going down, the gate was still submerged. He couldn't see the panel or the keyhole that Will had mentioned. It was underwater.

"I'm going in," Shane said, kicking off his boots. "We can't wait up here for the water level to drop. It'll be too late."

"I'm going with you," Luca said.

Daniel shook his head. "The crocodiles. You can't!"

Shane ripped off his shirt. "We have to find that key. We have to stop the pyramid."

Daniel began undoing his own buttons. "Then I'm coming with you."

"No. Stay with the Professor. Don't leave him."

Daniel opened his mouth to argue, but Shane sealed his lips with a kiss. Then he turned to Luca, who finished pulling off his own shirt and gave him a confident wink. "You ready?"

Luca nodded. Then, before anyone else could say another word, they both dived off the ledge and plunged into the turbulent water.

The current caught them almost immediately, dragging them precariously close to the crushing cogs of several submerged gearwheels.

Shane and Luca swam with all their strength against the tow of the water, kicking hard, pushing themselves deeper and deeper toward the submerged floodgate.

Shane's eyes scanned the walls at either side. His fingers

traced the rock. Then, in the dim depths, he caught a glint of gold. The key!

He gestured for Luca to follow and the two swam toward it. The key was firmly lodged in its place inside the wall.

Shane grabbed the end of it and tried to turn it, but it wouldn't give. He tried to pull it out. It budged an inch.

Out of the corner of his eye, Luca caught a glimpse of a large black shape moving through the tumultuous water above him. He looked up and saw the shadow of a monster croc, gliding through the water toward them. Its body was thick yet agile, its tiny legs now pressed against its torso, giving the beast the appearance of a mighty, prehistoric eel with giant fangs, slithering quickly through the water.

Luca tapped Shane on the shoulder and pointed to the massive shape moving through the water. Shane picked up the pace. He quickly turned back to the key and locked his fingers around the small, interlocked figures of Min and jerked as hard as he could. The key dislodged itself another inch.

Luca turned away to try to spot the croc. Suddenly the monster's massive tail whooshed past his head—the reptile had descended upon them faster than he anticipated. Luca grabbed Shane to try to pull him away.

Shane turned and saw the beast's crooked, killer teeth coming straight for him. He balked left. The croc snapped. Shane managed to spin out of its way—almost.

One jutting fang caught in his side.

It sank into Shane's torso.

The croc tried to snag its catch, but Luca laid the hardest punch he could manage into the beast's giant snout. At the same time, Shane twisted his body and the old, jutting tooth came loose.

Luca pulled Shane away.

The croc swirled through the water with one less tooth in its mouth, the fang now firmly stuck in Shane's bleeding side. But he wasn't about to give up that easily.

The pissed-off croc lunged again. Luca ducked low. Shane pressed himself against the wall and dipped down. The monster missed him by a fraction of an inch and pulled up fast before head-butting the wall. With a disgruntled sweep of its tail, it retreated once more a short distance through the water, then turned back again and opened its jaws wide, ready for one final attack.

Shane grabbed at the key and gave it one last tug.

The croc charged.

The key came loose.

Shane pulled with more force than he realized. The gold object shot out of the wall, then sailed clean out of Shane's hand—

—directly into the open jaws of the charging crocodile.

Luca and Shane stared, eyes bulging in horror, as the two golden Mins tumbled straight down the throat of the monster.

The croc swept out of its attack dive, then spluttered and swirled and thrashed through the water, choking on the unexpected object in its throat.

The monster tried to regurgitate the key, and for a brief moment Shane saw a flash of gold appear in the croc's mouth. For a brief moment he entertained the thought of reaching in to grab it.

But then the croc spasmed and lurched, its neck bulged, and with an unhappy jerk of its mighty body, the reptile swallowed the key whole.

In a horrified burst of bubbles, Shane let the last of his air escape his lungs. His chest was bursting, his lungs about to explode. Luca saw that he was in trouble. He seized Shane by the arm and began pulling him toward the surface.

At the same time, the giant croc floated to the floor of the cavern, belching and grumbling and unhappily trying to digest the gold in its gut.

From the ledge far above, Daniel saw Shane and Luca rising quickly from the dark, churning depths toward the surface. "It's okay," he told the Professor. "Here they come. I think it's going to be okay."

"Think again." The cold, snickering words didn't come from the Professor. They came from Mr. Goodwin, standing directly behind them, grinning as he punched his right fist into his left palm, warming up for the kill.

Will slid himself out across the churning, curling sea of eel-like earthworms and looping larvae, stretching out as far as he could to reach the first floating shirt.

His elbows and knees sank a little into the living mire, but as he dug one hand into the sticky pool, followed by the other, Will slowly began to paddle his way across the pit, sliding and wriggling across his own shirt first, then the dinner jacket, then Charles's shirt.

Within minutes his fingers locked onto the ledge at the far side of the pit. Swiftly he pulled himself to safety, up onto his feet, and danced around, shaking the worms and maggots out of his pants.

He shot a concerned glance back across the pit at his father and shouted, "Come on, Dad! You can do it!"

Visibly, a shiver shot down Charles's spine. He took a long, hard, painful gulp. "I'm not sure I can."

Will saw the fear in his father's eyes. It was something he'd never seen before. Suddenly he knelt at the edge of the pit. "What if I meet you halfway?"

Charles's fearful, blinking eyes filled with hope. Just a little.

"Come on, Dad. Meet me in the middle. We can do this. We'll do it together."

Charles nodded. "Yes." And slowly he knelt.

Like a mirror image, Charles Hunter followed his son's actions at the opposite end of the pit. Both men spread themselves low. Both men pushed themselves out over the pit. They stretched themselves flat over the swaying, lurching pool of grubs, Will splaying himself across Charles's shirt, Charles melting flat across Will's shirt.

Instantly, Charles began to sink and panic.

"Dad! Look at me! Stay calm, keep your eyes on me, and move your arms, one at a time!"

A faint smile, somewhat nervous, flickered across Charles's face. He looked at Will. "I remember telling you the same thing. Such a long time ago. Down at the ocean. I was teaching you to swim. You were only three years old. Your mother was still alive. We all went to the beach together, and I told you not to be afraid of the water. Water is life. Do you remember?"

Will smiled at the irony of his father's words and nodded, although for the life of him he couldn't recall that day. "Yes," he lied. "I remember, Dad. Now do as you taught me. One arm at a time."

The surface of the pit sucked and squelched with every digging motion of their hands, but slowly, surely, Will and Charles slithered and inched their way toward each other until finally Will's hand locked on his father's. Then, with even more careful, cautious movements, Will wriggled backward as Charles wriggled forward.

Soon Will's feet hit the far ledge.

He twisted himself around and pulled himself out of the pit and onto the stone floor, but not before securing Charles in his grip and hauling his father to safety too.

"Almost there, Dad. Come on. The stairs." Will helped his father to his feet and hurried him to the stairs, the beam of the sun shifting quickly across the steps as the pyramid continued to rotate and sink.

"I'm glad that's over," Charles sighed as Will helped him up onto the first of the steps. But as soon as the words left his mouth, the ground beneath their feet began to move once again. Will and Charles both jolted.

Will glanced down in panic. "I don't think we're done yet, Dad!"

He was right. The stone step beneath their feet was slowly tilting downward. Will looked up the length of the stairway and saw that every step ahead of them was doing the same, tilting downward inch by inch, slowly turning the stairway into a ramp. One that would soon be too steep to climb. If they didn't make it to the top before all the steps tilted into a diagonal position—

—they would simply slide all the way back down. Trapped forever. The fodder of worms.

"Dad, climb! Climb as fast as you can!"

Before Ra could reach the blowpipe in his coat pocket, Jake flew through the air and crashed directly into him. The two men hit the surface of the sinking column together, the air bursting from their lungs, their bodies toppling and rolling.

Jake tumbled over the edge of the column first. His fingers scraped along the surface and managed to snag the stony rim of it, catching him just before he plunged into the pit of hissing asps.

But with the momentum of Jake's lunge, Ra too came tumbling over the edge above him, crushing his fingers.

Jake didn't let go.

Ra rolled over the top of him, grabbing desperately at anything he could: Jake's hair, his head, his neck, his slippery, sweating shoulders and back. Frantically Ra clawed at Jake's body, trying to stop his fall. Then, suddenly, his clutching fingers hooked onto the waist of Jake's cargo pants.

He jolted to a halt.

Jake's fingers slipped another inch on the rim of the column with the sudden added weight. All he could do was hold on as tight as he could.

Ra glanced down, eyes wide in terror, fingers latching

onto Jake's pants. His feet were dangling mere inches above the pit, sinking closer and closer as the column descended. Asps were spitting at him, striking at him. He tried to lift his feet. He dug his hands into Jake's beltline.

Jake winced and gritted his teeth, trying to dig his fingers in deeper. But Ra squirmed and panicked. As the cargoes dropped down around Jake's ass, Ra tried to clamber his way higher up Jake's body.

Snakes continued to fall from the ceiling. One dropped into Jake's hair. Another landed in a tangled knot across Jake's slowly slipping fingers. It uncoiled itself, then began weaving its way down his forearm.

Jake shook the first snake out of his hair. It landed on Ra's left shoulder.

With a small jerk of his arm, the second snake slid down Jake's bicep, over his shoulder, slunk down his back, and landed on Ra's other shoulder.

Ra fidgeted frantically, trying to get rid of the asps. One fell into the pit, the other one vanished.

Ra hooked one arm tightly around Jake's waist, then managed to hoist himself high enough to hook one hand over Jake's shoulder.

The jagged stone edge of the column began to cut into Jake's fingertips. He felt trickles of blood run down his fingers and palms.

Ra managed to get his other hand higher still, grabbing the top of Jake's skull to pull himself up, using him as a human ladder.

Jake roared in pain, feeling the locks of his hair tug and pull in Ra's clenched fist. He felt Ra's sticky, gasping breath on the back of his neck. He saw Ra's other hand reach up toward the edge of the sinking column. He felt Ra's heavy, hot body paw and clamber and slide over the top of him.

And then the weight was gone. Ra's boot disappeared

above him, and Jake realized Ra had reached the top of the column safely.

He glanced back and saw that his own boots were hanging only inches above the pit now. An asp spat its venom and lashed at him. Jake swiftly hoisted his legs as high as he could, but he was sinking lower and lower into the pit. It was only a matter of moments now before the column would take him down with it into that hissing hollow of serpents.

And then, from above, came a crunch and a terrible pain.

He winced and looked up to see Ra towering over him, his boots grinding down on Jake's desperately clutching fingertips.

With a leering grin, Ra opened his coat and reached for his blowpipe, pulling the long, slender black weapon from his pocket.

"You should thank me," he said, smirking, gesturing to the churning mass of snakes below Jake. "My poison will work much faster than theirs. I'll do you the honor of a quick death."

Ra lifted the pipe to his lips.

Then, suddenly, his eyes bulged.

His jaw dropped open.

In a final moment of horror, Ra realized it was not his blowpipe he had pulled from his pocket, but an angry, evil-eyed asp.

He unlocked his hand to let it go, his fingers flew open. But it was too late.

The snake struck like lightning.

Its head flew straight into Ra's gaping mouth.

It latched onto his tongue.

Ra let out a shrill, open-mouthed scream.

He ripped the snake off his tongue and hurled it across the chamber. But the asp's fangs had already pierced the flesh, injecting its deadly poison into Ra's instantly swelling tongue.

He reeled backward, stunned, horrified. His hands shot up to his open mouth, trying to squeeze his tongue, trying to extract the venom.

But his fingers struggled to get inside his mouth.

His tongue had instantly turned purple and was now so engorged it took up all the room in his mouth, cutting off the air.

Ra began to make choking, gagging noises. He clutched at his throat, trying to breathe. But his poisoned tongue had completely filled his air passage.

As Jake swiftly managed to pull himself up onto the edge of the column—first onto his elbows, then his stomach—hauling himself out of striking distance from the pit below, he watched Ra take one dying, staggering step backward and plummet into the ferocious pit of fangs below.

There was a frenzy of hissing and slithering, as Ra's spasming body became tangled in the swirling mass. Slowly he melted into the twisting pit of snakes, and within seconds he vanished completely. Gone forever.

"Sam!" Jake pulled himself quickly to his feet, knowing that soon he and Sam would face the same fate.

At the end of the pit he saw Pierre Perron's rotund shape pulling himself up the far wall and rolling onto the floor of the passageway, exhausted but safe.

The Frenchman scrambled to his feet and raced for the shaft at the end of the passage. The light shining down from the shaft was now obscured by a constant, moving shadow. Sand, Jake realized. Sand was beginning to pour in through the shaft. The pyramid was sinking below the desert surface as fast as the columns were sinking into the pit of snakes.

Perron vanished through the entrance to the shaft, into the speckled light.

Hurriedly, Jake jumped across onto the column where Sam lay.

He dropped to his knees and took the young man's head in his hands and glanced at his watch. "No, no, no!" he shook his head. A tear slipped down his grimy, exhausted face. Sam only had fifty-two seconds left to live—Fifty-one—Fifty—

The columns sank lower and lower. Only a foot or so to go now.

"I'm not leaving you," Jake whispered to Sam, knowing there was no way he could get him out now. No way he could possibly save him.

In those final seconds, Sam's eyelids fluttered open.

His breath was shallow but his gaze steady.

He looked into Jake's eyes, his face streaked with tears.

Jake held him tight in his arms, and remembered one of the first things Eden had ever said to him. "Close your eyes," he whispered. "When you open them again, you'll feel better. I'll look after you, I promise."

Sam closed his eyes.

So did Jake.

He heard the rumble of the stone carrying them down to their deaths. He heard the hiss of the snakes. He heard—

"Open your eyes!"

—Eden's voice.

"Sam! Look at me! Open your eyes!"

Jake's own eyes shot open. "Eden?"

As if he had dreamed him up, Eden was suddenly kneeling next to Jake. He was checking his watch, pressing a finger to Sam's almost nonexistent pulse. "I need you to open his mouth, right now."

Jake quickly did as he was told while Eden reached into his pocket and frantically unscrewed the cap of the cryogenic cylinder containing the orchid. He quickly pulled the small, potent flower from its container and snapped off one of its chilled petals.

Jake caught a glimpse of the time counting down on

Eden's wristwatch.

They had twenty seconds left to save Sam's life.

Eden pushed the petal inside Sam's mouth.

He quickly pressed it under the boy's tongue.

He clamped Sam's jaws shut tight.

Eden and Jake held their breath. For an eternal moment, nothing happened.

And then—Sam's eyes blinked open and the young man stared around him.

"Sammy?" Jake gasped, smiling. He grabbed Sam by the shirt and sat him up abruptly, unbelieving, unable to say anything more.

Sam simply looked all around him, dizzy and disoriented, then inhaled deeply as a single word escaped him:

"Snakes!"

His legs flew out from under him as he pulled himself desperately to his giddy feet. He swayed precariously from side to side, still groggy and weak, his legs bowing beneath him. Jake caught him in his arms. "Easy!"

The stone column was only inches from the snake pit now. Asps began to flick and coil and slither their way onto the surface of the step.

"Where are we? And how the hell do we get outta here?" Sam asked, panicked and petrified and sucking in lungfuls of air.

"That way." Jake jerked his head in the direction of the disappearing columns between themselves and the far end of the pit, at the same time kicking the encroaching snakes away from his boots.

Eden sized up the distance and the odds. "We'll never make it!"

"Dad, climb! Now!"

Will leapt into action, seizing his father's arm and hauling as fast he could up the stairs. Charles's black leather shoes—

now scuffed and splitting at their Italian seams—slipped on the steps as they tipped on an ever-increasing angle.

"Come on, Dad!" Will looked ahead and saw a shadow move across the light up ahead. Then, in the next moment, the first trickles of sand began to pour in through the opening above them. "Faster, Dad! Faster!"

The steps sloped down ten degrees— Twenty degrees—

Charles clutched at his breath, frantic and fretting. They were only halfway up the tilting stairs. Sand began to cascade down past them. The trickles quickly turned into streams, the stream into rivers, and soon it seemed as though the entire desert was flooding in.

Will tried to keep his sights on the opening above them, but the sand was stinging his eyes. His feet were angled sharply as he climbed now. The steps were closing too quickly. And it dawned on him with a terrible sense of finality. "We're not gonna make it."

Shane and Luca broke the surface of the water and instantly saw that Daniel and the Professor had some unwanted company. They swam as fast as they could to the nearest flat gearwheel and pulled themselves out of the water, only to be greeted by a croc spinning on the huge stone turntable. Its jaws sprang open and it lunged straight for them.

On the ledge, Daniel put himself between the grinning Mr. Goodwin and the Professor, shielding the older man. He eased both of them backward, away from Perron's hulking henchman, but the Professor's foot began to slip and slide off the edge of the ledge. They were out of places to go.

"Shane!" Daniel shouted down over the ledge, calling for help.

"We're coming!" Shane called back, at the same time jumping out of reach of the lunging crocodile. He landed with Luca on the next gearwheel and quickly sized up the fastest route to the upper ledge, his eyes tracing a path from one wheel to the next, then onto the giant vertical gear-wheel.

It would carry him up directly to the ledge—

—if only they could get to it in time.

The giant pyramid continued its rumbling descent.

On the ledge, Daniel glanced down and saw the vertical gearwheel a few feet below them, its cogs rising up and then plunging into the water, turning like a Ferris wheel. It was their only escape. "We're going to have to jump!"

But Mr. Goodwin shook his head. "You're not going anywhere."

Suddenly he came for them. Daniel pushed the Professor clear off the ledge, then jolted, his knees quivering, as Mr. Goodwin's fist clocked him square in the face.

Behind him, the Professor landed with a thump on one of the cogs of the vertical gearwheel. It carried him over the top of the wheel and quickly down the other side.

Down below, Luca and Shane leapt from one wheel to the next, catching sight of the Professor on the giant Ferris wheel, about to plunge into the water and be pulverized by two interlocking cogs.

On the ledge, Daniel shook the stars out of his head, straightened the glasses on his nose, and threw his hardest punch at Mr. Goodwin. His fist connected with Mr. Goodwin's chin, but the giant man barely flinched. He simply responded by slamming Daniel with a right hook that lifted him off his feet.

On the wheel, the Professor felt himself begin to fall. He slipped off the wheel, and plunged toward the crushing cogs. Then, suddenly, he felt Luca's and Shane's arms beneath him.

It was a clumsy catch, one that spared the Professor from the cogs but knocked all three of them off the spinning wheel and into the water. The current began to drag all three back into the crunching mechanics of the wheels.

Up on the ledge, Mr. Goodwin smiled at the sight of it—Shane, Luca, and the Professor about to be sucked to their deaths, and Daniel at his feet, about to meet his own match.

With a satisfied chuckle, Mr. Goodwin bent down and picked Daniel up by the scruff of his shirt. He stood him on his unsteady feet and smiled as he said, "I'm gonna tear you limb from limb!"

With that, he lunged once more at Daniel—

—when his rushing feet snapped short in their steps.

The colossal bully glanced down to see his shoelaces tied together.

Unable to stop his mighty momentum, Mr. Goodwin stumbled and tumbled straight over Daniel and headfirst over the ledge. With a thud he landed between two huge stone cogs on the turning gearwheel. Desperately he tried to pull himself free, but his bulky frame was wedged firmly between the cogs.

The wheel turned.

Mr. Goodwin screamed.

He spun around on the wheel, over the top, then down the other side. Down toward the thrashing water. Down to the point where the cogs connected.

And then—

Scrunch!

Mr. Goodwin was sandwiched, his body caught like a wrench in the works.

The gearwheel groaned and grated to a halt.

In a chain reaction, all the wheels stopped turning.

Then, with an almighty shudder, the giant sinking pyramid came to a grinding halt.

The current stopped, just as Shane, Luca, and the Professor were about to be dragged to their deaths. They swiftly swam clear of the cogs, Shane and Luca pulling the Professor up onto a gearwheel.

As Shane and Luca helped the Professor up the shuddering, straining Ferris wheel, Daniel peered over the edge to see the crocodiles come rushing toward the trapped Mr. Goodwin and hungrily begin chomping on his limbs.

The steps tilted down to a forty-degree angle.

Will couldn't hold on much longer. Above him he gripped one of the slanted steps as tightly as he could. Below, he grasped his father's hand. He could no longer climb. All he could do was face away from the flood of sand pouring in through the opening. They were close to it now—only a few steps away—but not close enough.

Any second now the steps would close completely, turning the stairway into a slide.

Will looked down at his father as the sand filled his hair and bounced off his shoulders.

"Dad?" Will called over the thunderous deluge of the desert.

"What?" Charles shouted back up to him, spitting the gushing sand from his mouth and blinking it out of his eyes.

Will took a deep breath and said, "You know I love you, right?"

Charles caught sight of his son through the torrent of sand streaming in, then took a breath to say something. "William, I—"

Then, suddenly—

—the entire world rocked to a halt.

The pyramid stopped groaning and grumbling and turning and sinking. The steps stopped tilting downward. Even the river of sand sliding in on top of them suddenly reverted back to a stream.

Charles gasped.

Will looked up, wide-eyed and full of hope.

This was their window of opportunity. A window that might not be open for very long. Will seized their chance.

"Come on, Dad! Quick! We can do this!"

Gripping the sloped steps in one hand and hauling mightily with the other, calling on every ounce of strength and courage he had, Will dragged them both toward the light.

One step higher. One step closer. Until he felt the sunlight in his hand.

The entire chamber—the entire pyramid—jolted to a halt.

Jake held on tight to a dizzy, disoriented Sam, then quickly realized the pyramid wasn't the only thing that had stopped moving.

The columns had stopped sinking as well.

But for how long?

Jake wasn't about to stick around and find out.

He pulled Sam's weakened form off his feet and threw him over his shoulder, then turned to Eden. "Go! Quick! Jump now!"

At the crack of Jake's panicked voice, Eden sprang instantly onto the next step, then the next and the next, trying frantically to avoid landing on the snakes that attempted to slither up onto the surface.

Jake followed close behind with Sam slung over his shoulder, grunting with the effort of every launch and landing.

Snakes hissed. Some lashed at them. Others spat their venom into the air.

But the men were too fast.

At the end of the pit, Eden kicked a large black asp off the toe of his boot, then leapt onto the far wall, clinging to the rock face. "Pass him to me!"

Eden was already reaching back and Jake jumped onto the column. He pulled Sam off his shoulder and eased him to his feet. "Sammy, you're gonna have to help us get you outta here."

"I can do it," Sam said, nodding, his eyes still dazed but determined.

Hastily Jake scooped Sam up and passed him awkwardly over to Eden's reaching hand. Eden grabbed his arm and swung him toward the wall. Sam latched on as best he could, then, with his fingers finding every tiny crevice and handhold and Eden's fist clutching his arm and hauling him upward, they spidered their way up the wall.

Behind them, Jake hurled himself into the air, hit the wall, and started climbing. Soon, Eden reached the top and pulled Sam up and over the edge. They crawled onto the floor of the passageway on their stomachs, then both leaned back to help Jake.

"You okay?" Jake grabbed Sam's face in both hands once all three of them were safely out of the pit.

Sam nodded. "Better. Yeah."

"Come on." Jake rushed Sam and Eden quickly through the final doorway, into the exit shaft.

Sunlight pushed through a small opening at the top of the long vertical shaft with protruding stones like rungs up one side, leading all the way to the surface. Now that the pyramid had stopped sinking, the stream of sand pouring down the shaft had turned to a trickle, but already enough had poured in through the vent to create a large sand dune on the floor.

Just then, Jake noticed the chubby fingers protruding from the mountain of sand, barely wriggling, trying to reach for freedom.

Reluctantly, Jake grabbed the fat hand and pulled hard. Pierre Perron's arm emerged from the dune, followed by his fat, gasping, sand-spluttering face.

"Jake! Oh, Jake!" he coughed and gagged. "Pull me out of here, please!"

"What the hell for? You were happy to leave us behind."

"I was going to find help!"

"Bullshit!" Jake said, stepping back and folding his arms across his chest, watching as the Frenchman squirmed and struggled, trying in vain to pull himself out of the sand hill.

"Please!" Perron begged, then started to cry. "Please, help me! Help me! I'll give you anything you want! Name your price!"

Jake turned to Sam and Eden with a suddenly enthusiastic grin on his face. "Gentlemen? Any suggestions?"

Tails thrashed and jaws splashed as water and blood and chunks of flesh flew high into the air. When there were no limbs or head left to devour, the crocodiles began to rip into the fleshy torso of what remained of Mr. Goodwin. As they pulled and snatched at the meat, reducing its bulk, the gearwheel groaned and the lodged body finally began to flatten and expand under the immense weight of the cogs, until—

Crunch!

The crocs were thrown clear as the pent-up pressure of the jammed gearwheel finally gave way in an explosion of water and minced body parts. The remains of the corpse splattered everywhere. The cogs locked together, free of debris, and rolled into motion once more. With an enormous rumble, the pyramid began sinking again.

Jake leaned forward and offered Perron a handshake. "Do we have a deal?"

For a stubborn moment, Perron refused, pouting and huffing bitterly.

"If you don't take my hand, I can't pull you out," Jake said, smiling smoothly.

"All right, all right! Deal!" Perron snatched Jake's hand. Suddenly, the pyramid rocked into motion once more, grinding and groaning and sinking.

The light above vanished behind a cascade of sand flooding down the shaft faster than ever.

"Go!" Jake yelled to Sam.

Hand over hand, Sam pulled himself quickly up the rungs, fighting against the deluge of sand. Eden swiftly followed. Jake hurriedly hauled Perron out of his prison of sand and jerked him to his feet.

As Perron began to whimper and cry in a dithering panic once more, Jake pushed the fat Frenchman's ass up the shaft ahead of him as fast as he could.

"Move it!" he grunted, jamming his shoulder up into Perron's rump and pushing as hard as he could.

At the top of the shaft, Sam didn't so much as climb out through the opening—he was yanked out. When Eden reached the top, several more pairs of arms reached in and pulled him up into the bright daylight.

Perron began to smile and babble euphorically. "We're saved!"

As he fought against the incoming tide of sand, mostly with the help of Jake beneath him, he reached the top of the shaft and was hauled—with a great deal of effort—to safety.

The second Perron was gone, the sand flooded in over Jake. It filled his eyes, then, suddenly, he felt hands grabbing at him. He felt himself lifted into the sunlight. When he rubbed the sand from his vision, he saw them all. All the faces he trusted and loved—and even a couple he didn't—pulling him off the sinking pyramid and up the sandy slope to safety.

Luca and Eden helped the Professor to the top of the embankment. Shane helped Daniel. Will helped his father. Jake and Sam helped each other. Even Perron, trailing behind, managed to stagger and bumble his way to safety.

At the top of the slope, they all turned to watch the capstone of the Lost Pyramid twist and turn and sink back into the earth, spouting one last gust of air before the desert sands slid over the top of it.

And then it was gone. Consumed by the almighty desert once more.

"As though it never existed," Will whispered.

"But it did," said Daniel, smiling at Will. "The world will know it."

Shane reached around to his side, and with a pained look on his face pulled a two-inch-long croc tooth from a gash in his torso. "Till then," he said with a grimace, "I say we go home."

"All except you," Jake added, hauling a still whimpering Pierre Perron to his feet. "Monsieur Perron, you're going to jail."

"Personally, I think that ought to go for all of you!" exclaimed Charles, plucking a tattered handkerchief from his dusty dinner jacket and patting the grime and sweat from his brow.

"Dad!" Will exclaimed angrily.

"William, this incident is going to take a fair amount of explaining, to say the least! I suppose I'll do my best to skirt around the details when the Department of Foreign Affairs comes knocking on my door, but in the meantime, who's going to pay for my dinner jacket! And my shirt from Rome!"

Charles gazed down his nose at them all with a very displeased look on his face.

"I'll be happy to," the Professor spoke up. Quite diplomatically.

But Charles was already walking off.

Will watched him and sighed, not in frustration, but resignation.

The Professor stepped up behind the young man and patted him on the shoulder. "I think that's just his way of saying he loves you."

Will shrugged. "I don't know. He seemed kinda fond of that shirt from Rome."

As if to give Will another reason to sigh, Charles turned around and asked, "Where shall I send the bill?"

XVI

The Island of San Sebastián, Caribbean Sea

THE HOUSE WAS A BEAUTIFUL TWO-STORY COLONIAL mansion which sat on a vast green lawn, bordered on either side by towering palm trees. The large, open windows were framed by white shutters, and an ocean breeze tugged gently at the light, shimmering curtains, inviting them out onto the wide veranda. On the warm grass, several large, scattered coconuts—hairy, hard, and oddly masculine—lazed in the sun.

Lining the edge of the lawn was a shining white beach with an old wooden jetty stretching out over the water. Rays of light glittered on the turquoise sea. At the end of the jetty, a thirty-foot yacht bobbed gently on the sparkling water.

Shirtless and shoeless, Shane lay dozing on the bow of the boat, his hands tucked behind his head, his cowboy hat shading his face from the sun and, around his neck, a two-inch-long crocodile's tooth attached to the end of a leather necklace. The pages of an open newspaper fluttered gently on his lap. On the front page, just beneath the masthead of the *London Town Crier*, was the headline THE RIDDLE OF THE SANDS SOLVED. Underneath, in large, proud print: *Egypt's Secret Gay Genius Rises from the Lost Chambers of History—Exclusive story by Daniel West.*

From below deck, Eden emerged wearing sunglasses, shorts, and an unbuttoned shirt which had slipped from his muscled shoulders and caught around his biceps. He was carrying a box containing the Professor's few worldly possessions. He plunked it down on the deck next to Shane and gave the Texan a nudge with his bare foot.

"Hey, cowboy! We're supposed to be unloading the Professor's things, not soaking up the sun."

Shane lifted his hat and gazed up at Eden with an impudent, crooked smile. "I'm recovering!"—he lifted the croc tooth from around his neck, then pointed to the gash in his side, as if to prove his point—"and you're blocking my light. Now, if you don't mind, the only thing I want to soak up right now is a little more well-earned peace and quiet."

Suddenly, the peace and quiet was shattered by the sound of a distant scream.

Shane sat bolt upright. "That sounded like Elsa!"

"She's at the house," Eden added. "Something's wrong!"

Like lightning, the two men leapt off the boat and bolted down the jetty, along the unblemished white beach, across the lawn, and up the steps to the porch. They burst into the house and found Elsa in the enormous kitchen, a wooden spoon in one hand and a carving knife in the other, squaring off against a large island woman with tightly braided hair, bare feet, and a basket full of freshly caught fish in her hands.

"Elsa! What's going on?"

"This woman tried to attack me!"

"With what?" Shane asked. "A basket full of fish?"

"She just appeared from nowhere, and when I told her to

leave, she came at me with a mackerel!"

"This is *my* kitchen!" the woman announced in a tone assertive enough to match Elsa's. "I should be telling you to get out!"

At that moment, the Professor guided himself through the kitchen door, feeling his way along the wall. "Elsa? Eden? Shane? What's going on?"

"Who the hell are you people?" the large black woman demanded.

"My name is Professor Fathom. This is Dr. Eden Santiago, Shane Houston, and, by the sound of it, you've already met Elsa, my housekeeper."

"Where's Monsieur Perron?" the large woman challenged, slamming her basket of fish down on the counter and standing with her hands on her bountiful hips.

"Monsieur Perron no longer owns this island," Eden happily informed her. "He signed the deed over to the Professor a few days ago. He won't have a need for private lodgings anytime soon."

"Why? How?" the woman exclaimed, incredulous.

Shane shrugged innocently. "Monsieur Perron needed a helping hand, and the Professor needed a home. Let's just say a friend of ours named Jake did a little bargaining."

"He's a very good negotiator," the Professor added with a smile.

"You mean, Monsieur Perron's gone?"

"All the way to jail, in fact."

The large woman gasped in shock, then slowly a wide, beaming grin spread across her face as she started dancing around the kitchen. "Praise the good Lord above!" she sang. "That man had the heart of a pig and the brains of a coconut!"

The Professor's face shone warmly. "I think I'm going to like you. What's your name?"

"I'm Big Zettie. From the small fishing village on the

other side of the island, just beyond the plantation. I'm Monsieur Perron's cook—or, at least, I was."

"Pleased to meet you, Big Zettie." the Professor stepped forward, feeling his way uncertainly along the counter and offering the woman his hand.

Before she could shake it, Elsa promptly snatched the basket of fish off the counter and grumpily dumped it back in Big Zettie's hands. "Yes, lovely to meet you. Now take your smelly fish and go! The Professor already has someone to cook for him!"

"Now, now, Elsa," the Professor said calmly. "We're not about to move into this house and push the locals out. We're not barbarians. There's plenty of work to be done and space enough for everyone."

"But Professor—!"

"Elsa, there's always room to grow and expand your horizons. You and Big Zettie could learn a lot from each other."

Elsa stared at him, stunned and distraught. "Are you asking me to share my kitchen?"

The Professor smiled diplomatically. "I'm sure Big Zettie would love a lesson in sausage making."

Big Zettie glowed at the idea. "And I'll show you how to fire up a barracuda barbeque with traditional Caribbean rum curry!"

All Elsa could do was cross herself.

XVII

San Diego, California

DAWN BROKE ACROSS THE SKY AND FELIX FRASER WAS already preparing breakfast when he stopped whisking eggs and said to himself with a smile, "Master Hunter's back." He picked up the remote and triggered it to open the garage door. A second later he heard Will's Ducati rev along the driveway, but instead of pulling into the garage it pulled up at the front door in a screech of tires.

Felix pulled open the door as Will took off his helmet, pushing his chaotic blond hair out of his eyes.

"Master Hunter! If you think I'm going to try to clean that skid mark off the driveway, you've got—"

"Shut up, Felix!" Will grinned, opening the helmet box at the back of the bike and tossing Felix his spare helmet. Felix instinctively caught it, then stared at Will, shocked.

"And what exactly do you expect me to do with this... thing!"

Will laughed. "I expect you to put it on and jump on the

back."

Felix gasped. "What on earth for?"

"For a bit of fun, that's what."

Felix was stunned and bewildered, but something told him if he didn't get on the back of Will's bike now—he'd regret it forever.

Felix pulled on the helmet.

Will, looking as shocked as Felix, whooped and laughed. "Felix, *you* are my main man!"

"Just don't scare the living daylights out of me."

"This isn't supposed to make you feel scared," Will said. "It'll make you feel *free*."

Will kick-started the engine and revved the bike along the driveway. Felix held on for dear life, but after a little while he began to relax.

Soon he forgot all about the sound of the engine, that awful roar he loathed so much. He forgot about the sharp corners and the winding bends and the road passing beneath them at speeds he had never gone before.

As they rounded a turn onto the coast road, the sun rose over the hills and cast a bright yellow glow over the Pacific, and in an instant Felix let all his fears go.

He shut his eyes.

He felt the wind and the warmth of the sun.

And in that moment, Will was right: Felix Fraser truly did feel free. He felt as though he was living the life that Charles Hunter—despite all his money—should have been living.

And Felix was pleased, beyond any measure of doubt, that *he* was the one who got to live it.

XVIII

Warsaw, Poland

OLD NEWSPAPERS BLEW ACROSS THE EMPTY COBBLESTONE square, launching themselves into the air, sailing high into the sky like kites that had run out of string.

Luca stood watching them, his feet in a puddle of rainwater in the abandoned square. This was where the Cirque des Trompettes had performed, only days before. Now they were gone, along with his hope of finding the clown named Valentino.

Suddenly the temperature dropped and the wind picked up. A piece of paper flew through the air and slapped against his leg. It wrapped around his calf, until he plucked it off. The flyer fluttered in his hand as he read the headline.

CIRQUE DES TROMPETTES
Now touring Warsaw, Krakow, Budapest,
Prague. Danger, beauty, excitement, thrills—
all your dreams come true!
Hurry, limited performances.
Don't miss the show of a lifetime!

Luca checked his watch. If he hurried now he could make the next train to Krakow. Racing as fast as he could, he splashed his way across the bleak, empty square, clapping across the cobblestones, the circus flyer scrunched tightly in his fist. He wasn't about to let it go now.

XIX

Meatpacking District, New York City

ON THE PLANE BACK FROM EGYPT, IN THE CAB FROM JFK, even in the freight elevator on the way up to his warehouse apartment, Jake didn't utter a single word the entire way home. Sam didn't even try to speak to him, not until they were inside the apartment and the door slammed behind him.

"So give. What the hell's put you in such a bad mood?"

"Nothing," Jake lied, refusing to look at Sam as he let his backpack slip from his shoulder. "I'm going to get some food. You want anything?"

"Yeah," Sam challenged. "I wanna know why you're pissed at me!"

It didn't take much for Jake to snap. Bottling things up was not his strong suit. "Fine, you wanna know what's got me pissed? I'll tell you. I thought you were dead! I thought I was gonna lose you, Sammy! I've done some crazy shit in my time, but I've never been so scared in all my life! And that pisses me off! Do you know how close you came to dying?"

"But I didn't die. You guys saved me!"

"And what if we hadn't? What then?"

Sam shrugged, then threw his arms in the air defeatedly. He wondered if this was what it was like to have a parent. Always arguing. Never seeing eye to eye. "If you're trying to act like a father to me, you're doing a crappy job of it!"

Jake stared in astonishment. "I'm trying to make you understand that life isn't a game."

"Like I don't know that! Do you know where I've come from? Do you understand what I have to do to survive?"

"Yes, I do! Because I came from the same place! You and I are the same, Sam."

"Bullshit! I never wanna be like you. You don't know how to talk, you don't know how to care. You don't know how to love anything, Jake. The only thing you know how to do is fight! I'm tired of it—I do enough of that on the street."

Jake threw the challenge back. "I care enough to put a roof over your head, kid. But if that's not enough for you, then maybe the street is where you belong. Back with your gang of crack whores and rent boys. You can trust them, right?"

Sam shook his head. "No, but there is someone else I *can* trust."

This time it was Jake who threw his hands in the air. "Fine. You do whatever you want. I'm going to get food. And don't think I'm getting enough for two."

Daylight was fading and Jake was furious, and his anger carried him all the way to the Chinese takeout two blocks down the street. While he waited for his order, he fumed over Sam's allegations. How dare Sam accuse him of not knowing how to love anything? Hadn't he just risked every-thing for Sam? Hadn't he just fought off man-eating crocodiles and a pit of snakes to save the damn kid's life?

Yes, he had.

And he had fought hard.

It was what he did best.

And suddenly it dawned on him: Perhaps Sam was right about one thing. Perhaps the only thing Jake really knew how to do was fight.

"Number ninety-one!" shouted the brash woman behind the counter of the takeout shop, thrusting a brown paper bag filled with steamed rice and Szechuan duck in Jake's direction.

Making his way back along the street to his apartment, regret filled his head as his empty stomach rumbled. He dug a fortune cookie out of the takeout bag and snapped it open with his thumb, cramming part of its cracked, sugary shell into his mouth and shoving the rest of it back in the bag for later. All the while he picked up his pace, beginning to fear that he had gone too far, that perhaps this time he had scared Sam off for good.

Suddenly, from behind him, he heard a terrified shriek.

The moment Jake turned, a frantic young kid, not much older than Sam, barreled into him. The takeout bag flew into the air and smashed onto the pavement as Jake stumbled, almost hit the ground, then caught his balance. Ahead of him, the kid was sprinting as fast as he could, a woman's handbag clutched in his fist.

Jake glanced behind him and saw a panic-stricken elderly woman, pointing a waving finger at the bolting boy.

Without a second's hesitation, Jake took off, his stride longer and stronger than the young bag snatcher. As the kid turned into an alley, Jake poured on the speed. He cut the corner tight. Ahead he saw the kid spring into the air and stick to a chain-link fence near the end of the alley. The handbag fell from his clutches and landed on the ground below. The young thief hesitated a second, glanced down at the bag, then saw Jake charging straight for him. He decided it was better to escape than to try and retrieve the bag and take on his pursuer.

With lightning agility, the kid scaled the fence, dropped to the ground on the other side, and disappeared around a dark corner of the alley.

Jake threw himself onto the fence, but gave up the chase when he realized the kid was truly gone.

Back on the street, the elderly woman quivered with fear yet managed a grateful smile as Jake handed back her bag.

"Do you need a doctor? Are you okay?"

"I'm fine," the old woman said, nodding. "It's not the first time. Those kids are trouble. They're good for nothing. Someday they'll wind up dead in a Dumpster and nobody will ever know they're gone."

"I guess they're just trying to survive," Jake said with a shrug.

"So am I," the old woman remarked angrily.

Jake saw her safely inside her apartment, two doors down, then returned to the remains of his Chinese meal in an attempt to salvage his dinner.

Back inside the warehouse, he saw the setting sun throw shafts of pink light across his apartment. Jake closed the door to the freight elevator and listened for any sign of life.

"Sam, are you here? Sam? I'm sorry. I'm sorry about what I said."

There was no reply. Jake's mind began to race. Where was Sam? What did he think he was going to do with his life? Become a bag snatcher? Somebody who was good for nothing? A kid who would someday wind up dead in a Dumpster and nobody would ever know he was gone?

Hurriedly Jake checked the bathroom; he snapped aside the shower curtain, his head spinning with the recent vivid memory of an injured Sam lying helpless in the tub. Now there was nobody there. He stormed through the sparse apartment, looked through the windows for any sign of Sam outside.

Nothing.

No trace at all.

Like the street kid in the alley, Sam was truly gone.

So was his backpack.

And so was his passport.

Jake sighed and dumped his takeout meal on the kitchen counter. As he regarded its now cold, unappetizing contents, for a moment he entertained the thought of heading straight back out onto the street. Then he suddenly caught sight of his fortune.

It was still tucked in the half-eaten shell of the cookie.

He pulled out the slip of paper, and a terrible feeling sank deep into the pit of his hungry stomach as he read his fate—

Beware the curse that will one day take your life.

Coming Soon

THE CURSE OF THE DRAGON

China. A land of ancient wonders. A history of tradition, triumph, and tyranny. As it casts a shadow across the entire globe, this once forbidden country awakens as the dominant force in a new world economy.

Business empires will rise, deals will be made, lives will be lost as money changes hands, but one treasure will remain the most precious in all of China: a diamond known as the Eye of Fucanglong, the Dragon God of lost jewels and buried treasures. The diamond is flawless. It is priceless. It is cursed. And it is about to be stolen in the heist of the century.

Can Professor Fathom's team of gay adventure-seekers find the diamond before this perfectly executed crime leads to a cataclysmic event of mass destruction?

From the towers of Hong Kong to the diamond mines of Shandong; from the streets of San Francisco to the deserts of Dubai to the male strip clubs of Beijing; from China's mystical past to the boardrooms and back rooms of a modern industrial giant, take the high road to China and join in the sizzling action and page-turning adventure of *The Curse of the Dragon*.

About the Author

From palace-hopping across the Rajasthan Desert to sleeping in train stations in Bulgaria, from spinning prayer wheels in Kathmandu to exploring the skull-gated graveyards of the indigenous Balinese tribes, Geoffrey Knight has been a traveler ever since he could scrape together enough money to buy a plane ticket. Born in Melbourne but raised and educated in cities and towns across Australia, Geoffrey was a nomadic boy who grew into a nomadic gay writer. His books are the result of watching too many matinee movies in small-town cinemas as a child, reading too many Hardy Boys adventures, and wandering penniless across too many borders in his early adult life. He currently works in advertising and lives in Paddington, Sydney, and can't wait to buy his next plane ticket.